WHITE MAGIC

WHITE MAGIC

A NOVEL

BY

DAVID GRAHAM PHILLIPS

ILLUSTRATED BY

A. B. WENZELL

D. APPLETON AND COMPANY

NEW YORK AND LONDON

1910

CONTENTS

WHITE MAGIC

I

A TASTE FOR CANDY

WHEN Roger Wade's Aunt Bella died she left him forty thousand dollars in five-per-cent railway bonds and six hundred and ninety acres of wilderness extending from the outskirts of Deer Spring village to the eastern shore of Lake Wauchong, in northern New Jersey. She had contrived to quarrel and break with all her other relations. This was no easy undertaking, and in its success was a signal tribute to her force of character; for, each and everyone of those relatives knew of her possessions and longed and hoped for them and stood ready to endure, even to welcome, any outrage she might see fit to perpetrate. Roger she had not seen in fourteen years—not since he, a youth of eighteen, a painter born, long and lean, with a shock of black-brown hair and dreamy, gray-brown eyes, left his native Deer Spring to study in Paris. He and she had not communicated, either directly or indirectly—a for-

1

tunate circumstance for him, as several of Arabella Wade's bitterest quarrels had begun and had progressed to the irreparable breach altogether by mail. Besides not knowing him she had but one other reason for choosing him as her heir: a year before her death and a week before her last will she happened to read on the cable page of a New York newspaper an enthusiastic note about his pictures and his success in Paris. So the bonds and the land went to him instead of to a missionary society.

Much American newspaper puffery of Americans abroad is sheer invention, designed to give us at home the pleasing notion that *we* are capturing the earth. But this notice of Roger Wade's career had truth in it. He was doing extraordinarily well for so young a man. His sense of color and form was lifted toward genius by imagination and originality. His ability had no handicap of cheap and petty—and glaring—eccentricity, such as so often enters into the composition of an original and boldly imaginative temperament to mar its achievement and to retard the recognition of its merit. Thus he speedily made a notable place for himself. He could count on disposing of enough pictures to bring him in fifteen to twenty thousand francs a year; and that sum was about as much as he, simple of tastes, single-hearted in devotion to his work and indifferent to pose and pretense, could find time and opportunity to spend. He knew that in a few years far more money than he needed would be forced upon him—a prospect which he had the good sense to view with distrust when he thought of it at all. About the only thing that had stood in his way was his personal appearance. As one of his friends—Berthier, whose panels will be admired so long as the pale, mysterious glories of their elusive colors persist—said in a confidential moment: "Roger, you look so much like a man of genius that it's hard to believe you are the real thing."

Big is the word most nearly expressing that unusual appearance of his. He was tall and broad and powerful. His features were large, bold, handsome. The dark coloring of skin and hair and eyes added to the impression of bigness. It was in part a matter of real size, but only in part. Not the most casual glance could have reported a judgment of mere bulk. He seemed big because his countenance, his whole body, seemed an effort of Nature adequately to express a big nature. Herbert Spencer uttered about the most superb compliment one human being ever paid another when he said of George Eliot that she suggested "a large intelligence moving freely." There was in Roger Wade this quality of the great bird high in the blue ether above the grime and littleness of conventional life.

His looks had caused him more than a little trouble—of which he was not in the least aware. For a large part of his charm lay in his childlike unconsciousness of himself—a trait less rare in painters and sculptors than in any other class of men of genius, probably because their work compels them to concentrate constantly upon persons and things external and in no way related to their own ego. Had Roger been physically vain, beyond doubt his good looks would have ruined him. The envy of men and the infatuation of women would have made escape impossible. As it was, he did his work, ignored his enemies, and neither enslaved nor was enslaved by such women as drifted into his life—and out again. It is fortunate for men—especially for men who are striving for careers—that women are bred to feebleness of purpose and much prefer being loved to loving, being admired to admiring.

His long stay abroad and his success there had touched his Americanism only to idealize it. The dream of his life continued to be building a career at home. He was too able to be given to the fatuities of optimism. He had no delusions on the subject of the difficulties that would confront and assail him. He had observed that those Americans who had the money to buy pictures usually lacked the breadth to appreciate their own country, considered it " crude and commercial,"

4

whatever that might mean, and preferred foreign painters and foreign subjects. But, like many another
American artist of ability, he longed to have a personal
share in bringing about the change toward national
pride and confidence that must come sooner or later.
So, when his aunt left him a competence, he felt free to
engage in the hazardous American adventure. Two
months after he inherited his little fortune he landed in
New York with his Paris career a closed incident; a few
days later he was installed in the old farmhouse on the
edge of his wilderness estate and within a mile of the
post office and railway station at Deer Spring. On a
hill near the Lake Wauchong end of his estate—a hill
that seemed a knoll in comparison with the steeps en-
compassing it on all sides—he got the village carpenter
hastily to build for him a house of one large and lofty
room, admitting light freely by way of big windows in
the walls and an enormous skylight in the roof. Such
small impression as his return made was wholly confined
to his native Deer Spring. There the gossip went that,
having failed to make art pay, he had come back home
to " laze round " and live off his aunt's money. As he
had the doing sort of man's aversion to discussing his
plans, such of the villagers as succeeded in drawing him
into lengthier parley than polite exchange of greetings
heard nothing that contradicted the gossip.

Toward the end of an April afternoon, not long after the studio was finished, Roger reached it in the midst of a tremendous storm of rain and wind. Just before he gained the shelter of the north wall a swooping gust blew into his face a heavy cloud of wood smoke; so when he strode in he was not altogether unprepared for the sight that met his eyes as he dashed the water and smoke out of them. A fire had been built with generous hands in the fireplace in the south wall. Upon the long, low bench parallel with the outer edge of the broad hearth lay the intruder who had doubtless sought the one refuge within a radius of a mile when the storm came on suddenly about half an hour before. Roger had assumed he would find a man; but he was not much surprised to see that it was a woman for whom his roof was doing this good turn.

As he divested himself of dripping hat and waterproof he said genially: " I'm glad you made yourself at home! "

No answer came and the figure did not move. He flung his wraps on one of the heavy plain chairs which, with the bench, were all the furniture he had—or wanted. He advanced to a corner of the hearth to take a look at his guest. She was a girl—a young girl, sound asleep. Her head was comfortably pillowed on one slim, round arm and her folded jacket. Her sweet,

6

Then he went to the huge closet in the west wall where he kept, under strong lock, everything of value he had to have at the studio. He changed his boots for shoes. He took out and opened a collapsible table. Having noiselessly set upon it pots and dishes, including an alcohol stove and two cups and saucers, he proceeded to make chocolate. When it was nearly ready he opened a package of biscuit and filled a plate with them. All this with the expertness of the old, experienced bachelor housekeeper. He moved the table over to the hearth, to the corner nearer her feet, and seated himself. Luck was with him. Hardly had he got settled when her eyes —gray eyes—opened. She saw the table, the steaming pot of chocolate. She raised herself on her elbow—saw him. He met her amazed stare with a smile wholly free from impertinence.

"The chocolate is ready," said he. "I have no tea. You see, I didn't know you were coming." His voice carried the humorous suggestion of old and intimate friendship, of a conversation continued after a brief interruption.

She brushed her hand over her eyes, stared at him again, this time a little wildly. His expression—the kind eyes, the mouth with no suggestion of cruelty or guile, the smile of friendliness without familiarity—reassured her straightway. A merry smile drifted over

8

her features—charming, pretty features, though not beautiful. "You know I detest tea," said she. "Besides, I'm hungry."

"I've made enough for two large cups apiece," he assured her. "But I had only condensed milk. It's hard to get the other kind in the country."

She took the cup into which he poured first, tasted it. "Splendid!" she ejaculated.

"I've been famous for my chocolate for years," said he complacently.

"If you weren't so vain!"

"Everybody's vain. *I* have the courage to speak out."

"*I'm* not vain," replied she. "If I were I should be embarrassed at your catching me like this." And she glanced down at her wrinkled and mussy attire.

"Possibly you are so vain that you don't care," rejoined he. "You said you were hungry, yet you haven't tried the biscuit."

The storm howled and moaned and clattered about the house; the enormous fire poured out its gorgeous waves of color and heat, flung a mysterious and fantastic glow upon the gray-white canvas covering of the rough walls, beautified the countenance of the huge young man with the shock of black-brown hair and of the slim, fair girl with the golden-yellow crown. And healthily delicate face was toward the fire, and flushed from its warmth. She had abundant yellow hair, long lashes somewhat darker, a charming, determined mouth, a very fair skin. With such a skin a woman far less well-favored otherwise than she could have felt secure against any verdict of homeliness. His trained eyes told him that she was above the medium height and that her figure was good, arms and legs and body well-formed and in proper proportion to one another. She had—in texture of skin, in look of the hair, of the hands —those small but unmistakable indications that she had been brought up secure from labor and from those frettings and worryings about the fundamental necessities of life that react so early and so powerfully upon the bodies of the masses of mankind. Even her dress gave this indication of elevation above the common lot, though the felt hat pinned carelessly on her head, the plain shirtwaist, the blue serge short skirt, the leather leggings and shoes had all been through hard wear. There are ways and ways of growing old; the way of expensive garments is as different from the way of cheap garments as the way of expensively nourished bodies is from that of bodies poorly supplied with poor food.

He stood for several minutes, enjoying the engaging spectacle—enjoying it both as artist and as man.

they laughed and joked, keeping up their pretense of old acquaintance and drinking all the chocolate and eating all the biscuit.

"Such a strange idea of yours, to live all alone here in this one room," said she.

Roger did not undeceive her. "You must admit it's comfortable," said he.

"Except—I don't see how you sleep."

He waved his cigarette toward the closet. "I keep everything put away in there," he explained. "As for my bath—the tub's only half a mile away—Lake Wauchong."

She looked thoughtfully at him. "Yes—you would need a good-sized tub," said she. He saw that she was full of curiosity, but did not wish to break the spell of their fiction of old friendship. "What are you doing now?" she asked—the careless inquiry of an old friend after a brief separation.

"Same thing—always," said he.

"That's good," said she, and both laughed. She looked round carefully, noted the skylight, the canvas drapery, finally a broken easel flung into a corner. "How does the painting go?" inquired she, in her eyes a demand for admiration of her cleverness.

"Oh, so-so," replied he with a glance at the big skylight, then at the broken easel, to indicate that he did not regard her display of detective talent as overwhelming.

"It's a shame you've never painted me."

"You know I wouldn't touch portraits," rebuked he severely. "I leave that to the fellows who want to make money."

"But why not make money?" urged she. "I rather like money—don't you?"

"I'm married to my art," explained he. "In marriage the only chance for keeping love alive and warm is poverty. Show me a rich artist and I'll show you a poor one." He spoke lightly, but it was evident that he meant what he said.

The girl was not at all impressed. "You'd better never fall in love," laughed she, making a charming wry face. "You'll not find any woman who'd honestly marry you on those terms."

"What a poor memory you have—for what I say," reproached he. "Haven't I always told you I never should?"

"I remember perfectly," replied she. "But I've always answered that you can't be sure."

"Oh, yes, I can," said he, with irritating, challenging confidence. "As I said, I'm already in love. And I'm the most constant person you ever knew."

"That doesn't mean anything," said she, looking

11

shrewdly at him. And the gray eyes, with all the softness of sleep driven from them, were now keen rather
than kind. " You are young, for all your serious look;
and you are romantic, I suppose. Artists always are.
You will fall in love."

" Not impossible," conceded he.

" And marry," concluded she, with the air of having proved her case.

" If I loved a woman I wouldn't marry her. If I
didn't love her I couldn't."

" That sounds like a puzzle—a—a conundrum. I
give it up. What's the answer? "

" I've lived in France several years," said he, " and
I've learned the sound sense back of their marriage system. Love and marriage have nothing to do with each
other."

The gray eyes opened wide.

" Nothing to do with each other," pursued he tranquilly. " Love is all excitement; marriage ought to be
all calm. Marriage means a home—a family—a place
to bring up children in peace and tranquillity, a safe
harbor. Love is a Bohemian; marriage is a bourgeois.
Love is insanity; marriage is sanity. Love is disease;
marriage is solid, stolid health."

" I think those ideas are just horrid! " cried she.

He laughed at her with his eyes. In a tone of raillery he said: " And you—who love money, you say—do *you* intend to marry for love?—just love?—only love? "

Her eyes shifted. He laughed aloud. Her glance fell.

" Not a thought about his income—prospects? " he mocked.

She recovered from her confusion, laughed back at him a confession that she had been fairly caught in a refined, womanly hypocrisy—woman being the official high priestess of the sentimentalities. " But I don't approve of myself—not in the least," cried she. " In my better moments I'm ashamed of myself."

" You needn't be," said he cheerfully. " You're simply human. And one need never apologize for being human."

She was gazing earnestly into the fire. " Would *you*—marry a girl—say, for—for money? " she asked. And her color was not from the firelight.

" As I've told you," replied he, " I wouldn't marry for anything—not even for the girl."

" Wouldn't you despise anyone who did such a thing? " Still she was avoiding looking at him.

" I don't despise," replied he. " Everyone of us seeks that which he most wants. I, who devote my life to my selfish passion for painting—who am I to despise some one else for devoting himself to his passion for—

13

what you please—comfort—luxury—snobbishness—no matter what, so long as it harms no one else? "

" You aren't so very old—are you? " said she pensively. " You look and talk experienced. And yet—I don't believe you are *much* older than I am."

" A dozen years—at least."

" You aren't thirty-four ! " exclaimed she in genuine dismay.

" No, but I'm thirty-two. So you're ten years younger than I. I guessed you younger than you are."

" Yes, I'm twenty-two. But in our family we hold our own well—that is, mother does."

These discoveries as to age seemed to give both the liveliest satisfaction. Said he: " You look younger—and talk younger."

" That's because I don't make pretenses. People think that anyone who is still frank and simple must be very young—and very foolish. . . . I've been out four years. Do I seem ignorant and uninteresting to you? "

" No—very frank—naïve."

She smiled, flushed, glanced shyly at him. " Do you know, I feel I know you better than I ever knew any man in my life—even my brothers ! "

" Everyone says I'm easy to get acquainted with," said he, practical and unappreciative.

She looked disappointed, but persisted. " I feel

14

freer to talk with you. I'd tell you—anything—the things I think, but never dare say."

" There aren't any such things," said he, hastening away from the personal. " Anything one really thinks one can't help saying."

" Oh, that isn't a bit true," cried she. " I think lots of things I don't dare say, just as I want to do lots of things I don't dare do."

" You *imagine* you think them, you *imagine* you want to do them," he assured her. " But really, what you say and do—that is your real self."

She sighed. " I hate to believe so."

" Yes. It is unpleasant to give up the flattering notion that our grand dreams are our real selves, and that our mean little schemes and actions are just accidental—or devil—or somebody else besides self."

·She looked at him and he was astonished to see that there were tears in her eyes. " Don't—please!" she pleaded. " Don't make it harder for me to do what I've got to do."

" Got to do? Nonsense."

" No, indeed," said she, intensely in earnest. " Remember, I'm a woman. And a woman has got to do— what's expected of her."

" So has a man if he's the weak sort."

He studied her with an expression of sympathy bordering on pity, but without the least condescension ; on the contrary, with a radiation of equality, of fellow-feeling that was perhaps his greatest charm. " Don't mind what I've said," he went on in the kindliest, friendliest tone. " I'm not fit to talk with young girls. I've got my training altogether in a world where there aren't any young girls, but only experienced women of one kind and another. You've been brought up to a certain sort of life, and the only thing for you to do is to live it. I've been talking the creed of my sort of life, and that's as different from your sort as wild duck from domestic."

He rose, gave a significant glance toward the windows through which clear sky and late afternoon light could be seen. She felt rather than saw his hint, and rose also. She looked round, gave a queer little laugh. " Am I awake—or still asleep? " said she. " I'm· not feeling—or talking—or acting—a bit like my usual self." She laughed again a little cynically. " My friends wouldn't recognize me." She looked at him, laughed again, with not a trace of cynicism. " I don't recognize my present self," she added. " It's one that never was until I came here."

But Roger showed no disposition to respond to her coquetry. He said in matter-of-fact tones: " Do you live far? Hadn't I better take you home? "

" No, no! " she cried. " We mustn't spoil it."

" Spoil what? "

" The romance," laughed she.

He looked amused, like a much older person at a child's whimsicalities. " Oh, I see! Once I was in a train in the Alps bound for Paris, and it halted beside a train bound for Constantinople. My window happened to be opposite that of a girl from Syria. We talked for half an hour. Then—we shook hands as the trains drew away from each other. This is to be like that? A good idea."

She was listening and observing with almost excited interest. " Didn't you ever meet that Syrian girl again? " inquired she.

He laughed carelessly, shrugged his shoulders. " Yes—unfortunately."

The girl's face became shadowed. " You loved her? "

His frank, boyish eyes twinkled good-humored mockery at her earnestness. " As you see, I survived," said he.

She frowned at him. " You're very disappointing," said she. " You're not a bit romantic—are you? "

" I save it all for my painting."

She laughingly put out her hand. They shook hands ; he accompanied her to the door. She said: " I'd like to have a name to remember you by." And she looked at him with candid and friendly admiration for his handsome bigness. "Not your real name. That wouldn't be a bit romantic—and, as you see, I'm crazy about romance." She sighed. "Probably because I never get any. Don't laugh at me. You can't understand my taste for candy, because with you—it's been like keeping a confectionery shop."

"Yes—that's true," said he, looking at her with a new and more personal friendliness of sympathy.

"So," said she, with a wistful smile, "give me a name."

He reflected. "You might call me Chang. That was my nickname at school."

"Chang," said she. "Chang." She nodded approvingly. "I like it. . . . They called me Rix before I came out."

"Then—good-by, Rix. Thank you for a charming hour."

"Good-by, Chang," she said, with a forced little smile and pain in her eyes. "Thank you for—the fire and the chocolate—and—" She hesitated.

"Don't forget the biscuit."

"Oh, yes. And for the biscuit."

As she went reluctantly away he closed the door and, standing well back from the window, watched her gracefully descend the slope of the knoll. Just as she was about to lose sight of the little house she turned and looked back. She could not have seen him, so far back was he; but she waved her hand and smiled precisely as if he were in plain view, waving at her.

II

LAKE WAUCHONG is the crowning charm of that whole north New Jersey wilderness, rich though its variety is—watercourses hard to equal in sheer loveliness; lonely mountains from whose steeps look majesty and awe; stretches of stony desolation and of gloomy, bittern-haunted swamp that seem the fitting borderland of an inferno. At the southwestern end of the lake it receives the waters of a creek by way of a small cataract. In the spring, especially in the early spring, when there is most water on the cataract and when the foliage is at its freshest, most exquisite green, the early morning sunbeams make of that little corner of the lake a sort of essence and epitome of the lovely childhood of Nature.

On the next morning but one after the adventure of the studio in the storm, Roger was industriously sketching in a view of this cataract, his canvas on an easel before which he was standing—he always stood at his work. Across his range of vision shot a canoe, a girl kneeling in it and wielding the paddle with expert grace. He instantly recognized her. "Hello!" he called out friendlily—after a curiously agitated moment of confusion and recovery.

She turned her head, smiled. With a single skillful dip she rounded the canoe so that it shot to the shore within a few feet of where he stood. "Good morning, Chang," said she. "Did you miss me at tea—or, rather, chocolate—yesterday?"

"I didn't expect you," replied he.

"You didn't invite me."

"That was ill-mannered, wasn't it? But, no—I forgot. We said good-by forever, didn't we? Well, it was safer to prepare for the worst in a world as uncertain as this. Aren't you rather early?"

She looked a little confused. "I'm very energetic for the first few days after I get to the country," she explained. "Besides, I'm dreadfully restless of late. . . . Are you working?"

"I was."

"Oh—I'm disturbing you." She made a movement to push off. He smiled in a noncommittal way, but said nothing. She did not conceal her discontent with treatment of a kind to which she apparently was not used. "You might at least have the politeness to say no. I'd not take advantage of it," said she—a rebuke for his rudeness in her raillery.

"I was debating something. . . . I need you in my picture. But posing is tiresome work."

She brightened. "I'd be glad to. Will you let me? I do so wish to be of some use. How long would it take?"

"Not long—that is, not long any one morning," was his apologetic assurance.

"You mean — several mornings?" said she, a mingling of longing and hesitation in her expressive features.

"I work slowly." The more he considered the matter the more necessary she seemed to his picture. His artist's selfishness was aroused. "I'm sure you'd not mind," said he, deliberately using a tone that would make refusal difficult, ungracious.

A curious strained expression came into her eyes as she reflected. "I—I—don't know what to say."

"You think I'm asking heavy pay for my hospitality?"

"No—no, indeed," protested she earnestly. "I can't tell you what I was thinking."

The more he considered the idea the apparition of her in that graceful posture in the canoe had suggested the more it seemed an inspiration. He was regarding her now with the artist's eye only. She leaned on her paddle, lost in reverie; the look of the self-satisfied, over-petted American girl faded from her face; the sunbeams flung a golden glamour over her yellow hair and her delicate skin. He saw alluring possibilities of idealizing her face into the center and climax of the dreamy romance he was going to try to make of his first American picture. His original impulse to get rid of her as a useless, perhaps disquieting intruder had gone altogether. He was resolved to have this providential model. "I don't want to be disagreeable," said he, "but I really need you. It'd be a—a service to "—he smiled—" to art."

She seemed not to hear. Presently she compressed her lips, looked at him defiantly—a strange look that somehow disquieted him for an instant. "Where do you want me to put myself?" she asked, stepping into the canoe.

They spent half an hour in trying various positions and poses before he got just what he wanted. His impersonal way of treating her, his frank comments, some of them flattering, others the reverse, amused her immensely. But he was as unconscious of her amusement as of her personality or his own. She obeyed him without a protest, patiently held the pose he asked—held it full fifteen minutes. He had a way—the way of the man who knows what he is about—that inspired her with respect and made her feel she was at something worth while. "That'll do beautifully," he said at last. "You must be tired."

"I can stand it a while longer," she assured him.

"Not a second. I've enough for to-day. And I don't want to frighten you off. I mustn't tempt you to leave me in the lurch—disappear—never show up again."

"I've promised," said she. "I'll keep my word. Besides "—she flushed, with eyes sparkling; her smile was merry, but embarrassed—"I'm not doing this for nothing."

"We haven't talked business yet, have we?" said he, not a bit embarrassed. "You can have anything you like, within reason."

She laughed at him. "I want more than money. I want your valuable time. In exchange for my services as model you must amuse me. I'm lonely and bored—and full of things I want to forget."

"How much amusement per pose?" said he.

"Oh—I shan't be hard. Say—an hour."

"The bargain's closed."

She paddled ashore, seated herself on a log a short distance before him, and rested while he filled in his notes. He glanced at her after a few minutes, was about to speak; instead he gave a grunt of satisfaction, fell to sketching her face; for the thoughts that were gilding her reverie gave her features precisely the expression of exalted, ethereal longing which he wished to put into the face in his picture. He worked feverishly, hoping she would not move and dissolve the spell until he had what he needed—enough to fix that expression.

A quarrel between two robins over a worthless twig which neither wanted startled her, drove the spiritual look from her features.

"But I got it," said he. "Thank you."

She looked at him questioningly.

"You've given me a second sitting—much better, because you didn't realize it."

"May I see?"

His sudden alarm revealed the profoundly modest man, uneasy about the merits of his unfinished work. "Not yet," said he positively. "Wait till there's something to look at."

"Very well," she acquiesced.

A certain note in her voice made him laugh. "You don't care in the least about the picture—do you?"

"Yes, indeed," protested she. But the attempt to conceal his having hit upon the truth was far from successful. She realized it herself. "I care only about the pay," confessed she.

"We can talk while I work, now."

She protested. "No, that isn't honest. I gave you my whole attention. You must pay in the same way. You must do your best to amuse me."

"Well?"

"Come here, and sit on this log."

He obeyed. "You deserve better pay," said he. "I never had a professional model who behaved so well."

"Do you know, I never did anything so obediently in my whole life," declared she. "I don't understand myself." There was seriousness behind the mirth in the glance she flung at him. "I'm a little afraid of you. I half believe you hypnotize me. You—seem to —to put to sleep my ordinary, every-day self and to wake up one that's usually asleep—one I've only known —until—until recently—as a—a sort of troublesome ghost that haunts me from time to time."

He, thinking of his picture, was only half attending to her. "But you'll marry the man with the money, all right," said he absently.

She startled. "How did you know?" she demanded. "Have you found out who I am?"

"Certainly. You're Rix, model to Chang. . . . No, I was joking. I know only what you told me yesterday—or, rather, what you enabled me to guess."

"And you approve of my marrying—that way?"

" I'd hardly be guilty of the impertinence of either approving or disapproving."

" Frankness wouldn't be impertinence—between you and me. At least, that's the way I feel about it. Do you really approve of—of marriage for—for other reasons than love? "

" Heartily."

A long silence. Then she, with an effort: " When I got back home night before last all that happened up there seemed unreal—absolutely unreal—like a dream."

" Even the biscuit and the chocolate? "

" Even you," she replied.

Her tone made his wandering attention concentrate, made him glance swiftly at her.

She smiled. " Don't be alarmed," said she. " There's not the slightest cause."

" Sure? " inquired he jestingly. " You see, I'm not used to young girls—American girls. You talk so freely. If I weren't an American I'd misunderstand."

" What would it matter if you did? " retorted she.

" To be sure—it wouldn't matter at all," he admitted. " Do go on."

" If it weren't that my knowing you—this way— would always seem unreal—not at all a part of life— I'd not dare come. Now, don't misunderstand. That doesn't mean I'm falling in love with you—at least, I don't think it does." Dreamily—"No, I don't think so."

"Depressing," said he, with an awkward attempt at humor. He did not like these frank personalities from his model—these alarming skirtings of the subject he wished to discuss or consider with no woman. It was interesting, refreshingly interesting, this unheard-of, direct way of dealing with a matter invariably ignored by an unmarried, marriageable girl—that is, so far as his experience went, it was ignored—but, perhaps, in the America growing up during his absence—yes, this interesting audacity was disquieting.

"No—I've thought it out carefully, Chang," pursued she. "I'm not afraid of falling in love with you. It's simply that what you are—what you stand for—appeals to my other self—the self I'm soon going to wrap in a shroud and lay in a grave—forever. . . . Coming here is a kind of dissipation for me. But I shan't lose control of myself." She nodded positively, and there was a shrewd flash in her eyes.

"I'll back you up," said he. "So you needn't worry. Falling in love is entirely out of my line."

He saw that she had no more belief in this than the next woman would have had. For, little though he knew about women—the realities as to women, the intricacies of women—he had not failed to learn that

28

every young or youngish woman regards herself as an expert at compelling men to love, as a certain victor whenever she cares to exert herself to win. "You have your career, I mine," he went on. "They have nothing in common. So we needn't waste time worrying about impossibilities."

"That's true," exclaimed she with enthusiasm.

He changed the subject to safer things, acting as if the whole matter of their relations were settled. But, in reality, he was profoundly disturbed. If the scheme of his picture had not taken such firm hold upon him— the hold that compels an artist, in face of any debt to consequences, however heavy—he would have contrived to rid himself of her that day for good and all. He had had too many adventures not to know the dangers filling the woodland in the springtime for a young man and a young woman with no one to interrupt. He did not like his own interest in her; he was little reassured by her explanations as to her interest in him, though he told himself he must be careful not to judge American girls by foreign standards. But the picture must be made, and she was indispensable.

The bright weather held for several days. Every morning artist and model met near the cascade and worked and talked alternately until toward lunch time.

She came earlier and earlier, until it was hardly six when her canoe shot round the bend which divided off that end of the lake into a little bay. He was always there before her. "Do you spend the night here?" she asked.

"Why, this is late for me," he replied. "I have breakfast before sunrise and go up to the studio for an hour's work before I come down here. You see, light—sunlight—is all-important with me. So I go to bed with the chickens."

"You don't live at the studio?" Then she reddened and hastily cried: "No—don't answer. I forgot."

At her suggestion they had been careful about letting slip things that might betray their identity in the outside world. This had become a fetich with them, as if betrayal would break the charm and end their friendship. "I never had anything like a romance in my life before," she had said. "I suppose I seem very silly to you, but I want to do the best I can with this. You'll humor me, won't you?" And he agreed, with a superior smile at her folly—a smile not nearly so sincere as he fancied, for, like all men of his stamp, he was still the boy and would be all his life.

Though she came earlier she lingered later; once it was noon before she slowly paddled away in her

graceful canoe with its high, curved ends. His uneasiness about what was going on in her head ended
with her second visit; for she did not again speak of
personal things and treated him in a charming, com-
radelike fashion that would have quieted the suspicions
of a greater egotist than he. She made him do most
of the talking—about painting and sculpture, about
books and plays—the men he had known in Paris—
about his curious or amusing experiences in out-of-the-
way parts of Europe. It was flattering to have such
a pretty listener, one so tireless, so interested; her
many questions, the changes in her expressive countenance, the subtle sense of the sympathetic she radiated,
were all proof convincing of her eagerness to hear, of
her delight in what she heard.

After many days—not so very many, either—when
their friendship was well into the stage of intimacy,
she began to try to draw him out on the subject of
women. At first she went about it adroitly—and an
adroiter cross-examiner never put questions seemingly
more trivial in tones seemingly more careless or lay
in wait behind eyes seemingly more innocent. But she
set her traps in vain. Of the love affairs of other men
he would talk, taking even more than the necessary care
to avoid things a young girl was supposed not to know
or understand. Of his own love affairs he would say

nothing—not a hint, not so much as a suggestion that romance had ever gladdened his youth. That chance allusion to the mysterious Syrian woman was his first and last indiscretion, if anything so vague could be called an indiscretion. So, she abandoned the tactics of guile and attacked him frankly.

"You certainly are trustworthy," said she. "You have a wonderful sense of honor."

"What's this about?" inquired he, ignorant of her train of thought.

"About women," explained she.

"Oh, about women," repeated he. "It's time to begin work again."

"Not for twenty minutes. You kept me at it ten minutes' overtime—and you agreed I was to have double pay for overtime."

He sat down again, a little cross.

"As I was saying," pursued she, "you never talk about yourself and women—except the Syrian girl. Were you *terribly* in love with her?"

"That's been so long ago. I don't recall——"

"I'm sure she was crazy about you—and that you got tired of her—and broke her heart——"

He laughed. "She's married to a friend of mine, and she weighs a ton. They've got a rug shop and how they do swindle rich Americans! Did I ever tell you

32

about how two men in Paris bought a rug for eleven thousand francs and sold it to an American for——"

"Why do you always dodge away? Are you really a woman hater?"

"Not I. Just the reverse."

"And you've been in love?"

"Yes, indeed."

Her smile kept bravely on, but her tone wasn't quite the same as she said, "*Really* in love?"

"Madly. Lots of times."

"I don't mean that. I mean once—*the* once. I somehow feel that you've had a great love in your life —a love that has saddened you—has made you put women out of your life."

He was laughing frankly at her. "What a romancer you are," cried he. "It's very evident that you've had no experience. If you had, you'd know that isn't the way of love at all. Anyone who can catch it once can catch it any number of times. It's a disease, I tell you. You want to fall in love and you proceed to do it, taking whoever happens to be convenient."

This seemed to content her. "I see you've never been in love," said she. "You've simply had experience. I like that. I hate a man who hasn't had experience. Not that I ever thought you hadn't—no, indeed. In the first five minutes I knew you I said to myself,

'Here's a man who has been over the road.' I could tell by the way you took hold."

"Took hold!" cried he.

"That's it—took hold—made me like you—made me interested in you."

He looked uncomfortable—glanced at his watch.

"Oh, so much has happened to you. And nothing has ever happened to me—nothing but this," she sighed.

"But this!" laughed he. "Don't you call it something—to be clandestinely an artist's model? Think how horrified your prim, proper, pious people would be if they knew!"

"What kind of people do you think I come from?" she inquired, gazing at him quizzically.

"That's tabooed," he answered. "I've never speculated about it. When your canoe rounds that bend yonder I never follow. You begin and end at the bend."

"I don't see how you can help wondering," mused she. "I wonder a great deal about you. Not that I want to know. I'd rather wonder—fancy it as I please —differently every day. You see, I haven't much to think about—much that's interesting. Honestly, don't you wonder—at all—about me?"

"I've always been that way about my friends," re-

34

plied he, and went on to explain sincerely: "They interest me only as they appear to me. Why should I bother about what they are to other people—people I don't know and don't care to know?"

"Isn't that strange!" mused she. "Do you really mean it?" She blushed, hastily added: "Of course, I know you mean it. You mustn't mind my saying that. You see, the people I know are entirely different. That's why I feel this is all—unreal—a dream. . . . You honestly don't care about wealth—and social position—and all that? Not a bit?"

"Why should I?" said he indifferently. "It isn't in my game—and one cares only about the things that are in his game."

"That other game—it seems a very poor sort to you, doesn't it?"

He shrugged his shoulders.

"Yes, I know it does. It seems so to me, whenever I'm—here—and even when I'm not here."

"Why bother about such things?" said he in the tone that indicates total lack of interest.

After a pause she said: "You may not believe it, but I'm a frightful snob—out there."

"But not here. There's nothing here to be snob about—thank God!"

"Yes—I'm as different as possible—out there,"

she went on. "There are people I detest whom I'm sweet to because of what they are socially. I'm like the rest of the girls—crazy about social position and fond of snubbing people—and——"

"Don't tell me about it," he interrupted gently, but with an expression in his straight, honest eyes that made her blush and hang her head. "I'm sorry for what you are when the black magician who rules beyond the bend takes possession of you. But what he does to you doesn't change what the white magic makes of you here."

Her eyes, her whole face lighted up. "The white magic," she repeated softly. After a brief reverie she came back to the subject and went on, "I told you because I—I'm ashamed to be a fraud with you. . . . I wonder if you're really as big and honest as you seem? Nobody is—out there. They're mean and petty!— when you see through what they pretend to be—pretend even to themselves. I'm just as big a fraud as the rest. And I often convince myself I'm sweet and good and— If I could only—" There she stopped, leaving her wish unexpressed but easy to imagine.

"The way to keep the little things out is to fill one's mind with the big things," said he. "But you're not to blame for being what your surroundings compel."

36

"Do you think I could be different?" she asked, waiting in a sort of breathlessness for his answer.

"I've not thought about it," was his depressing answer. "Offhand I should say not. You're at the age when almost everybody does a little thinking. But that'll soon stop, and you'll be what you were molded to be from babyhood."

"I know I don't amount to much," said she humbly. "Out there—under the black magic—I'm vain and proud. But here—I feel I'm just nothing."

"You're a superb model," said he consolingly. "Really—superb."

"Please don't mock at me. Honestly, don't you think I'm commonplace?"

He gave her that fine, gentle smile of his, particularly fine coming from such a big, masculine sort of man. And he said, "Nothing that the sun shines on is commonplace."

She developed strong curiosity as to the general aspects of his affairs—as to his hopes and fears for the future. Her efforts to draw him out on these subjects amused him. His frank confession that he was unknown in America threw her quite off the track; it never occurred to her that he might be known abroad. "And you have worked many years?" she said.

" All my life."

She looked tenderly sympathetic distress. " Doesn't your not being recognized discourage you? " she said.

" Not a bit," declared he, with every indication of sincerity. " Everything worth while takes time. Anyhow, I don't much care. My living is secure. You see, I'm quite rich."

Her eyes opened wide. " Rich! " she exclaimed. " Really? Why, I thought—" There she halted, blushing.

" Oh, yes. I've got forty thousand—not to speak of my land."

" Forty—thousand—a year! That's *very* good." And her face revealed that her brain was busy and what it was busy about.

He laughed loudly. " Forty thousand a *year!* " he cried. " No—*two* thousand a year."

Her chagrin was pitiful. " Oh! " she exclaimed dismally. " I thought you said you were rich."

" And I am. Why, when I think of how I used to live on less than two thousand francs a year I feel like a Rothschild." He tried to keep his face and his tone serious as he added: " What's the matter? Why do you look so woe-begone? "

" Nothing. Only— You gave me such a shock! For a minute I thought you were—were different."

He took advantage of her mournful abstraction to slip back to his work. So absorbed was she that she did not observe how he was " cheating " her, though all his other attempts to do it had been promptly detected and stopped. From time to time he looked at her and puzzled over the cause of her deep gloom. Finally he decided to interrupt. A mischievous look came into his eyes. He said: " You thought of transferring yourself from that other rich man? "

She was overwhelmed with embarrassment. Then she met his laughing eyes with a brave attempt at mockery. " Well—I'd rather marry a rich man I liked than one I didn't."

" Naturally. But forget about me, please. I'm not a candidate, remember." He was glad of this chance to remind her of his views as to marriage.

" Never fear," said she, forcing a laugh and a look of coquettish scorn. " We're equally safe from each other."

On the eighth morning it began to drizzle at dawn, and by the time artist and model should have been at work a heavy, cold rain was falling. However, Chang in his waterproofs walked down to the lake shore. He had to take a walk—he always took a walk—no matter what the weather; why not in that direction? As he drew near the cascade he was amazed to see the canoe beached in the usual place. And there, huddled under a tree, as doleful as the shivering birds, stood Rix. He hesitated, started quietly back the way he had come. "No," said he to himself, "she might catch sight of me. Then she'd be offended—and what would become of my picture?" So he turned about—in obedience to these counsels of calm and unprejudiced good sense.

"What are you doing here?" he demanded with friendly severity as he came forward. "You'll catch your death of cold."

At sound of his voice her drooping form straightened ecstatically. At sight of him, looking more tremendous than ever in the big waterproofs, she gave a smile like a sunburst. "You're *frightfully* late!" she reproached.

"Late! We can't work to-day."

"You didn't tell me not to come if it rained," said she, with a convincing air of innocence. "And—I didn't want to lose a day's pay."

He was still frowning. "I came very near not coming at all," said he. "It was by the merest accident that I took my walk in this direction."

"But—you did," said she slyly.

"Why not?" was his carefully careless reply. "I walk, rain or shine."

"I don't mind rain, either—when I'm prepared for it," said she cheerfully. "You don't know how fascinating canoeing in the rain is."

But he was not convinced. He stood staring gloomily out over the lake, as if he were seeing formidable enemies approaching under cover of the thick, blue mist. "I've got to go in a few minutes," said he almost curtly. "I've arranged for a trip to town, as I can't work to-day."

"To sell a picture?"

"I haven't any. Those from the other side aren't here yet. Anyhow, I'm going to show only American work."

A long pause—an uncomfortable pause. Then she said in her artless, impersonal way: "I should think a wife would be of great assistance to an artist——"

"As a roper-in, you mean?" he interrupted fiercely. "No real painter would stoop to anything so degrading to his art and to himself."

"Yet you've told me of all sorts of queer schemes you've put up to lure in buyers," she said.

"An artist who marries is a fool—and worse," said he sourly. "If he's happily married his imagination is smothered to death. If he's unhappily married it's stabbed to death."

She listened sweetly and patiently. "The subject

4   41

of marriage is on my mind to-day," said she with con-
fiding and childlike innocence.

" It usually is on the minds of young girls," said he,
big and frowning.

" But my—my affairs are near the crisis," proceeded she. " And one reason I came through the rain
was that I wanted your advice."

He shook his big frame, making the water fly as
from the fur of a great, shaggy dog that has been in
swimming. " I don't give advice," said he ungra-
ciously. " When you give advice you make yourself
responsible for the consequences. Besides, I don't know
enough about you to be able to judge."

Her look up at him was the essence of implicit trust.
" You know more about me than anyone in the world—
more than I know myself."

He laughed shortly. " I know nothing about you.
Girls are not in my line."

Her pretty face, the prettier for the dreariness all
round, now took on an expression of hurt feelings.
" What's the matter, Chang? " she asked gently.
" You're not a bit friendly to-day."

His face could not but soften before this sweet appeal. He said in a kindlier tone: " I think you ought
to go home. I'm sure you'll catch cold."

She looked immensely relieved. " Oh, that's why

you're cross, is it?" said she gayly. "Don't worry about me, Chang. I'm as dry and snug as can be. Now, do be kind to me. I don't see how I'm going to marry Pete—that is, this man. He's a nice fellow— good-looking—has everything I want—but— Ye gods! He's such a rotter!"

"What's that?"

"It's a man—or woman, for there are lots and lots of female rotters—it's a person who—well, you always know just what they are going to do before they do it, and just what they're going to say before they say it."

"That sounds like good marrying material. You know, you don't want surprises in married life."

"Chang, how *can* I live through it?" she cried despondently.

"You say you've got lots of tastes, all expensive. So—marry him."

"He's really very good-looking," pursued Rix, watching him out of the corners of her eyes. "And he dresses beautifully—has everything just right. There isn't a thing against him—except—" And there she halted, as if she were not quite certain whether after all there was a positive objection to the man.

"Except—what?" inquired he, impatient at the long pause at the most exciting point in the recital.

She secretly delighted in the success of her ruse.

But she said plaintively: "Oh, you're not interested. You're not listening."

"I'm sure you're catching a hideous cold. Of all the absurd, silly performances——"

"Now, don't lecture on health. I simply can't stand it. As I was about to say when you interrupted me——".

"I didn't interrupt you," protested he.

"Not paying attention is interrupting," said she. "Anyhow, you're interrupting now. What I want to say is, the only thing against him is that I don't love him."

This seemed to cheer the big, dark, young man. With a certain gayety he replied: "But you soon will. You've been well brought up, haven't you? Well, that means you are—just girl—ready to be whatever your husband chooses to make of you."

"That's true of most girls, Chang"—he winced each time she gave him that name—"but it isn't true of me—at least, not any more. You've put all sorts of ideas into my head."

He started back in dismay before her accusing, reproachful face, so sad, so serious. "*I?* Put ideas into your head? Why, you were buzzing and boiling with 'em the first time I saw you."

"But they didn't amount to anything until you——"

"That's like a woman!" he exclaimed indignantly. "Trying to shift responsibility to some one else."

"But you have a tremendous influence over me."

"Rubbish! Have I ever tried to get influence over you?"

"I don't know how you got it," was her maddeningly feminine evasion.

He gave a kind of snort. "Next thing you'll be accusing me of advising you not to marry this rich man you're engaged to."

"Not quite engaged," corrected she. "He wants me to be. And," she went on with meek obstinacy, "while you didn't advise me against it in so many words——"

"Now, Rix," he almost shouted, pointing his finger at her, "you stop right there!"

"Please, Chang—come in out of the rain. And don't talk so loud; it makes me nervous. I'm almost hysterical as it is."

He looked at her in terror. All that would be needed completely to upset him would be for her to have hysterics. He moved nearer her, went on in a soothing, persuasive tone: "I advised you to marry him. I showed you it's the only thing for you to do."

"And such talk was unworthy of you," said she, like a rebuking angel. "You didn't really mean it.

You know *you* wouldn't stoop to do such a thing yourself."

His frank countenance had quite a wild look, so agitated and confused was he by her swift twistings and turnings, so alarmed was he as he felt the awful danger approaching. "We're not talking about me. We're talking about you and your affairs—or, rather, *you* are talking about them. Keep *me* out of this."

"But how can I?" argued she gently, looking admiringly up at him. "You've become the big influence in my life. If I had known you earlier I'd have been very different. Even now I feel as if a great change were coming over me——"

"It's the cold you're catching," interrupted he, in desperate attempt to be jocose and create a diversion. "You must go straight home."

"Chang," she said, laying her hand on his arm, "if you were rich, instead of poor, would you talk to me like this?"

"Now, Rix—stop that nonsense."

"Don't, Chang," she pleaded. "You realize, just as well as I do, that we've made a frightful mistake."

He did not venture an answer.

"You knew it as soon as you saw me this morning—didn't you?" continued she. "Yes, I saw it in your eyes. I felt it in your——"

He suddenly seized her by both shoulders, looked into her eyes searchingly. "This isn't a bit like you, Rix. What are you up to?"

She simply gazed at him—a gaze he found it hard to withstand; yet he could not shift his charmed eyes.

"You're trying to lead me on. Why?" he demanded.

"Because we love each other, Chang," she said as simply and sweetly as a child.

He laughed gently. "What a romancer you are! Fortunately, I'm a man. I don't take advantage of a baby."

"I'm twenty-two."

"And as ignorant of the world as a baby," declared he, like grandfather to grandchild.

"I know what I want when I see it, just as well as you do, Chang," she replied steadily. "Better—because you're making me do all the talking—which isn't gentlemanly of you." Her eyes filled with tears—and very lovely they looked—like dew-drenched violets. "If it wasn't that you're holding back simply because you're poor I'd not forgive you so easily."

He dropped his hands from her shoulders, turned away abruptly. He strode to the edge of the lake and debated with himself. When he came back to her he was serene though grave. At sight of his expression, which she had eagerly awaited, she shivered. "Rix," he said—and all the fine frankness and simplicity of his nature were in his eyes and his voice—"it's lucky for you that I've lived a little, or we might be dragging each other into a fearful mess. You think you've fallen in love—don't you?"

"I know it, Chang," she answered, undaunted.

"Well, I know you haven't fallen in love with me. You've simply fallen in love with love. Your imagination has been giddied by this little adventure that seems so romantic to you. And the day'll come when you'll thank me for having had the sense to understand you and to understand that my own strong liking for you isn't love, either."

"It's what *I* call love," said she, a solemn, wistful look in the eyes she fixed on him. "Don't you miss me and think of me all the time when we aren't together—just as I do? Don't you come earlier and earlier—just as I do? Didn't you fight against coming in the rain to-day, just as I did? Weren't you dreadfully afraid you'd be disappointed, just as I was? And didn't you simply *have* to come——"

He suddenly lost his temper. "This is too exasperating!" he cried. "I've done wrong to let you come here. I was innocent enough in it——"

"You couldn't have kept me away," she interrupted

with a kind of childish glee. " The mischief was done the first day—over the chocolate. Wasn't it, Chang?— honestly, wasn't it? "

" You're a nice little girl, but——"

She cut him off again: " If you knew how I fought that evening and night and all the next day and night— and how early I started out to find you. Had you be- gun to hunt for me? "

" No," said he, more curt than convincing.

" Then what were you thinking about—that first morning down by the waterfall? "

He flushed guiltily. Very poor, indeed, at all kinds of deception was Chang—except, possibly, self-decep- tion.

" I watched you for half an hour. You were sketch- ing a face, Chang—instead of the waterfall. Whose face was it? "

" Yours," he admitted, as if the matter were of no consequence. With a smile of patient indulgence he went on: " Oh, if you'd had experience! But you haven't. That's why you're carrying on like this. Now, listen to me, child——"

" I like Rix better," she interposed.

" No matter," he said, with a gesture of impatient brushing away. " I don't love you. I won't marry you. And you've got to stop proposing to me. I never

49

heard of such vanity! What would people think of you?"

"You've taught me not to mind what people think. You said you despised——"

"No matter what I said! What will you think of yourself? What will *I* think of you?"

"Why, that I love you," said she sweetly.

He looked hopelessly at her, threw out his arms in a gesture of despair. "A baby—just a baby. Go home and grow up!" he cried, and strode swiftly away with a great swashing of the skirts of his long coat and a great swishing of the disturbed undergrowth of the wilderness.

III

A LESSON IN WOMAN

TOWARD four the next afternoon Wade, at the studio, heard a knock on the door. He recognized it so promptly that one might almost have suspected he had been expecting it—or, would hoping for it be a more exactly accurate phrase? By way of answer he tiptoed across the floor, rested his full weight against the door, as there was no bolt, indeed no ·fastening of any kind but the unused outside bar and padlock. If that assault was to be repelled he must rely wholly upon his own unaided strength. He was not content with resting his weight; he braced himself and pushed.

The knock came again—right between his shoulder-blades with only the inch plank between.

It was as if those pretty knuckles of hers were tapping him on the back, on the spinal cord, which, as everyone knows, immediately radiates sensation to all parts of even such a huge body as was Chang's. He grew quite pale, then an absurdly boyish red. He muttered something that sounded like " damn fool "—and it certainly must have been addressed to himself.

51

The knock came the third time, quickly—a triumphant knock, seeming to say, "So you're in there, are
you? Well, surrender at once!"

He wondered how she had found out, for he certainly had made no sound she could have heard. With
the fourth and most vigorous knock he discovered the
secret. He noted that his body against the door made
the knock sound differently. He hastily lifted himself
away, put his hands against the door high up above
where she, merely a person of medium height, and woman's medium height at that, could reach. When she
knocked again he felt absurd. For the sound, hollow
once more, must reveal to her that there was indeed
some change of conditions within, proving beyond
doubt the presence of some intelligent—or, at least,
brain-using—being.

His poor opinion of himself and his fear of her
sagacity were forthwith justified. "It's only I," she
called. "So you can open."

The impudence! As if he were eager to see her,
would instantly open for her! Why, she was positively
brazen, this sweet, innocent young girl. No—that was
unjust. Just because she was innocent she did these
outlandish, outrageous things. Yet how could a girl of
twenty-two, out four years, extremely intelligent—how
could she be thus unaware of what was proper and mod-

est for a young woman dealing with a bachelor? How could she venture upon—no, not merely venture upon, but boldly tackle, grapple with—the subject which the maiden should never so much as hint until the man has forced it upon her? "I don't understand it," he muttered. "She's some queer mixture of craft and innocence. And where the one begins and the other ends I'm blessed if I know. There's some mystery in this. She's got some notion—some false notion—or something—Heaven knows what. All I know is, she's got to stop hounding me—and she's not going to get in."

As if she had heard these angry but cautious undertones she said: "Now, Chang, don't be a silly. I know you're against the other side of the door. I could tell by the way the knocks sounded. Besides, I've just peeped through the crack underneath and I saw your big feet."

Then he did feel like an ass! Caught holding a door, like a ten-year-old boy—he, a great, huge, grown man, no less than thirty-two years old! Still, of the two absurd courses open to him—to let her in and to continue to bar her out—the less absurd was the latter. To face her with a red and sheepish countenance—to face her mocking smile—that was not to be thought of.

"Don't be afraid, Chang," she scoffed. "I haven't got a clergyman with me."

"Run along home, you foolish child," he cried. "I'm busy and mustn't be interrupted."

"I must see you—for just a minute," she pleaded—the kind of pleading that is command. "Don't be so vain. Don't take yourself so seriously."

That voice of hers—it sounded sanely humorous. And he certainly was putting himself in the position of having egotistically believed to the uttermost her remarks of yesterday, which were probably nothing but a fantastic mood. But he simply could not open that door and face her plump off. He made three or four steps away from it on tiptoe, then walked heavily, calling out in a tone of gruff indifference: "Come on! But don't forget I'm busy." Luckily he happened to glance at the picture; he had just time hastily to fling a drape over it. He went to the fireplace and busied himself with the fire—for the day after the heavy rain was of an almost winter coolness. He heard the door open and close.

"Your manners are simply shocking," came in her voice.

He turned round to face her. No, she was not in the least abashed, as one would have expected her to be on seeing him for the first time after her proposal. What did it mean? What was in that industrious, agile mind? She was much better dressed than she had been

54

as his model. She was wearing a most becoming gray gown with a small, gray walking hat to match. Yes, she looked prettier, more ladylike, but—

"How do you like my new suit?" asked she.

"Very good," replied he. "But while you've gained something, you've lost more."

"I know it," admitted she. "I saw it the instant I looked at myself in the glass, and I've felt it all the way here. I've lost what you like best in me. That is, I've not exactly lost it, but covered it up. But it's still here." This last in a tone gay with enjoyment in teasing him.

He stood with his back to the fire, and waited. She came slowly toward him, halting at every second step. Her smile was mysterious—and disquieting. It was a mocking smile, yet behind it there lurked—what? *What* was the mystery of that proposal?

"Well, I suppose you'll be satisfied now," said she. "I'm engaged."

"I don't care anything about it," declared he. "Let's talk of something else."

They were facing each other now, not many steps apart; and the sight of her, in such high good humor, made it simply impossible for him to remain grumpy, or to pretend that he was. She went on: "I did it this morning—instead of coming to pose for you. I hope I didn't put you out too much. I couldn't think of any way to send you word."

"I wasn't there," said he. "I can finish the picture up here."

"Then you don't need me any more?" inquired she. And the little hands she was stretching out to the blaze dropped pathetically to her side and up went her face to gaze into his mournfully.

"I've done with models in America!" said he, laughing—not in very mirthful fashion, however.

Her eyes—they were innocent to-day—remained serious. "I don't see why you were upset by what I said," observed she reflectively, warming her palms. "You can't have had much experience with women or you'd not have been."

It was a notable proof of Chang's fundamental simplicity of character that this usually sure thrust at masculine vanity did not reach him, though he was only thirty-two. "You're not a woman," replied he. "You're a girl—a child—a stray from the nursery."

She shook her head. "No, I'm a woman. You've made me a woman."

"There you go again!" cried he. "Blaming me!"

"Thanking you!" corrected she gently. "But please don't get excited about—yesterday. How can we be friends if you begin to fuss and fume every time you think of it? Really, I didn't do anything out of the ordinary."

He dropped into a chair and laughed heartily.

" I simply proposed to you," said she.

" So you think it is ordinary for a girl to propose to a man—and to insist on it, in spite of his protests? Well—maybe it is—in America."

" I don't know," said she reflectively. " I never did it before."

" Really? "

" No," she answered him unsmilingly. " But I'm sure I'll do it again—if I feel like it."

" I wouldn't—if I were you. The next man might misunderstand."

" *You* didn't? " The gray eyes were not interrogative, but affirmative.

" Certainly not. I'm not so vain; and, besides, I knew you."

" That had a great deal to do with it—I mean, the fact that we knew each other so well. I shouldn't, of course, do such a thing to a perfect stranger." There was no suggestion of irony, of any kind of humor, in her voice. But he felt uneasy. She proceeded tranquilly: " I suppose any girl would—in the same circumstances—any sensible girl."

" I've never heard of it," confessed he. What did

she mean by " in the same circumstances "?   There
seemed a chance to penetrate into the mystery, but he
would venture no questions.   He contented himself with
repeating: " No, I never heard of it."

" Naturally," observed she.   " A girl wouldn't tell
it afterwards—and the man couldn't—if he were a gentleman.   I'm sure if anyone ever asks me whether I ever
proposed to a man I'll say no.   And, in a way, it is true.
Really, you were the one that proposed to me."   She
nodded slowly.   " Really, it was you."

" I ? " he exclaimed in derision.

" Yes, you," she affirmed, meeting his gaze gravely.

His eyes wavered; he confusedly sought and lit a
cigarette.

" Of course," pursued she, " I never could have
done such a thing if I hadn't known it would be—agreeable."

That word agreeable struck him as being a peculiarly happy choice.   He chuckled.   Her smile showed
that she herself regarded it as a rhetorical triumph.
" You'll have a chocolate—won't you? " said he.

" Thank you," she accepted, with eager gratitude.
" Won't you let me make it? "

He was already busy.   " I can't have you mussing
in my closet," he laughed.   " Though, Heaven knows, I
feel as if you were at home here."   It slipped out, be-

fore he realized what he was saying. He hoped she had not heard.

But she had. " That's it! " cried she. " *Don't* we feel at home and at ease with each other! I never felt that way with anybody in my life before. And I've an instinct that you never did, either—never so much so. . . . What's the matter? "

He had turned in the closet doorway, was gazing gloomily at her, and, being so big and so dark, his gloom was indeed somber—suggested the darkness of an enchanted forest. " After all my resolutions! " he exclaimed, with bitterness of self-reproach. He shut the closet. " No chocolate," he said firmly. " You must go home and let me work."

" Why, what are you afraid of? " cried she, an angry light in her eyes. " You told me yesterday you wouldn't have me. And now I'm engaged."

" You must go."

She stamped her foot, and in poise of head, in curve of brow and lip showed for the first time the imperious-ness she had told him about. " If I didn't like you so well! " she cried. " Do be sensible. You're always calling me a baby. It's you that are the baby."

" I think so, myself," said he, the more quietly but also the more strongly for her threatening outburst of temper. " Listen to me, Rix. This nonsense has got to stop. We're going to keep away from each other. We're not in love—and we're not going to put ourselves in the way of temptation." He looked reproachfully at her. " Why in thunder did you have to go and spoil everything with that chatter of yours yesterday? We were getting along beautifully, and the idea of you as a girl in the ordinary sense never had entered my head."

" You didn't understand yourself," said she. " Women are wiser about those things than men—the most foolish women than the wisest men. Besides, if you knew the circumstances as I know them, you'd not attach so much importance to what was perfectly natural."

He puzzled for an instant with this second mysterious reference to the " circumstance," dismissed it. " Anyhow, the milk's spilled," said he with determination. " And you must go and not come back."

" But now that I'm engaged——"

" Engaged be hanged!" exclaimed he violently. " I'm not as stupid as you think. Can't I see that you're up to the same tricks as yesterday? What do you mean by it? What's going on in the back of your head? No—never mind. I don't want to know. I want you to go."

She sat on the long, low bench and began to cry.

"You're brutal to me," she sobbed. "Here I went and got engaged just to oblige you and so that we could be friends. And now you won't be friends!"

He fretted about, glancing angrily at her from time to time until he could endure her unhappiness no longer. He rushed for the closet and began rattling the pots and dishes. "You are making an ass of me!" he cried. "I never heard of such a woman! No matter what I say or do, you put me in the wrong. . . . Dry those tears and I'll give you chocolate. But, mind you, this is the last time."

She removed the traces of grief with celerity and cheerfulness. She beamed on him. "I simply won't let us not be friends," said she. "I never had a friend before. I couldn't get along without you. You teach me so much, and give me such good advice."

"Which you take," said he, grumpily ironical.

"All of it that's good," replied she. "You wouldn't want me to take the bad advice, would you, Chang? No, certainly you wouldn't."

In the end he let her help him make the chocolate, guided her as she investigated the secrets of the closet—the easels and paints, the canvases and drawing paper. And she laughed at his pair of big, old slippers, and insisted on trying on a working coat full of holes and smelling fiercely of stale tobacco. Before he realized what was going on he was submitting joyously while she combed his hair in a new way—" one that'll bring out the artist in you." And then they had a picnic before the fire, and neither said a single word that would not have sounded foolish from the lips of twelve years old—foolish, mind you, not silly; there's a world of difference between foolish and silly, between folly and flatness. They had a hilariously good time, like the two attractive grown-up children that they were—both brimming with the joy of life, both eager for laughter as only intelligent, imaginative people with no blight of solemn-ass false dignity upon them are. And how thoroughly congenial they were! He did not awaken until she cried: " Good gracious! What time is it? Six o'clock? I must go this minute."

" Don't hurry. I'll take you home," said he. Then, with sudden virtue, " You know, this is to be the last."

She shook her head, laughing. " Oh, no. I'll be down at the lake, as usual, to-morrow morning."

" I'll not be there."

" Then I'll come on here."

" Now, Rix, that isn't square."

" Square? To whom? "

" To me—to yourself—to that chap you're engaged to."

"Are you afraid of falling in love with me?"

"No—not in the least," replied he, hasty and vigorous. "I don't think of you at all in that way."

"You think you'll hurt my vanity and make me angry."

"Nothing of the kind!" protested he crossly. "You simply can't get it through your head that I don't love you—that my life is settled along other lines."

"Then why shouldn't I come?"

His mouth opened to reply, closed again. His expression was foolish.

She laughed. "You *are* vain!" she cried. "You think the more I see of you the more I'll love you. Oh, Chang, Chang—what a peacock!"

"You've got a positive genius for putting me in the wrong. You——"

"Now, isn't it sensible," she interrupted, "for you to let me come—and get cured of my romantic nonsense, as you call it?"

"I don't need you any more. You only interrupt my work. And I've got a hard fight, making a career in this country. I——"

"You know you do need me. The picture isn't done."

"Why do you say that?"

63

"I saw it in your face when I first came and spoke about the picture."

She had him there. The picture did indeed need several days more with the model. He took another tack. "It's a mean trick for you to play on that—that fellow you're going to marry."

"He and I understand each other," said she with dignity.

"Does he know about—about this?"

"As much as is good for him. He isn't the kind of man that can be told the whole truth. A person has to be careful, you know, and judge the character of the person she's dealing with."

Her manner was so wise and serious that he could not but laugh. "I'm afraid Rix is—just a little deceitful."

"You seem very much interested," said she. "Well, I'll tell you all about it. Perhaps you can advise me better, if——"

He put up his hands. "Not a word!" he cried. "I don't want to know. I don't care anything about it."

"Please let me say just one thing. If you'll let me come——"

"But I won't."

"Oh, yes, you will," cried she, looking mockingly at

64

him, her head on one side. "You say you are devoted to your art. Then you've no right to sacrifice your picture to your vanity."

"My vanity! Well, I like that!"

"Your vanity. Your idea that on acquaintance you are more and more fascinating, instead of less and less so."

"I can take care of the picture."

"Oughtn't I to pose till it's done? Honestly, Chang?"

He could not lie when she put it to him that way. "Well, I will admit," he conceded with much reluctance, "the picture would be the better for a few more sittings. But they're not absolutely necessary."

"I have my right, too, Chang," continued she. "We're doing that picture together. I've got a share in it—haven't I?"

He had grown still and thoughtful. He nodded.

"So I insist that it must be done right. . . . Have you noticed I haven't once to-day said anything about loving you?"

"For Heaven's sake, Rix, don't talk that way. It gets on my nerves. It makes me feel like a jumping idiot."

"But have I said anything?" persisted she.

"Not in so many words," he admitted. "But——"

65

" I'm not responsible for what you may have read into my looks and voice, Chang. You know, you are so vain! . . . I haven't said anything, and I'll promise not to—to get on those shaky nerves of yours when I come to pose."

" That's a bargain? "

" Shake hands."

And they shook hands. " Now, I must go," said she. When he began to get ready to accompany her she forbade him in a tone that admitted of no discussion. " It's an hour from even dusk," said she. " Anyhow, I'm afraid of nothing."

" I should say ! " laughed he.

" Because I'm not afraid of you? Oh, you *are* vain ! "

" Till to-morrow? "

" To-morrow."

" And no more nonsense? "

" I thought it all out last night," said she. " I understand that you haven't got the money to support a wife——"

" Stop right there ! " commanded he. " Can't you ever get it straight? I don't love you—and you don't love me. That's all."

" Is my hat on straight? . . . I must hurry. . . . Well, I've no time to discuss. Only I do admire and

66

respect you for not wanting to marry a girl when you couldn't support her properly. Now, don't get red and cross and begin to bluster at me. I must go. Good-by."

And, without giving him a chance to collect words for a reply, she darted lightly and gracefully away.

IV

THE picture progressed steadily. There were no interruptions from the weather, and a paid model would not have been so regular as was Rix. But progress was slow. Roger blamed himself in part for this; he was a slow workman, growing slower always as his work neared completion. " I never saw anybody so painstaking," said Rix. " And you're just the opposite in everything else but your painting." The chief reason, however, for the snail's pace of this particular work was the model. Rix came early and stayed late; but, after their plain talk and agreement, her strength seemed to fail rapidly. She looked just the same; she had every sign of perfect health; but after ten or fifteen minutes of posing she would insist on a rest—a good, long rest. As he had no right to criticise or control this voluntary model, he could not protest. And, it being essential to the picture that the model keep on till the end, was he not merely doing his simple duty by his picture in trying to amuse and interest her during the long pauses? Not that talking with her

was a disagreeable task—no, indeed, or a task at all.
But his conscience, as a serious man bent upon a career,
needed constant reassurance that he was really not
trifling away the gorgeous lights of those long mornings in dawdling with a foolish, frivolous girl who
cared only for laughter—that he was not encouraging
his liking for her and failing in his duty as an honorable man, as her friend, to discourage her liking for
him.

"Don't be cross with me," she said one morning
when he fell into an obviously depressed reverie during
a rest. She had the habit of observing him as a woman
observes only the man of whom she believes that he is
more worth while as a subject for thought than herself.

"I'm not cross with you," replied he.

"Then, with yourself."

"Can't help it. I work so infernally slow—slower
all the time."

He thought he saw the diaphanous gossamer of a
smile flit swiftly across her face. But he could not be
sure; it might have been an imagining of his own sen-
sitiveness. "I read somewhere," observed she, "that
genius is the capacity for taking infinite pains."

"I'm hanged if I know whether I'm taking pains,
as I hope, or am just dawdling, as I fear and as you
believe. However, we'll soon be done."

"You say that as if you were glad."

"Oh, of course I'm pleased to work in such charming company," said he politely. His face took on the expression that always made her uneasy as he added: "Still, I never lose sight of my career."

"No danger of that," declared she, with a conviction of tone which she could have found it in her heart to wish insincere. "I never saw anyone so persistent and so—so hard."

He laughed at the absurdity of her calling him hard. What would she think if she knew what a relentless taskmaster he usually was!

"How much longer do you think you'll need me?" asked she.

"Not many days. Three or four, perhaps."

It was her turn to drop into depressed abstraction. She roused herself to say, "Won't you use me in another picture?"

He frowned—it was nearly a scowl. "No, indeed," said he. "I've—that is, I've imposed on you enough."

"You sounded as if you were going to say *I* had imposed on *you* enough," she reproached, with an air of aggrieved suspicion that was perhaps a trifle overdone.

"What are you laughing at?"

"I?" cried she with the utmost innocence. "I feel like anything but laughing."

He subsided. "Well, if you weren't laughing you ought to have been."

She rather disappointed him by refusing to take the bait. Instead of asking why, she returned to her original point. "Don't you think pictures with figures in them—especially women—are more interesting than just grass and leaves and things?"

"Undoubtedly."

"Then you've got to have *some* model. Why not me? Haven't I been giving satisfaction?"

"Indeed, you have. But I'll get a model who isn't so interesting to talk with—one who doesn't demand such high pay. Time is the most valuable thing in the world."

"Not mine. It's dirt cheap." She sighed. "I don't know what I'll do with myself when you get through with me," she said dolefully. "I've always been restless before. I see now I was right in thinking it was because I didn't have something to do— something useful."

The subject dropped. While he was as inexpert as the next strongly masculine man in the ways of women, he had intuitions that more than replaced analysis. And there was something in her increasing tendency to reverie that made him uneasy—that made him wonder whether this idle child were not plotting some new device for stealing more of his time from his career. " She'll get left, if she is," he said to himself. But he continued to have qualms of nervousness. She was crafty, this innocent maiden; she was always taking him by surprise.

There came a stage in his work when it did not especially matter whether he had a model or not. He let her continue to come, however—while he evolved how best to effect the separation. He felt certain she was simply making use of him in whiling away leisure hours that would otherwise bore her; still, courtesy demanded that, in ridding himself of her, he show consideration for her. After all, she had been most valuable to him, had helped him to make what he hoped would be regarded as far and away the best picture he had ever produced. " Never again! " he swore solemnly. " Never again will I work with anyone I can't pay off and discharge. Free labor is the most expensive. Something for nothing takes the shirt off your back when you come to pay."

She was posing in her canoe, well out from the shore. He was laboring at an effect of luminous shadow that would better bring out the poetry he had been striving to put into the expression of her face. A slight sound made him glance at the other shore of the lake—about two hundred yards away, in that little bay. At a point where his model's back was full toward them, two young men were standing staring at her. The expression of their faces, of their bodies, made them a living tableau of the phrase, " rooted to the spot." At first glance he was angered by their impertinence; but directly came an intuition that something out of the ordinary was about to happen. Swift upon the intuition followed its realization. One of the young men— the shorter, much the shorter—shouted in a voice of angry amazement:

" Beatrice ! "

That shout acted upon Roger's model like the shot from a gun it so strongly suggested. She glanced over her shoulder, lost her balance. Up went her arms wildly; with a shriek of dismay she rolled most ungracefully into the water. Her flying heels gave the capsized canoe a kick that sent it skimming and bobbing a dozen yards away. Roger lost no time in amazement at the sudden and ridiculous transformation of the serene tranquillity of the scene. The girl was head downward; her agitated heels were more than merely ludicrous, they were a danger signal. He flung down palette and brush, dashed into the shallow water, strode rapidly toward where Rix was struggling to right herself. He soon arrived, reached under, seized

6 73

her by the shoulder and brought her right side up. She splashed and spluttered and gasped, clinging to him, he holding her in his arms. It would have been impossible to recognize the lovely and charming model of two minutes before in this bedraggled and streaming figure. Yet it was obvious that for Roger there was even more charm than before. He was holding her tightly and was displaying an agitated joy in her safety out of all proportion to the danger she had been in.

"What a mess!" she exclaimed, as soon as she could articulate. "Where are those two?"

He glanced across the bay, located them running along the shore, making the wide detour necessary to getting to where he had stood painting her. "They're coming," said he. He spoke gruffly and tried to disengage himself.

Still clinging to him she cleared her eyes of water and looked. "Yes, I see," gasped she. "How cold it is! The one ahead is my brother. About the only thing he can do is sprint. So he'll get here first. You must act as if you knew him—must call him Heck—that's the short for Hector. I'll prompt him all right."

"Come on. Let's wade ashore." Again he tried to release himself from her. "The water's not four feet deep."

"Don't let go of me," pleaded she. "I'm a little weak—and oh, horribly cold!" And she took a firmer hold.

He did not argue or hesitate, but decided for the most expeditious way ashore. That is, he gathered her up in his arms as easily as if she had weighed thirty pounds instead of nearly one hundred and thirty— making no account of the hundred pounds or so of water she was carrying in her garments. As she had predicted, Hector distanced his taller and heavier companion and arrived well in advance of him. When he came panting to within a hundred yards or so of where she was wringing out her skirts Roger sung out, loudly enough for his voice to reach the ears of the still distant other youth: "Hello, Heck. She's all right."

"Heck" stopped short in astonishment. Then he came on, but at a slower gait. "Who are *you?*" he said to Roger.

Rix looked up from her clothes-wringing. "Call him Chang," she said tranquilly to her brother. "Hank mustn't know."

"What the dev—" began Heck.

"Shut up, Heck," Beatrice ordered in the tone members of the same family do not hesitate to use to one another in moments of extreme provocation.

"Don't try to think. You know you can't. You've certainly got sense enough to see that Hank must be made to believe that Chang and you are old friends." She added in a still lower tone: "Drop that hit-on-the-head look. He's not ten seconds away."

Hector had barely time for an indifferently successful but passable rearrangement of his expression when up dashed Hank, puffing, all solicitude. "You're not hurt very much, dear—are you?" he panted. "Might know—Heck's such an awful fool."

"Mr. Chang, Mr. Vanderkief," interrupted Beatrice.

Vanderkief, big and heavy, red and breathless, mechanically bowed. The effort of that conventional gesture seemed suddenly to recall to him the state of mind suspended by the catastrophe. He gave the big artist a second and longer and unpleasantly sharp stare. Roger returned it with polite affability of eye. "We must build a fire," said he, "and dry this young lady. Come on, Heck." The way "Heck" winced seemed to delight him—and Beatrice and he exchanged one of those furtive looks of sympathetic enjoyment of a secret joke that proclaim a high degree of intimacy and understanding. Said Roger to the stiff and uneasy "Hank": "Will you help, Mr. Vandersniff?"

"Mr. Vanderkief," corrected Beatrice. "While

76

you three are building the fire I'll retire into the bushes and squeeze out all I can of the lake."

Not without making Hank's eyes glint jealously and her brother's eyes angrily, but without either's overhearing, she contrived to say to Roger, " You'll help me out, won't you? "

" Sure," said he. " But my name's Roger Wade—not Chang."

" And mine's Beatrice Richmond."

" That's plenty to go on. Now, hide in the bushes. We must hurry up the fire." And he cried to Hank: " Come on, Vanderkief! "

Miss Richmond's teeth were chattering; but she delayed long enough to engage her brother aside a moment. " His name's Wade, not Chang."

" Good Heaven! " muttered Heck. " What's the meaning of all this? Beatrice, who on earth is the fellow? Why, you aren't even sure of his name! "

" Mind your own business," said Beatrice tranquilly. " He's an old friend of yours—of mine—of the family—an artist we met in Paris. Don't forget that."

Heck clinched his fists and drew his features into a frown that would have looked dangerous had his chin been stronger. " I'll not stand for it. I'm going to take you bang off home."

" And put Hank on to the whole business?—and

77

end the engagement?—and disgrace me?—and yourself?—and the family?" Everyone of these cumula-
tive reasons why Heck could not refuse to conspire she
emphasized with a little laugh. She ended: "Oh, I
guess not. I care less about it than you do. Be careful, or I'll give it away, myself. It would be such
fun!"

Hector, despite his anger, gave an appreciative
grin, for he had a sense of humor.

"Behave yourself," said Beatrice. "Go help get
wood."

"But what'll mother say—and father! Holy cat!
How father will scream!"

"Don't you worry. Do your part!" And Beatrice vanished among the bushes and huge glacial rocks.

Roger conducted his part in the deception with signal distinction. He so busied himself collecting huge
pieces of wood and bearing them to the central pile they
were making in an open space that he had no breath
or time for conversation; and as the other two men
could not but follow so worthy an example, not a word
was said. Besides, a glance at the face of either big
Hank or little Heck was enough to disclose how industriously they were thinking. Once Hank, finding
himself near the picture, began to edge round for a
look at it. He thought Roger was busy far away. He

literally jumped when Roger's voice—authoritative, anything but friendly—hurled at him: "I say there, you! Keep away from that picture! I don't let anybody look at my unfinished things."

"I—I beg your pardon," stammered Vanderkief, hastily putting himself where no suspicion of even peeping could possibly lie against him.

The fire was a monster, and Roger and Beatrice—who addressed him alternately as Chang and Mr. Wade —were soon drying out. They talked and laughed in the highest spirits, not unmindful of the gloominess of the silent, listening brother and fiancé, but positively enjoying it. Presently Beatrice turned to her brother and said, "I've persuaded Mr. Wade to accept mother's invitation."

Roger smiled agreeably. "Not exactly, Miss Richmond," parried he, as skillfully as if the stroke had not come without the least warning. "I couldn't be sure, you know."

Beatrice looked at the watchful Vanderkief—a handsome fellow, almost as big as Roger, but having the patterned air of a fashionable man instead of Roger's air of unscissored individuality. "Chang is still the toiling hermit," said she. "Mother's having hard work to get him even for dinner." She turned to Roger. "You must come, this once, Chang," pleaded she. In an undertone she added, "You owe it to me—to help me out."

"There's no resisting that," said he, but he did not conceal his dissatisfaction.

Vanderkief's jealousy would no longer permit him to be silent. He blurted out: "I don't see why you annoy Mr.—Mr.——"

"Wade," assisted Roger easily.

"I thought it was Chang," said Vanderkief with a slight sneer.

"So it is," cried Beatrice gayly. "But only for the favored few whom Mr. Wade admits to friendship. You know he's not like you and Heck, Hanky. He's a real personage. He can do things."

Hanky looked as if he would like nothing on earth or in Heaven so much as a chance at this big, impressive-looking mystery, with bare fists and no referee. "I was about to say," he went on, "it's a shame to annoy so busy and important a chap with invitations."

Roger looked at him in a large, tolerant way that visibly delighted Beatrice. "Much obliged, Vanderkief," said he. "But I'm fond of the Richmonds, and it's a pleasure to break my rule for them." He beamed on Heck. "I *am* glad to see you again!" he exclaimed. "I didn't realize how much I had missed you till I saw you once more. Isn't this like old times?"

"Well, I guess," said Heck on the broad grin. "It *is* old times!"

"But you'd better take your sister home now— walk her briskly every inch of the way. Really, she ought to run."

"No," said Beatrice. "I'm going back as I came."

"But who's to wade into that icy water for your canoe?" inquired Roger. "Not I, for one."

"Certainly not," cried she. "I spoke without thinking. I'll send one of the servants for it in a boat."

"Now, hurry along," said Roger; "and walk fast. And if I can arrange to come to dinner I'll send up a note this afternoon."

Beatrice was eying him reproachfully; but as Hank was watching her she did not venture to protest. "I'll see you to-morrow morning," said she.

"Oh, no—don't bother to come. I'll let you know when I need you."

"So this is where you've been spending your mornings?" said Vanderkief.

"Some of them," replied Beatrice. "It was to have been a surprise. Still— You didn't let them see it, did you, Chang?"

"Not a peep," he assured her.

Vanderkief's tension somewhat relaxed. Roger admired the innocent Miss Richmond. Really, she had been displaying a genius for deception—whose art lies in saying just enough and leaving it to the dupe's own imagination to do the heavy work of deceit. The parting was accomplished in good order, Vanderkief showing a disposition to be apologetically polite to Roger now that he had convinced himself he was mistaken in his first jealous surmises. "If you make a good job of Miss Richmond," said he graciously, "I'll see that a lot of things are put in your way."

Roger thanked him with a simple gratitude that put him in excellent humor with himself. After the three set out Beatrice came running back. "You saved me," she said. "I'm so ashamed for having dragged you into such a mess. But you must do one thing more. You *must* come to dinner."

"Can't do it," said Roger. "Here's where I step out."

This seemed to astonish her. She looked at him doubtfully, was so agitated by his expression that she hastily cried, "Oh, no, you'll not desert me. I admit it's my fault. But you wouldn't be so unfriendly as to get me into trouble!"

"How would I get you into trouble? It's just the other way. If I came to your house it'd make a tangle that even Vanderkief would see."

"No—no, indeed," protested she. "I can't stop

to explain now. *Don't* be so suspicious, Chang. I'll be here to-morrow morning—no, at the studio. Pete —that is, Hank—might follow me here. And now that you know who we are, don't you see there's no reason for——"

She laughed coquettishly, and away she sped, before he could repeat his refusal. To call after her would be to betray her.

As he was working in the usual place near the cascade the next morning she came upon him from the direction of the studio. "What a fright you've given me!" exclaimed she, dropping to the grass a few yards away. "I went up to the studio as I told you I would."

He had bowed to her with some formality. His tone was distinctly stiff as he replied: "My work compelled me to be here. Anyhow, Miss Richmond, it's clear to me, and must be to you, that our friendship must cease."

"You don't look at me as you say that," said she, obviously not seriously impressed.

"It isn't pleasant to say that sort of thing to you," replied he. "But your coming again, when you ought not, forces me to be frank."

"Why?" said she, clasping her knees with her hands. "Why must our friendship cease?"

"There are many reasons. One is enough. I do not care to continue it."

"How nasty you are this morning, Chang!"

He took refuge in silence.

"Surely you're not jealous of Hanky?" said she, with audacious mischief.

He ignored this.

"Don't look so sour. I was merely joking. Are you cross because I made you help me tell—things that weren't quite so?"

"I don't like that sort of business," said he, unconvincingly industrious with his brush.

"Neither do I," said she. "But what was I to do? You know, you forced me into engaging myself to him."

He stopped work, stared at her. The light—or something—that morning was most becoming to her, the smallish, slim, yellow-haired sprite—most disturbingly becoming.

She went on in the same sweet, even way: "And if it hadn't been for my coming here to act as your model I'd not have got into trouble. And, having got in, what was there to do but get out with as little damage to poor Peter's feelings as possible?" Then she looked at him with innocent eyes, as if she had uttered the indisputable.

Roger surveyed her with admiration. "You are—the limit!" he exclaimed. "The limit!"

"But isn't what I said true?" urged she. "What else could I have done?"

"True? Yes—true," said he, making a gesture of resignation. "I admit everything—anything."

"Now, do be reasonable, Chang!" she reproached. "Where isn't it true?"

"If I let myself argue with you I'd be running wild through the woods in about fifteen minutes. Tell me, does anyone in your family—or among your acquaintances—does *anyone* ever dispute with you?"

She reflected, ignoring the irony in his tone. "No," said she, "I don't believe they do. I have my own way."

"I'd have sworn it," cried he.

"You are the only one that ever opposes me," said she.

"I? Oh, no. Never! But in this one thing I must." He changed to seriousness. "Rix, I'll have nothing to do with your deceiving that nice young chap. That's flat and final."

"Isn't he nice, though!" exclaimed she. "I've always liked him since he was a little boy at dancing school with such a polite, quiet way of sniffling. He hates to blow his nose. You know, there are people

85

like that. I wouldn't hurt his feelings for the world. You see, everybody can't be harsh and hard like you. Now, you take a positive delight in saying unpleasant truths."

" I'm nothing of a liar," said he curtly.

" I like that in you," cried she with enthusiasm. " It makes me feel such confidence. You're the only person I ever knew whom I believed in everything they said."

He gave her a look of frank surprise and suspicion. " What are you driving at? " he demanded. " Now, don't look innocent. Out with it! "

" I don't understand," said she, smiling.

" Pardon me, but you do—perfectly. What are you wheedling for? "

" How *can* we be friends," pleaded she, " if you're always suspecting me? "

" We're not going to be friends," replied he positively. " This—here and now—is the end."

It was evident that his words had given her a shock —a curious shock of surprise, as if she had expected some very different reception to this proffer of hers. However, after a brief reflection she seemed to recover. " How *can* so clever a man as you be so foolish? " expostulated she. " You know as well as you're sitting there that we simply can't help being friends."

"Friends—yes," he conceded. "But we're not going to see each other."

"And what would I say to Pete?"

"Something clever and satisfying. By the way, how did you manage to get away with it when you reached home?"

She laughed delightedly. She was looking her most innocent, most youthful. "Oh, *such* a time!" cried she. "Mother— You don't know mother, so you can't appreciate. But you will, when you do know her. It was a three-cornered row—Heck and mother and I. Heck took a shine to you, so he was really about half on my side. I told just how I met you— the whole story—except I didn't tell the exact truth about the picture."

Her look was so queer that he said in alarm: "What did you say about it?"

"We'll talk of that later," replied she—and his knowledge of her methods did not allow him to receive with an eased mind this hasty insistence on delay. "Mother wanted to know who you were, and, of course, I couldn't tell her—not anything that would satisfy a woman like mother. She forbade me ever to see you again. I told her that, on the contrary, I'd see you this morning. She raved—my, how she did rave!" And Rix burst into peals of laughter. "You ought to have heard! She's so conventional. She accused me—but you can imagine."

"Yes, I can," said he dryly. "And she's right—absolutely right. We'll not see each other again."

"Oh, but she wants to see you," rejoined Miss Richmond. "She can hardly wait to see you, herself. She's badly frightened lest you'll not come."

Roger let his absolute disbelief show in his face. There must somewhere be bounds to what this resourceful and resolute young person could accomplish. These assertions of hers were beyond those bounds—far beyond them.

"It was this way," pursued Miss Richmond with innocent but intense satisfaction in her own cleverness. "I pointed out to her that, if I didn't go to you and keep on with the picture, Hanky—that's Peter Vanderkief—would realize I'd been flirting *wildly* with a strange man I had picked up in the woods and would break the engagement. And mother is set on my marrying Peter. So she sent me off herself this morning and took charge of Peter to keep him safe. Am I not clever?"

"I can think of nothing to add to what I have already said on that point," observed Roger mildly. "I am actually flabbergasted!"

"So was mother," said she with innocent, young

88

triumph. " And she used just that word. Here's a note from her to you."

Miss Richmond took a letter from the pocket of her jacket and held it toward him. He made no move to advance and take it from her. Instead he made a gesture that was the beginning of a carrying out of the boyish impulse to put his hands behind his back.

" Do you want me to get up and bring it to you? " said she.

" I want nothing to do with it," said he coldly. " I don't know your mother. I've no doubt she's an estimable woman, but I've no time to enlarge the circle of my acquaintances."

Miss Richmond once more seemed astounded by this unmistakable evidence of an intention on his part to end their friendship absolutely. She looked at him incredulously, then questioningly, then haughtily. She put the note in her pocket, rose and stood very straight and dignified. " That is rude," she said.

" Yes, it is rude," admitted he. " But you have left me no alternative. There is only the one way to avoid being drawn into deceptions that are most distasteful to me."

She eyed him as if measuring his will. She saw no sign of yielding. " You think I'm contemptible, don't you? " said she, her tone friendly again.

" I do not presume to judge you. You have your own scheme of life, I mine. They are different—that is all. I don't ask you to accept mine. You must not ask me to accept yours. You must not—shall not—entangle me in yours."

She leaned against a tree, gazed thoughtfully at the rainbow appearing and disappearing on the little waterfall. When she returned to him her face was sweet and sad. He glanced up from his work, hastily fixed his gaze on it again. " You are right—absolutely right," she said. " I've always done as I pleased. And everyone round me—the family, the servants, the governesses—everyone—has humored and petted me and encouraged me to take my own way."

" I understand," said he. " The wonder is—" But he deemed it wise not to say what the wonder was.

" You really can't blame me, Chang, can you, for having got into the habit of thinking whatever I please to do is right? "

" Certainly I don't blame you, Rix," said he gently. " Considering what you've probably been through, you're amazing. In the same circumstances I'd have been unfit to live."

" You don't despise me? " asked she eagerly.

" Despise you? Why, I couldn't despise anybody. It's a roomy world—room for all kinds."

"You like me? Not love," she hastened to explain, "just like. Do you?"

He smiled his friendliest. "Sure! You're about the nicest girl I ever met—when you want to be."

"Thank you," she said, tears in her eyes; and she dropped back into her reverie, he resuming his work. There was a long pause between them—a pause filled by the song of birds thronging the foliage above and around them, and by the soft music of the falling waters. "Sometimes I think it's an awful bad thing for people to have all the money they want—to be rich," said she pensively. "That's one trouble with our family."

"Why, you told me you had to marry for money," said Roger, much surprised. He hated liars; he was loath to believe that she had lied to him.

She looked miserably confused. "You didn't understand quite," she replied hastily. "And I can't explain—not now. You mustn't ask me."

"Ask you? It's none of my business."

"I didn't mean—I didn't mean to deceive you," pleaded she. "But—I can't explain now."

"Don't think of it again," said he, with a careless wave of one of his long brushes. It was no new experience to find that people supposed to be rich were merely struggling along on the edge of the precipice of poverty. Poor child, making one of those hideous sacrifices on the altar of snobbishness!—or, rather, being sacrificed, for she was too young to realize to the full what she was doing. Still, Peter Vanderkief did not size up so badly, as husband material went.

Silence for several minutes; she, seated again and studying his strong, handsome face with its intent, absorbed expression—concentrated, powerful. She did not venture to speak until he happened to glance at her with an absent smile. Then she inquired sweetly: " May I ask you something? "

" Go ahead."

" Won't you please come to dinner to-morrow night? That's what mother's note's about. It would be a great favor to me. It would straighten everything out. You won't have to do any further deceiving."

He went on with his work. After a while he asked: " Does your Peter think you love him? "

The color mounted in her cheeks. But it was in the accents of truth that she replied: " He knows I don't."

" And if I came I'd not be helping to deceive him as to what you think of him? "

" No—on my honor."

He looked at her. " No's quite enough," said he, in a tone that made her thrill with pride. " I think you · are truthful."

"And I am—with you," said she, her expression at its very best. "I'd be ashamed to lie to you. Not that I've always been quite—quite—painfully *accurate*——"

"I understand. You and I mean the same thing when we say truthful."

"Will you come?"

"Yes. Where do you live?"

She laughed. "Why, we're *the* Richmonds. Didn't you guess?" She nodded as if a mystery had been cleared up for her. "Oh, I understand now why you've acted so differently from what I thought you would when you found out."

He smiled faintly. "I suppose I ought to know. But I'm a stranger here. When I was here as a boy the city lawyers and merchants hadn't got the habit of coming up and taking farmhouses for the summer. Are you boarding or have you a place of your own?"

She had got very red and was hanging her head. Evidently she was suffering keenly from embarrassment.

"What's the matter, Rix?"

"I—I rather thought—after yesterday—you sort of—understood about us," she stammered.

He laughed encouragingly. "Good Lord, don't be a snob," cried he. "What do I care about where you live? I don't select my acquaintances by what's in their

93

pockets, but by what's in their heads. A while ago you said you were rich—and then you said you weren't——"

"Oh, I'm all upset," interrupted she. "Don't mind the way I act. We live on Red Hill. The house up there belongs to father."

"That big, French country house?" said Roger, surprised. "I've seen it. I'll be glad to see it closer." He painted a few minutes. "I suppose you put on a lot of style up there. Well, I've got evening clothes somewhere in my traps. I used to wear them occasionally in Paris, but not much. Paris doesn't go in for formalities—at least, not the Paris I know. . . . What time's the dinner?"

"Half past eight."

He groaned and laughed. "Just my bedtime. But I'll brace myself and show up awake. . . . I wonder if I've got an evening shirt." He happened to glance at her, was struck by a queer gleam in her gray eyes. "What now?"

"Nothing—nothing," she hastened to assure him. "Just some silliness. I'm full of it."

He went on painting, and presently resumed his soliloquizing: "May have to come in ordinary clothes. But that wouldn't be a killing matter—would it? . . . This isn't town—it's backwoods. . . . I've heard some sorts of Americans have got to be worse than the Eng-

lish for agitation about petty little forms. Are yours
that sort?"

"Mother's a dreadful snob," said she weakly.

"Well, I'll do the best I can," was his careless
reply. "Perhaps it'll be just as well if I have to hor-
rify her." He laughed absently.

"I hope you'll do the best you can," pleaded she.
"For my sake."

He looked amused. "You don't want her to think
you picked up a hooligan—eh?"

"Oh, I don't care what she thinks—not deep down,"
cried the girl. "I don't care what anybody thinks
about you—not really. But on the surface—I'm—I'm
a horrible snob, too."

"All right. I'll try not to disgrace you utterly."

She reflected absently. Presently she interrupted
his painting with "Heck and father are both small.
But Hank—I might send you down one of Hank's
shirts. He's almost as big as you—in the way of size.
And I could get my maid to borrow one from his
valet——"

His expression—amused, intensely, boyishly amused
—halted her. She had been blushing. She flamed scar-
let, looked as if she were about to sink with humiliation.
Then she lifted her head proudly and a strange light
came into her eyes—a light that made him quail.

" Anyway you please," she said—and the words came jerkily—" Anything *you* please." And she fled.

He stared after her until she was lost to view among the rocks and bushes. He held the brush poised before the canvas—laid it down again—gazed at the radiant figure he was conjuring in the midst of his picture. He drew a huge breath. " Well, to-morrow night will be the finish," he muttered. " And it's high time."

V

AN ATTEMPT TO DAZZLE

At a quarter past eight the following night Roger drove up to the vast entrance to Red Hill in the buggy he had hired from Burke, the Deer Spring liveryman. Five lackeys in gorgeous livery, with powdered hair and white silk stockings—five strapping fellows with the dumb faces and the stalwart figures the rich select as menial showpieces—appeared in the huge doorway. Three of them advanced to assist Roger. A fourth disappeared—to telephone the stables about this unexpected, humble equipage. The fifth stood upon the threshold, ready to take the hat and coat of the evening's one guest from without. The moon was high, almost directly above the towers of the great, gray chateau. By the soft, abundant light Roger surveyed the splendid, broad terraces that broke the long and steep descent to Lake Wauchong; the enormous panorama of untouched wilderness covering little mountain, big hill and valley far as the eye could reach—all of it the property of Daniel Richmond. Nearer, in the immediate neighborhood of the house were the elaborations of the

97

skilled landscape gardener. It was indeed a scene of beauty—beauty as well as magnificence—an interesting exhibit of the grandiose style of living wherein the rich sacrifice practically all the joys of life and most of its comforts for the sake of tickling their own vanity and stimulating the envy of their fellow beings.

As Roger advanced into the lofty, gloomily paneled entrance hall—its carvings had cost a fortune—he drew off his overcoat, disclosing evening dress that would have passed muster on a figure far less in need of ornamentation than his massive yet admirably proportioned frame with its climax of godlike head. And the most impressive feature of that head was the frank simplicity of the expression of the face—that expression which marks the man who is something and lifts him high above the flocks and herds of men who are trying—not too successfully—to seem to be something. The modern evening dress for men is one of the few conventions—perhaps the only one—not designed to bolster up insignificance by reducing all to the same level of smooth elegance. It is one of the curiosities of the history of manners how such a blunder came to be firmly established as a propriety. In evening dress, as in no other kind of costume or lack of costume, the personality, the individuality, of the wearer obtrudes itself to every eye. At a glance one may classify any number of men by their qualities and quantities of head and heart. Beatrice Richmond, coming along the corridor leading into the entrance hall from the east, stopped short at sight of her artist.

She herself, in an evening gown of pale silver, with lovely shoulders bare and graceful head looking exquisite under its crown of simply arranged, yellow hair, was quite a different person from the rather hoydenish elf of wood and stream whom Roger had been painting. But she had lost, instead of gaining, in the transformation. She was more beautiful, but much less fascinating. She had been leveled down toward the conventional. She merely looked what the newspapers call " a beautiful, young, society girl." Roger, on the other hand, had gained. He was retaining all his charm of the large, the free, the sincere, the natural; he now had in addition a certain refinement that yet had nothing of conventionality's cheapness. It was somewhat like the difference between a thoroughbred uncurried and curried. His natural proportions showed to better advantage in this sleekness than they had in the rough.

" What's the matter? " demanded Roger, as he took her hand. " Am I late, or is it the wrong evening? "

" Neither," she assured him, and it delighted her to note that he did not dream of taking to himself her pale and trembling joy in his splendor of manhood. " Noth-

99

ing much. Just—I was thinking this is the first time we've seen each other in civilized dress."

"Oh!" Roger evidently thought this not worth pursuing. "This is a wonderful place you've got here. It'd be hard to blame anybody for making any sort of sacrifice to keep it." He glanced round with the expression of a man used to such surroundings. In fact, there was nothing about him which in the remotest degree suggested the ill-at-easeness she had anticipated and feared. She felt humbled. He was again—and where she had least expected it—rebuking her nervousness over trifles and exaggeration of them. As they stood in the corridor, talking, she could discover not a trace of the awe she had confidently expected and hoped for. He treated her precisely as he had in the woods. But she was not discouraged. She felt that he must be deeply impressed, that he must be understanding now why she had taken the proposing upon herself—and must be appreciating what a fine thing that proposal was. He was concealing his feelings, reasoned she—was perhaps unconscious of them; later on they would show in results.

"I'll take you to mother," said she.

They turned in at one of the several doors, were facing a roomful of the sort of people one always finds in houses of that kind—carefully dressed, carefully patterned people, leading the monotonous life fashion imposes upon the upper class throughout the world. Beatrice looked round, then looked proudly up at the huge, young man whose expression made him seem to tower and loom, even among those physically his equals. "Father isn't here," she explained. "He hates this sort of thing for himself, though he tolerates it for us."

Roger found himself being welcomed by a youngish, shrewd-looking woman with a cold, discontented face. Beatrice's mother was merely a type—one of the kind the development of great fortunes is turning out by the score in every city and large town from New York to San Francisco: an indefatigable and not unintelligent seeker after the correct aristocratic pose. She was in simple black velvet. Her graying hair made her too-sharp face softer and more youthful. Her figure was as slim and straight as her daughter's, though not without evidences of toil and corset manipulation to give it that girlish appearance. Peter Vanderkief—Hanky—was beside her.

"So, you are really here?" she said cordially to Roger, as she gave him a warm hand clasp and the smile of an old friend. "I can hardly believe my own eyes."

"Impossible to resist," said Roger. "It's indeed a pleasure to see you again. How d'ye do, Mr. Vanderkief?"

101

Vanderkief forced a smile to his lips and extended a
tardy hand. But his brow remained sullen—not the
sullenness of suspicion now, but of jealousy.

" How is the picture coming on? " asked Mrs. Richmond of Roger.

" Oh, you know how those things go with me," was
Roger's subtly noncommittal reply.

" I remember," laughed Mrs. Richmond. " You
are the true artist. You're to take in Beatrice. She
tells me you still have your old horror of strangers."

" Not horror—shyness," protested Roger, with no
more shyness or suggestion of it than a well-brought-up
child.

Then a small, slim, dark man—obviously a Conti-
nental foreigner—joined the group. In dress and bearing he was a most elegant-looking person—or, rather,
personage. His fine, sensitive face was exceedingly
handsome. " Ah, my dear Wade! " cried he, pronounc-
ing the name as if it were spelled Vahd.

Roger's face lighted up. " D'Artois! " exclaimed
he, and they shook hands with enthusiasm.

" How are you in this country without my hearing
of it? " said Count d'Artois. " I'd not have believed
one so famous could move about quietly."

Mrs. Richmond and Beatrice—and Hank—were intensely interested spectators and listeners. D'Artois

turned to Mrs. Richmond. "Vahd must be extremely fond of you, that you are able to get him. In Paris they run after him in vain. He keeps himself hidden."

Mrs. Richmond smiled nervously. Peter stared despondently at the big man thus suddenly disclosed as a great man. As for Beatrice, her eyes sparkled and her cheeks flushed proudly. Roger's expression was good-natured tolerance, perhaps touched with annoyance. Dinner was announced and Beatrice took his arm. "I might have known!" she exclaimed, gazing up at him.

He reddened and frowned. "Known what?" said he.

"That you were famous."

"Trash!" observed Roger carelessly. "D'Artois is polite. Also, he is my friend."

"Oh, I know," said the girl. "At lunch he was talking about you—what a great painter you are—how rapidly you, though an American, were making yourself famous in Europe. We didn't dream he was talking of you. He pronounces your name peculiarly."

"I'm enormously hungry," said Roger. "Where do these people come from? I had no idea this was such a fashionable neighborhood."

"Oh, they're stopping in the house. Most of them came last night and to-day."

Roger ate and listened to the girl on his left—Alicia

Kinnear, the tennis player. Mrs. Richmond had Count d'Artois on her right, and he talked steadily of " Vahd." She listened sourly and from time to time shot a glance down the table at him—the glance of the alarmed and angry mother of a rather unmanageable heiress. Peter—directly opposite Roger—was as silent as he, but instead of covering his silence with appreciation of the Richmond chef he stared at the lace insertion of the tablecloth and crumbled and messed his roll. Beatrice was the happiest of the thirty-two at that table. She was radiant, ecstatic.

" Aren't you going to say a single word to *me?* " she inquired of Roger when he had finished the game course. " You can't still be ravenously hungry."

" I've eaten too much," replied he. " I'm stupid."

" It really doesn't matter, as I'll see you to-morrow morning."

" I'm not working to-morrow. I've got to go to town."

" Then the day after? "

" I may stay in town several days."

Her expression was so hurt, so depressed, that he felt guilty, mean.

" It's terribly hard to be friends with you, isn't it? " said she.

" Because I refuse to spend my time idling about?

You must choose your friends in your own class. No good ever comes of going out of it."

" I'm surprised at *your* talking about classes in this country."

" There are classes everywhere—and always will be. A class simply means a group of people of similar sympathies, tastes, habits and means."

" Means!" said she. " I was under the impression you despised money!"

" I?" He laughed. " No more than I despise food. Money is a kind of food. I want—and I try to get—all of it I need. My appetite is larger than some, smaller than others. I take—or try to take—in proportion to my appetite."

She nodded thoughtfully. It was in a queer, hesitating voice that she went on to ask: " And you really don't care to be rich?"

" No more than I want to be fat. And I want to be poor no more than I want to be emaciated."

Again she reflected. Suddenly she asked: " Do you like this house?"

" Certainly. It is beautiful of its kind."

" I mean, wouldn't *you* like to have such a house?"

" God forbid!" said he, and she knew he was speaking sincerely. " I've other things to do in my brief life than take care of property."

" But one can hire those things done."

" Yes, I suppose so," said he to close the subject; but unconsciously his glance traveled round the room, rested here and there for an instant on the evidences of slovenly housekeeping which always disfigure any great house for a critical observer. Her glance followed his. Presently she colored, for she understood. " You are a terrible man," said she. " You see everything."

" I wish I did," replied he, not realizing what she had in mind. " Then I'd paint the picture I dream about."

" Do you like these people? " asked she.

" Certainly. They seem very nice. They're most attractive to look at."

" But you wouldn't be friends with them? "

" Couldn't be," said he. " We have too little in common."

" Don't you want *any* friends? " she said wistfully.

" I have friends. I shall have more. People of my own sort—people who can give me what I want and who want what I have to give."

" You despise us—don't you? " cried she.

" Haven't I told you," protested he, " that I don't despise anybody? Why should I think people despicable because they are different? "

"You'd despise my sister Rhoda, who married the Earl of Broadstairs for his title."

"Not at all. I approve of her for taking what she wanted. Why should she have been a hypocrite and married for love when she didn't want love, but splurge?"

"Do you know why I was so anxious to have you come here?"

"How you do jump about!" laughed he. "Well—why? To smooth down——"

"No," she interrupted, coloring furiously. "I *must* be truthful with you. I wanted it because I thought you'd be impressed."

"And I am," he assured her, a friendly smile of raillery in his eyes. "I had no idea you were such a grand person."

"Don't jeer at me," she pleaded. "I'm in earnest. It isn't fair to mock at anyone who's in earnest—is it?"

"No. It's contemptible," said he. "But I understand you better than you understand yourself."

In defiance of conventionality she looked at him with eyes whose meaning no observer could have mistaken. He glanced hastily round. "Don't do silly, sensational things," said he. "You're making us both ridiculous."

"I don't in the least care," she declared.

He said sternly: "Now, my friend, I'm getting

107

just a little tired of this. You've always had your own way. You are piqued because you can't make a fool of me. So, you are willing to go to any lengths. I understand you perfectly."

Her gaze was steady and earnest—not at all proper for a public place. "Do you think I'm simply coquetting? Don't you realize that I'm in earnest?"

"Perhaps you think you are," admitted he. "You're so wrought up by your game of make-believe that you have partly convinced yourself. Luckily, *I* remain cool."

"If I were a poor girl you wouldn't act like this!"

"How did I act when I thought you were a poor girl?"

That silenced her for the moment. He went on: "You and I are going to be as good friends as our separate lots permit. And you are going to marry in your own class—are going to do your duty. I'll admit I did think it strange that a girl like you should be deliberately marrying for money. But at that time I thought you were poor. Now that I have seen what your life is, I don't blame you. I can see how you simply couldn't give up all this magnificence that has become necessity to you. It'd be like asking me to give up my painting."

She looked at him with a puzzled expression. "But

I'm not marrying to keep it. My father's much richer than Hank. Hank's not so very rich."

Over his dark features slowly crept a look like the fall of a winter evening. "Oh," said he coldly. "I thought— No matter."

"What did you think?"

"Naturally, I assumed—from your saying so much about your duty—I assumed your father had lost, or was about to lose, his money."

"Mercy, no!" exclaimed she, brightening hopefully. "I meant my family—my social—duty."

His expression was quizzical. "To be sure—to be sure. I never thought of that."

"You see, we're newcomers among fashionable people, while the Vanderkiefs—they're right at the top of the heap."

He nodded smilingly. "Of course—of course. A very sensible marriage."

"But I'm not going to marry him," cried she. "I never intended to."

He forgot where he was for a moment in his astonishment. "Then why did you engage yourself to him?"

"It isn't that kind of engagement," she explained sweetly. "I did it because *you* acted so. But I was square with Peter. I warned him I didn't love him and

109

couldn't. Our engagement is simply that he is having a chance to make me care for him if he can."

" You'll be married within six months," said Roger lightly; and he lifted a glass of champagne to his lips.

" Not to him," replied she. " If to anybody, to the man I love—the man who loves me."

Her words, so direct, and her tone, so simple, disconcerted him to such an extent that he choked upon the champagne. While he was still coughing Mrs. Richmond rose, and the men were left alone. Roger went with the first man who rejoined the women. He made straight for Mrs. Richmond, bade her good night and got himself out of the house before Beatrice, hemmed in by several people, could extricate herself and intercept him.

He did the homeward drive slowly, preyed upon by swarms of disagreeable thoughts. His experience of women had taught him to be more than suspicious of any feminine show of enthusiasm for a man; women were too self-centered, too prudent by nature and training, to give themselves out freely, even when encouraged —unless there were some strong, sordid motive. In this case sordid motive simply could not be. Nor could he conceive any practical reason why Beatrice should pretend to care for him—any practical reason why she should wish to marry him. He felt like a fool—as a normal man not swollen with conceit is bound to feel in circumstances such as Beatrice had made for him. And what vanity she had!—to fancy herself so fascinating that it simply could not be that he did not love her. And how poor an opinion she had of him! How little respect for him!—to believe that his reason for hiding his love was awe of her wealth and social position. " What can I have said or done to give her such an impression of me? " He could recall nothing that might have been twisted by her into a suggestion of that sort. No, the mystery was without a clew. " Am I crazy, or is she? " he demanded of the moonlit night. . . . And when was this thing to stop? Could Fate have dealt more irritatingly with him? He had come back home to make the grand effort of his life—to concentrate his whole being, every power of mind and body, every thought and feeling, upon the realization of his lifelong dream. And here was this girl, a nice enough girl, no doubt, an unusually attractive girl, as girls go, but still a mere idle, time-wasting woman with no real seriousness—here she was, harassing him, retarding his work, distracting his thoughts, involving him with a lot of people who had neither importance nor interest for him. In spite of himself he was being dragged into her life, whirled about by her caprices. He felt not only like a fool, but like a weak fool. "And what the devil can I do about it? How can I be insulting to a sweet, friendly girl who doesn't realize what she's doing and has been so brought up that she can't be made to realize?"

The only hopeful course that suggested itself was flight. "Yes—if she keeps this up I'll have to take to my heels." There his sense of humor came to the rescue and he jeered at himself. "A delightful person I'm becoming!—discussing what to do to escape from a girl who is madly in love with me!"

About the time that Burke, the liveryman, was once more in possession of his "rig," Beatrice, undressing for bed with the aid of her maid Valentine, received a peremptory summons from her mother by way of her mother's maid, Marthe.

Mrs. Richmond was established in splendor in five big rooms on the second floor of the east wing. She received her daughter in her office—a luxurious, library-like room with few signs that it was the seat of the administration of a household of forty-two servants. Indeed, Mrs. Richmond was little of an administrator. She nagged at and criticised Pinney, the superintendent, and Mrs. Lambert, the housekeeper. She picked flaws in accounts, usually in the wrong places. She delivered sharp talks on economy and extravagance. But things were run sloppily, as is bound to happen where the underlings learn that there is no such thing as justice, that criticism is as likely to fall upon good work as upon bad. The stealing and the waste grew apace; and though Richmond, each year, largely increased his wife's allowance for the maintenance of their various establishments, she was never able to put by more than twenty-five thousand or thereabouts for her own secret, privy purse.

Yet she was a most industrious woman, up early, to bed late. How did she occupy her time? Chiefly in taking care of her person. She was not highly intelligent about this. She wasted much of the time and most of the money she invested in the tragi-comic struggle for youth. Still, she got some results. Perhaps, however, most of her success in keeping down fat and wrinkles, and holding in her hair and her teeth in spite of self-indulgence as to both food and drink, was due to the superb constitution she had inherited. Mrs. Richmond came originally from Indiana; and out there they grow—or, in former days grew—a variety of the human species comparable to an oak knot—tough of fiber beyond belief, capable of resisting both fire and steel, both food and drink.

There was small resemblance between mother and

113

daughter save in the matter of figure. Beatrice's sweet and pretty face was an inheritance from the Richmonds, though not from her father direct. Her shrewdness and persistence were from her father direct. The older woman in the pale-blue dressing gown looked up sharply as the younger, in pink and white, entered. But the sharp, angry glance wavered at sight of the resolute little face wearing an expression of faintly amused indifference. She had long since taken her daughter's measure—and she knew that her daughter had taken hers.

"What did you send for me about?" Beatrice asked.

"You know very well."

"Chang?"

"Chang! What does *that* mean?"

"It's my pet name for our dear old friend Roger—Roger Wade. He calls me Rix. I call him Chang."

Mrs. Richmond seemed stupefied for the moment by this cool and candid shamelessness.

"I hate beating round the bush," pursued Beatrice. "So, I might as well tell you at the outset that I intend to marry him."

"Beatrice!" exclaimed her mother, electrified into panic.

"You know *me*, mother. You know I always do

114

what I say I'll do. Didn't I cut off my hair close to my head when I was eight because you insisted on those foolish curls? Didn't I——"

"You have always been obstinate and troublesome," interrupted her mother. "I've warned your father you would make a wreck of your life. But he wouldn't heed me."

"Father and I understand each other," said Beatrice.

"You think he will consent to your marrying that common, poor artist?" demanded her mother excitedly. "Well, for once you are mistaken. In some ways I know your father better than you do. And when it comes to any such insanity as that——"

"Don't agitate yourself, mother."

"He'll cut you off if you do it. I shouldn't be surprised if he should turn against you as soon as he hears you have thought of such a thing."

Beatrice listened calmly. "That remains to be seen," said she.

"I think you've lost your mind, Beatrice," cried her mother, between railing and wailing.

"I think so, too," replied Beatrice, dreamy-eyed. "Yes, I'm sure I have."

"This isn't a bit like you."

"No, not a bit. I thought I was hard as—as you've

brought me up to be. I thought I cared only for the material things."

" What *is* the matter with you? "

" I want *him*," said the girl, lips compressing resolutely. Presently she added, " And I'm going to get him—at any cost."

" Trapped by an adventurer! You! "

Beatrice laughed. " You ought to hear Chang on that subject."

Her mother started up. " You don't mean it's gone as far as that? "

" As what? "

" You haven't talked about such things to him? "

" Long ago," said the daughter coolly.

Mrs. Richmond, all a-quiver with fright and fury, moved toward the door. " I shall telephone for your father at once! "

" Do."

" We will have you put away somewhere."

" I'm of age."

Mrs. Richmond could not altogether conceal how this terse reminder had discomfited her. " Your father will know how to deal with this," said she, trying to cover the essential weakness of the remark by a savagely threatening tone.

" I hope so," said the girl, unmoved. " You see—

the fact is—Chang has turned me down. I've got to get father to bring him round—some way."

Her mother, at the door into the anteroom where the telephones were, halted and whirled round. "What are you talking about?" she demanded.

"I asked Mr. Wade to marry me. He refused. He is still refusing."

Mrs. Richmond, hand on the knob, seemed to give careful thought to each of these three highly significant little sentences. Her comment was even more compressed; she laughed harshly.

"I saw that he was an unusually clever, experienced man."

Beatrice looked quickly at her mother with shrewd, inquiring eyes. "You think he's afraid father will cut me off?"

"Of course that's it."

"I wonder?" said the girl thoughtfully. "I hope so—yet I'm afraid."

Mrs. Richmond's mouth dropped open and her eyes widened with horror. At last she said witheringly: "You—*hope*—so!"

The girl did not answer; she was deep in thought.

Her mother sat down near the door. "You *know* so. I see you are more sensible than I feared. You know he's simply looking for money."

"You don't understand me at all, mother." Beatrice leaned toward her mother across the arm of the sofa. "Haven't you ever wanted anything—wanted it so intensely, so—so fiercely—that you would take it on any terms—would do anything to get it?"

"Beatrice—that is—shocking!" As the word shocking had lost its force in the general emancipation from the narrow moralities that is part of fashionable life, Mrs. Richmond decided to bolster it up with something having real strength. "Also, it is ridiculous," she added.

"Father would understand," said the girl pensively. "He has that sort of nature. I inherit it from him. You know, they've almost ruined and jailed him several times because he got one of those cravings that simply have to be satisfied."

No loyal wife could have taken a better air and tone than did Daniel Richmond's wife as she rebuked: "You are talking of your father, Beatrice!"

"Yes—and I love him—adore him—just because he *does* things. He's good—good as gold. But he isn't afraid to be bad. He doesn't hesitate to take what he wants because he hasn't the nerve."

"Your father has been lied about—maligned—enviously slandered by his enemies."

"Don't talk rot, mother," interrupted the girl.

118

"You know him as well as I. You're afraid of him. I'm not. He knows he can rule you through your love of luxury—just as he makes Rhoda and her earl crawl and fawn and lick his boots—and the boys—even Conny, who's only fourteen. Oh, I don't blame him for making people cringe, when he can. I like to do that, myself."

The mother regarded this daughter, so mysterious to her, with mingled admiration and terror. "You are frightful—frightful!"

Beatrice seemed to accept this as a rare, agreeable compliment. "I've got the courage to say what I think. And—really, I'm not so frightful. I used to imagine I was. But "—she paused, laughed softly, a delightful change sweeping over her face—" just ask Chang!"

To Mrs. Richmond the words and the manner of them were like an impudent defiance. They drove her almost beside herself with alarm and anger. "Your father'll soon bring you to terms! You'll see, miss! You'll see." And she nodded her head, laughing viciously, an insane glitter in her bright, brown eyes. "Yes, you'll find out!"

Beatrice was not in the least impressed.

"All father can do is to cut me off. I've got five thousand a year in my own right—enough to keep body and soul together. So, he knows he's powerless with me."

" What a fool he was," cried her mother, " to give you that money."

" It isn't altogether the money," pursued Beatrice. " You've got nearly half a million put by out of the household allowances. And your jewels make as much more. Yet you're afraid of him."

Instead of becoming furious, Mrs. Richmond sank weakly back in her chair. " He's my husband," she said appealingly. " You don't understand how much that means—not yet."

Beatrice laughed softly. " No, but I'm beginning to," said she. However, she did not pursue that branch of the subject—did not force her mother into the corner of admission that the real source of Richmond's power over her was not wifely duty nor yet motherly feeling, but love of the vast and costly luxury which being Richmond's indulged wife got for her. All the girl wished to accomplish was to reduce her mother to that pliable state of mind in which she would cease to be the active enemy of her projects. Mrs. Richmond was now down to that meek weakness; through the rest of their talk her manner toward her daughter was friendly, sisterly, remonstrant rather than denunciatory.

"You don't realize what is the matter with you, Beatrice," said she.

"What *is* the matter with me?"

"You wouldn't understand— I couldn't explain— You have had no experience. If you had, you'd realize and control yourself."

"All I know is, I *must* have *him*."

"That's it, exactly," cried her mother. "That's the way it affects anyone who gets possessed by it. If you married under a spell of that sort you'd wonder at yourself afterwards—when you had got enough."

"But—I wouldn't ' get enough,' as you call it."

"Oh, yes, you would. They always do."

"*Always?*"

Mrs. Richmond shifted ground. "You will never get your father to consent—never!"

"That's the least of my troubles," said Beatrice confidently. "The only question is: How could he help me to bring over Roger?"

"How can you be so silly, child!" exclaimed the mother. "That fellow would jump at you just as soon as he found your father consenting." Mrs. Richmond smiled. "And when he did jump at you— Oh, I know you so well! You'd laugh at him and turn your back on him then."

"I wonder," said Beatrice absently. "I wonder."

" I'm sure of it," cried her mother with energy.

" I—don't—know," replied the girl. " It isn't a bit like me to marry out of my own class. At first I laughed at myself for even imagining I'd really marry Chang. I was fascinated by him—everything he said and did—and the way he said or did it—the way his hair grew—the way his clothes fit—the way he blew smoke out of his mouth—the way he held his palette— and his long brushes— You see, mother, I was infatuated with him. Isn't he *splendid* to look at? "

" He certainly is strikingly handsome," admitted Mrs. Richmond. " But hardly more so than Peter."

" Oh, mother! " laughed out Beatrice. " You are not that undiscriminating. There's all the difference between them that there is between—between a god and a mere mortal." Contrasting the two men seemed to fire the girl afresh. " Yes, I do want Chang," she cried. " I'd be enormously proud to have such a man to exhibit as my husband."

" But think, my dear! He's nobody! "

" You heard d'Artois——"

" Yes—but if he were to try to marry d'Artois's sister——"

" I know. I understand," said Beatrice impatiently. " I wish he were a *real* somebody. Still, he probably comes of as good a family as we do." She rose and faced her mother. "When I'm with him I'm ashamed of being so—so cheap. When I see him beside Peter I'd laugh at anybody who talked such snobbishness. But— Oh, I've been so rottenly brought up! No wonder he won't have me! If he knew me as I am he'd spurn me." Her expression softened to loving tenderness. "No, he wouldn't. He's big and broad. He'd understand and sympathize—and try to help me to be worthy of him. And I will be!"

Her mother looked at her with the uncertain expression one sees on the faces of the deaf when they are making pretense of having heard and understood. "You're very queer, Beatrice," said she.

"Ain't I, though!" exclaimed the girl. "I guess you were right a while ago. I guess I'm crazy."

"Don't you think we'd better go abroad right away, instead of waiting till June?"

"I've thought of that. But the idea of getting out of reach of him sets me wild. I'd not be able to stand it to Sandy Hook. I'd spring overboard and swim back to see what he was about. . . . Were you ever in love, mother?"

"Of course," replied Mrs. Richmond. "But I didn't fall in love with a nobody with nothing—at least, a man with no prospects."

"Then you don't know what *love* is! Oh, it was

delicious—caring about him—crazy about him—trembling all over if he spoke—shivering if he happened to look at me in that calm, big way of his—and that when I felt he might be little more than a tramp, for all I knew."

There was no sympathy in the mother's face, nothing but plain aversion and dismay. Yet she dared not speak her opinion. She knew Beatrice. " I'm afraid he's very artful, dear," she ventured to say. " He seems to understand exactly how to lead you on."

" I don't think so," replied Beatrice. " I may be wrong. I often doubt. I'm like father—very suspicious by nature. Of course, it's possible he is playing with me. If he is, why, it's the most daring, splendid game a man ever played, and he deserves to win. . . . No, mother. He's not playing with me. I tried to win him when he thought I was a poor nobody. It didn't go. Then I thought he was holding back because he was poor; and I tried to win him by showing him what he would be getting. I'm still trying that. But it doesn't seem to be working any better than the other."

" Beatrice, I'm amazed. What *must* he think of you? "

" Now, you know very well, mother, that a girl in my position has to do the courting if the man's poor

124

and has any self-respect. In fact, I've got a notion that the women, in any circumstances, do a lot more courting than is generally supposed."

"I don't know how it is in this day," said her mother stiffly. "But in *my* day——"

"You wouldn't own up, mother dear," laughed the girl. "And your manner is suspiciously like an attempt to hide guilt."

"I'm sure of one thing," said Mrs. Richmond tartly. "In my day children did not insult their parents."

"Now, don't get cross at my joking, dear," cajoled the daughter, kissing her mother's well-arranged, gray hair so lightly that there could be no danger of disarranging it.

As if it had all suddenly come over her again Mrs. Richmond cried despairingly, "What *will* your father say! He'll blame me. He'll say things that will prostrate me."

"If you'll not mention it to him," said Beatrice, "I'll guarantee that he'll not blame you. Hank is going away in the morning. You and Hector can pretend to know nothing. I'll take it up with him."

Her mother looked somewhat reassured, but said dubiously, "He'll give it to me for not having guarded you more closely."

"I'll fix all that," said Beatrice with infectious confidence. "Trust me."

Mrs. Richmond gave her a look of gratitude so deep that it was almost loving. "If you'd only be sensible and put this foolishness out of your mind," she said plaintively.

Rix laughed gayly, then softly. "It isn't in my mind," said she. "It's in another place—one I didn't know about until I met him." She looked at herself admiringly in a long mirror that happened to be at hand. "Don't you see how much better looking I've grown of late? You understand why. Oh, I'm so happy!"

Her mother gave a sigh of helplessness. Rix laughed again and went away to her own rooms—to try to write poetry!

VI

THE following morning it was not yet half past six and Chang had just reached the lake when her canoe shot round the bend. He stood a few yards from the water's edge, observing her graceful maneuverings. She controlled that canoe as perfectly as if it had been part of her own body. He was too much the artist to be able to keep a stern countenance in face of so enchanting a spectacle. Also, her features—her yellow hair, the ever-changing, gray eyes, the mobile and rosy mouth, the delicate skin—had too much of the soft and dazzling loveliness of the morning. " If a man wished to let himself be bewitched," thought he, " there would be an ideal enchantress." She was one of the few women he had known who had worn well—about the only one, indeed. When he first knew her he had not thought that she was especially attractive, beyond the freshness that is the almost universal birthright of youth. But as he had studied her, as he had observed and felt her varied moods, her charm had grown. Even things about her, in themselves unattractive, were

127

fascinating in the glow and throb of her naturally vivid personality—not an intellectual personality, not at all, but redolent of the fresh fragrance of the primal, the natural. "An ideal enchantress," he muttered, and the lot he had sternly marked out for himself seemed bare and lonely, like a monk's cell beside the glories of the landscape beyond its narrow window.

"How can you be out of humor on such a morning?" cried she, as the prow of her canoe slid gently out of the water and she rose to her feet.

"On the contrary, I'm in a fine humor." And his look and voice bore him out. "Didn't I tell you I was going to town to-day? I simply took my walk here."

She laughed. "Neither did I expect you. I simply took my outing here." And when he blushed in confusion and annoyance, she laughed the more gayly.

"You are so amusing," she said tenderly.

"I'll admit," said he, "that I thought there was a chance you might come. And I thought, if you did, it would be the best opportunity to have a plain talk with you."

She seated herself, or, rather, balanced herself, on the forward curve of her canoe. He occupied a big bowlder near the maple under which he always painted.

"I see," observed she, "that you are getting ready to say a lot of things you don't mean. How you will thank me some day for having been patient with you!" He averted his eyes, muttered something incoherent, searched confusedly for his cigarettes. "You always keep the case in your lower left-hand waistcoat pocket," said she. And sure enough, there it was—to his increased confusion. But, when their glances met, the twinkle in her gray eyes—merry as the sunbeams that were changing the yellow of her hair to the reddish yellow of the finest gold—proved irresistible.

"It's simply impossible to be serious with you," cried he, in what he would have liked to think a vexed tone.

"And why should you be?" inquired the girl. "You used to warn me that I took everything, myself included, far too seriously. Now, you're getting into the habit of taking yourself, oh, *so* solemnly!—which is far worse than seriously. You're more like a dismal preacher, a man with a mission, than an artist with the joy of living laughing in his heart. You made a great hit last night."

He, off his guard, looked as pleased as a boy that has just got a present of a gun. "Glad I didn't disgrace you. You remember how nervous you were about it."

" Your talk about that shirt was a little disturbing. It came out well. At least, I think it did. People don't notice your clothes. They look at *you*."

" Now, how am I to say what I've got to say, if you keep on like that? " demanded he. " Oh, but you are crafty! "

" I don't want to be lectured, Chang."

He settled himself with an air of inflexible resolution. " I'm not going to lecture," said he. " I'm going to deliver myself of a few words of good sense and then say good-by."

She looked upon the ground, and her expression wrenched his tender heart. In vain he told himself that he was an egotistical fool; that the girl was probably more than half faking, to work upon him; that the other half of the feeling in her expression was the flimsiest youthful infatuation, certain to disappear in a few days, a few weeks at most. There, before him, was the look of suffering. And when she lifted her eyes for an instant they said more touchingly than her voice could have said it: " Why don't you strike and have done with me? I am helpless."

He got up, tossed his cigarette far into the lake. " This is too rotten! " he cried. " How in the devil did I ever get into such a mess? "

She waited, meek, silent, pathetic.

"I've about decided to go away—to go back to Paris," said he.

"Maybe we can cross together," said she. "Mother and I are going soon. She wants me .to go right away—there, or anywhere, wherever I wish."

He dropped to the bowlder again, a sense of helplessness weakening his backbone and his knees. Of what use to fly? This girl was free—had the means to travel wherever she chose, to stay as long as she liked. In his excitement he saw visions of himself being pursued round and round the earth—till his money gave out, and he, unable to fly farther, was overtaken and captured. He began to laugh—laugh until the tears rolled down his cheeks.

"What is it?" asked she. "Tell me. I want to laugh."

"You are making me into an imbecile," replied he. "I was laughing at myself. I'm glad I had that laugh. I think I can talk sensibly now—without making myself ridiculous." Once more he put on a highly impressive, highly ominous air of sober resoluteness. He began: "A short time ago you did me the honor of telling me you were in love with me."

"Yes. Do you—do you think poorly of me for having been frank?" And the gray eyes looked innocent anxiety.

"No, I don't," confessed he. "As a general proposition, I think I should have thought—well, queerly—of a girl who came out with such a startler on no especial provocation. But in this case the effect is puzzlingly different. Probably because I can't in the least believe you."

"Oh, no—that's not the reason," cried she. "It was only right that I should speak first. You see, when the girl's poor, and marrying her is going to put the man to great expense—it'd be—be—downright impertinent for her to say such a thing. It'd be as if she asked him to support her for life."

"Maybe so," said he. "The money side of it didn't occur to me. Naturally, you, who have much money, would think more about it than I, who have little."

"Would you be afraid to—to marry—a woman who had a lot more money than you?"

"Not in the least," declared he. "How ridiculous!"

A chill of suspicion crept into her face.

"I don't want to marry, and I shan't marry," continued he. "But if I did want to marry, and wanted the woman, I'd not care who she was or what she was or what she had or hadn't—so long as she was what I wanted. And I don't think even you, crazy as you are about money, could suspect me of having the same mania."

His tone and his manner would have convinced anyone. They convinced her. She drew a huge sigh of relief. "I'm glad you said that—in just that way," said she.

"I'm sure I don't see what difference it makes," replied he. "You don't mean to say you've been suspecting me of wanting your money?"

She hung her head foolishly. "I've got a horrid mind," confessed she. "It came to me that maybe you might be holding out for fear father'd cut me off."

"You *have* got your nerve!" ejaculated he. "I never heard of the like!—never!"

"Now you're disgusted with me," cried she. "I know I oughtn't to have told you. But I can't help telling you everything. It isn't fair, Chang, to think I'm worse than most girls, just because I let you see into me. You know it isn't fair."

"You're right, Rix," said he impulsively; and the sense that he had wronged her pushed him on to say, "It's your frankness and your courage that I admire so much. I wish you weren't attractive. Then it'd be easier for me to do what I've got to do."

Her face became radiant. "Then you do care for me?"

133

"Why, of course I do," said he heartily—but in a tone most unsatisfactory to ears waiting to drink in what her ears longed for. "Do you suppose I could stand so much of anyone I didn't like?"

"You aren't frank with me!" said she a little sullenly.

"Why not?"

"You've some reason why you won't let yourself say you love me. And you won't tell me what it is."

"How many times have I got to tell you," cried he heatedly, "that I don't care for you in that way—any more than you care for me?"

She was all gentleness and freedom from guile. "But every time you say that, you say it angrily—and then I know you don't mean it."

"But I do mean it!"

Her face looked stubbornly unconvinced.

"I tell you, I do mean it!" he repeated with angry energy.

"You are mad at yourself for liking me so much."

He made a gesture of despair. "Well, have it your way—if it pleases you better to think so." He rose and stood before her, his hands thrust deep into the outside pockets of his loose sack coat. "Whatever I may or may not think of you, I am not going to marry anybody. Do I make myself clear?"

134

" But everybody gets married," said she innocently. " Oh, Chang, why do you want to be eccentric? " And up into his gazed the childlike eyes. " You told me yourself that eccentricity was a stupid caricature of originality."

" Eccentric—eccentric," he muttered, for lack of anything else to say. What an impossible creature to talk seriously with! She was always flying off at a tangent. Controlling his exasperation he said in a low, intense voice: " Eccentric or not, I am not going to marry. *Do* you understand? I—am—not—going —to—marry."

" Why do you get angry? " she pleaded sweetly. " It's unreasonable. I can't *make* you marry me—can I? I don't want to marry you if you don't want to marry me—do I? "

He strode away, back again to where she sat in graceful ease on the end of her canoe. " I'm not so thundering sure of that! " he cried. " By Jove, you sometimes make me feel as if I had a halter round my neck. Where did you get this infernal insistence? "

" From my father," said she, quiet and calm. " I can't help it. When my heart gets set on a thing I hold on like grim death."

He looked round, like a man dreaming. " Am I awake? Am I really awake? " he demanded of lake and trees and stones. Then he addressed her, "What are you up to? I know you don't love me. I know you don't want to marry me. Then *why* do you do it?"

"I don't know," she said. "I just can't help it. Sometimes when I'm alone and think over things I've said to you I can't believe it was really I—or that such words really were uttered. . . . There can be only one explanation."

"And what is that? For Heaven's sake, let's have it."   ·

"That I know beyond the shadow of a doubt that you love me."

"Really!" exclaimed he, with a fantastic attempt at scornful irony; and away he strode, to halt at his former seat, the big bowlder under the tree. "Really!" he repeated.

"You must see it yourself," urged she, serious and earnest. "Honestly, Chang, could a girl talk to you as I have—a girl as proud and as modest as I am—and with no experience—could she do it, unless she were absolutely sure she was talking to a man who loved her?"

There was something akin to terror in his eyes—the terror of a man who feels himself sinking in ocean or quicksand and looks about in vain for aid. Down he sat, to stare out over the shining, sparkling lake.

"You know I'm right," said she with quiet conviction.

Up he started again in agitation. "I must be getting weak-minded!" he cried. "Or are you hypnotizing me?"

"If anybody's done any hypnotizing I guess it must be you that have hypnotized me."

"Maybe so," said he, with a confused gesture. "Maybe so. Lord knows. I don't."

"And now," pursued she, "that it's settled that we love each other——"

"What!" he cried, with some of his former energy. But it subsided before her calm, surprised gaze. He stared stupidly at her feet, extended and crossed. "Is it settled?" he muttered. "Is it?" And then he straightened himself—a kind of rearing, insurgent gesture—the gesture of the last fierce stand in the last ditch.

"Yes, Chang, it's settled," said she soothingly. "You are such a big, foolish dear! But—as I was about to say—" She hesitated.

"Go on," he urged, with a large, ironic gesture matching the boisterous irony of his tone. "Say anything you like. Only, don't keep me in suspense."

"Have you had your breakfast?" she asked solicitously.

"I take only coffee. I had it."

"But that's not enough for such a long morning as you have," protested she.

"Isn't it? All right. I'll eat whatever you say—eat till you tell me to stop."

"It really isn't enough," said she, refusing to relax her seriousness. "But, to go on—now that it's settled that we love each other—the question is: What shall we do about it?"

"Yes," said he, nodding his head in solemn mockery. "That's it. What shall be done about it?"

"How queer your voice is, Chang," observed she, with a look of gentle, innocent worriment. "What's the matter?"

"I had only coffee," said he.

"You mustn't do that again. . . . Have you any suggestion to make?"

"None. Have you?"

"Chang!" she said reproachfully. "You have a suggestion."

"Have I? What is it?"

"The only possible suggestion. You know very well that the only sensible thing to do is to get married."

"I'm dreaming," jeered he. "Yes, I'm dreaming."

"You're laughing at me, Chang!"

"Am I?"

"Oh, I don't care. I'm so happy! The only thing that stands in the way is father."

"Oh, father! Yes; there is father!" And he nodded ironically, repeating: "Father — there's father."

"But I'll soon bring him round," cried she. "His will's very strong, but mine's much stronger."

"I believe that!" said he with energy. "You've got the strongest will we've had since Joshua ordered the sun to stand still and the sun did it."

"You're laughing at me again!" reproached she with an injured air.

"No, no! How could I?" protested he. "But suppose father refuses his consent. What then?"

"But he won't," she said with an emphatic little nod.

"But he might. He doesn't know me as well and love me as dearly as his daughter does."

"Chang, I feel as if you were laughing at me!"

"How can you!" said he. "But let's go back to father and stick to him. Suppose he refuses—absolutely refuses! What then?"

"I hadn't thought. It's so unlikely."

"Well—think now. You'd give up your romantic dream, wouldn't you?"

She beamed, happy, confident. " Oh, that won't happen. He's sure to consent."

" He's sure *not* to consent," said Roger, dropping his irony. " What then? "

She was silent. Her face slowly paled. A drawn look came round her eyes and mouth. He laughed— a sarcastic laugh—a sincere sound that indicated to her acute ears an end of the irony she had been pretending not to suspect. She glanced up quickly. Her eyes fell before his.

" You see," said he, a little disdain in his jocose mockery, " I've shown you your own true self. Now, you will be sensible. Go back to your Peter and let the poor artist alone." He rose, came to her, held out his hand. " Good-by, Rix. I must catch my train."

She did not take his hand.

" Surely you'll shake hands," said he gently, friendlily. " I understand. I like you for what you are, not for what you ought to be. Come, give me your hand, my friend."

She sighed, gazed up at him. " Suppose I said I'd give up everything for you. What then? " she asked.

" Why, you'd be saying what isn't true."

" Chang," she said earnestly, " I *think* I'd give up

140

everything for you. But since it is you who ask me—
you to whom I feel I must tell the exact truth—I had
to be honest. And the honest truth is I don't know.
And any girl, in the same circumstances, would say
precisely the same thing—if she weren't lying—or just
romancing."

"You are a trump, Rix!" he exclaimed. There
was a look in his eyes that would have thrilled her, had
she seen it. But before she turned her gaze upon him
again, he had controlled his impulsive self-revelation.
In his usual manner he went on: "I'm proud of your
friendship. It's always good to be reminded that there
are people of the right sort on earth. But you see
yourself now that I was right from the beginning. We
don't belong in the same class. We couldn't comfortably travel the same road. We——"

"Would you marry me if I gave up everything
for you?" she interrupted.

"No," was the prompt reply. "Any man who did
that to your sort of girl would be a fool—and worse.
But don't forget another fact, my dear. I wouldn't
marry you in any circumstances. I'm not marrying.
I'm married already, as I told you before. I don't believe in any other kind of marriage—for my kind of
man. I love my freedom. And I shall keep it."

There was no mistaking the ring of those decisive

words. The girl shrank a little. She began in a choked, uncertain voice: " But you said——"

" Rix, my dear friend, I said nothing that contradicted what I've always told you—what I believe in as I believe in my work. You knew perfectly well that I was merely ironic a few minutes ago. I didn't want to part from you with you imagining you were broken-hearted. That's why I let you run on and on—until you came that fearful cropper. Oh, *what* a cropper for romantic Rix! "

She laughed with a partial return of her old gayety. " I do feel cheap," said she—" dirt cheap."

" Not at all. Just human. But—really I must be going," said he briskly.

" When shall I see you again? " And she tried to speak steadily, with smiling eyes.

" Let me see. I'll be back in two or three days. In a week or ten days I'll have that picture about done. I suppose you'd like to see it. I'll send your mother a note, asking her to bring you. Well—good-by, Rix."

He took her hand, released it. She stood, paling and flushing and trembling. " Is that—all? " she murmured. " Won't you—" Voice failed her.

He bent and kissed her hair at her temple. Suddenly she flung her arms round his neck, kissed him passionately, her embrace tight; and a shower of tears rained upon his cheek. With a hysterical cry more like joy than like grief, yet like neither, she flung herself free, sprang into the canoe and pushed off. And she went her way and he his without either looking back.

VII

Roger was working in the studio, with doors and windows wide. It was fiercely hot. He had reduced his costume to outing shirt and old flannel trousers—the kind they make in the Latin Quarter—baggy at the hips, tapering to a close fit at the ankles and hanging with a careless, comfortable, yet not ungraceful looseness. He was working at *the* picture. He had not decided on a name for it. Should he call it April?—or Dawn?—or The Water Witch? Or should he give it its proper name—Rix? That title would mean nothing to anyone save himself. But to him the picture meant nothing else. True, there was landscape in it; the play of early morning light on foliage, on leaping water, on placid water made it the best landscape he had ever done —incomparably the best. The canoe, too, was a marvel in its way. But the girl—*there* was the picture! He made another infinitesimal change—it would have been impossible to count the number of those changes he had made. Then he stood off at a little distance to look again.

144

"Is it in the canvas—or is it in my mind?" said he aloud.

He could not tell. He rather feared he was largely imagining the wonders he thought he saw in that pictured face and form.

"It may be rotten, and I a fool hypnotized by her and by my own vanity, for all I know. But—what do I care? I am getting the pleasure."

Pleasure? Never before had he taken such deep, utter joy in his work. Not merely joy in the doing—that was his invariable experience—but joy in the completed work. Never before had he brought anything so near to the finish without a feeling of dissatisfaction, sense of failure, of having just missed his aim. He viewed the picture from a dozen points. And each time he beheld in it something new, something yet more wonderful.

"I'm damned if it's there! It simply can't be. Not the greatest genius who ever lived could produce what I imagine I see."

He took a dozen new positions, standing long at each view point. But the illusion—it must be illusion!—refused to vanish. The work—the figure part of it—persisted in appealing to him as a product of transcendent genius.

"That business didn't stop a minute too soon—not

a minute! For it's evident I was on the verge of falling in love."

"On the verge?" . . . What was the meaning of the illusion of a picture greater than ever artist made? . . . On the verge?

"Why, hang it all, I've done nothing but think about her since we kissed. I'm bewitched! I'm in love!"

The kiss was a week old now—ought to have lost its power long ago; for there is power in a kiss from a pretty woman, even though a man does not love her. But this kiss had an extraordinary, an unprecedented quality. Other kisses—in days gone by—had given their little sensation and had straightway drifted into the crowd of impressions about the woman or about the general joyousness of life when the senses are normal and responsive. But this kiss—it had individuality, a body and soul of its own, a Jack's bean-stalk kind of vitality. It was more vigorous day by day. He could feel it much more potently to-day than on the day it was given. Really, it did not make a very powerful impression then. He had experienced much better kisses. He had felt awkward—a little ridiculous—rather uneasy and anxious to escape. Now——

"Not a minute too soon—not a minute! As it is, I'm going to have the devil's own time forgetting her."

146

What had become of all his projects for a career, for rapid striding into fame? Gone—quite gone. He simply wanted to stay at the studio and work on and on and yet on at the one picture—at the one figure in that picture. He had vaguely decided on a scheme for another picture when this should be done. What was it? Why, a picture of a woman sitting under a tree, her hands listless, her whole body relaxed and inert—except her eyes. Her eyes were to be winging into the depths of the infinite. He had planned out the contrast between the eyes, so intensely, so swiftly alive, and the passive rest of her. And who was this woman? Rix! He had still more vaguely planned a third picture. Of what? Rix again.

"Not a minute too soon? By Heaven, a minute too late!"

"Well, what of it?" demanded he gloomily of his gloomy self. Why, pay the bill. Pay like a man. "I couldn't marry her if I would. I wouldn't marry her if I could. But I can pay the bill for making a fool of myself." He glowered savagely around. "The next time a good-looking woman comes here," he muttered, "I'll take to my heels and hide in the woods till she's gone. I see I'm no longer to be trusted in female society. At my age—with my plans—after all I've been through—to make such an easy ass of myself!" He

147

sat down despondently on the bench—sprang up—for was it not there—lying there—just where he had seated himself—that he had first seen her? He glanced round the studio. He groaned. Everything in it reminded him of her; and there, in the center, in the most favorable light, on the easel—was she herself!

He rushed outdoors. Sunshine shimmering and sparkling on the foliage—he could see her, the yellow hair aflame with sunbeams, flitting gracefully through the aisles of the forest! A heavy bill it was to be! But he set his teeth. " She is not for me, nor I for her. If she were here now I'd talk to her just as I did. But, thank God, I didn't realize until I had done the only thing that's sane and honorable. I wonder how long it will be before I can begin to forget? "

Every morning he awoke vowing he would not touch or look at her picture that day. Every morning he cut short his walk that he might get to the studio earlier and busy himself at the picture. He partially consoled himself with the reflection that at least he was improving it, was not altogether wasting his time. And he found evidence of real strength of purpose in the fact that he kept away from the waterfall. For two weeks he daily feared—or hoped—whether fear or hope or both he was not sure—that she would come to the studio. As the days passed and she did not appear he felt that she was getting over her infatuation; to stay away thus long unless her enthusiasm had cooled was wholly unlike her impetuous and brave nature. This thought did not make him happier exactly, but athwart its gloom shot one sincerely generous gleam: " Anyhow, I'm paying alone," said he to himself. " And that's as it should be. It was altogether my fault. I am older, more experienced. I ought to have seen that the strangeness and novelty of our meetings were appealing to her young imagination—and I ought to have broken off at the very outset. If she had been a poor girl leading a quiet, dull life the consequences might have been serious. Yes, and I might have been weak enough to marry her out of regret—and that would have been misery for us both."

He tried fighting against the desire to spend his days with that picture. He tried yielding to the desire. But neither abstinence nor excess availed. He tried savage, sneering criticism—found that he loved her for her defects and her weaknesses. He tried absurd extravagance of romancing—found that he had quite lost his sense of humor where adulation of her was concerned. The kiss flamed on. He decided to leave—to fly. But he discovered that if he went he would surely take the picture; and of what use to go, if he lugged his curse along with him?

149

One afternoon late he went to the door to get the full benefit of a cool breeze that had sprung up. He saw, a few hundred yards away, Rix and a man climbing up through the dense woods toward his workshop. He wheeled round, rushed in and put the picture away —far back in the depths of the closet, behind a lot of other pictures. In its place on the easel he set a barely begun sketch—one of his attempts to distract his mind. Then, with no alteration in his appearance—his hair was mussed this way and that, and his negligee shirt was open at the neck and rolled up to the elbows—he lit a cigarette and sauntered to the door again. His not making any effort to improve upon his appearance was characteristic and significant; rarely indeed has there been a human being habitually less self-conscious than he. It would take a very vain person to continue to think of himself or herself on becoming suddenly a spectator at some scene of tremendous interest. Roger was in that state of mind all the time. His senses were so eager, his mind so inquisitive, his powers of observation so acute that his thoughts were like bees on a bright, summer day—always roving, and returning home only to unload what had been gathered and quickly depart again in quest of more from the outside.

As the ascent was steep he had ample time to compose his thoughts and his expression. She must not see or feel anything that would make it, however little, harder to pursue the road Fate had marked out for her. The man beside her was obviously her father—obviously, though there was no similarity of face or manner or figure. The relationship was revealed in that evasive similarity called family favor—a similarity which startlingly asserts itself even in dissimilarities, as if the soul and the body had a faint aureole which appeared only at certain angles and in certain lights. He was a little, thin man—dry and dyspeptic—with one of those deceptive retreating chins of insignificant size that indicate cunning instead of weakness. He had a big, sharp nose, a rough skin and scraggly mustache, with restless, gray-green eyes. He was very slouchily dressed in dusty gray. When he took off his straw hat to wipe his brow Roger was astonished by the sudden view of a really superb upper head which transformed his aspect from merely sly to dangerously crafty—the man with the nature of a fox and the intelligence to make that nature not simply a local nuisance but a general scourge. "I'd like to paint him," thought Roger —and compliment could no further go in an artist who detested portrait work.

As the two drew near Rix waved her sunshade at him and nodded. He advanced, holding to his cigarette. When she extended her hand—a gloved hand, for she was in a fashionable, white, walking costume—her eyes did not lift and her color wavered and her short, sensitive, upper lip trembled slightly. "Mr. Wade, I want you and father to know each other," said she. As her voice came the thrill that shot through him dropped his cigarette from between the fingers of his left hand. He and Richmond gave each other a penetrating, seeing glance, followed by a smile of immediate appreciation.

Richmond gave and took back his hand quickly— the hand shake of the man who is impatient of meaningless formalities. "I've come to look at the picture," said he, in his voice the note of one who neither wastes his own time nor suffers others to waste it.

Roger froze instantly. "I'm sorry you've had your journey for nothing," said he.

Richmond looked at him aggressively. Roger's tone of the large, free spirit that does as it wills was to Richmond, the autocrat, like a challenging trumpet. "It's here—isn't it?" said he.

"But it's not finished," replied the big artist, gentle as the voice of a great river flowing inevitably on its way.

"No matter," said Richmond graciously. "We'll take a look at it, anyhow."

"Oh, no, we shan't," said Beatrice, laughing. "He

has a rule against it, father. And he's like iron where his rules are concerned. But you'll give us some chocolate, won't you, Mr. Wade?"

"Delighted," said Roger, with a gesture inviting them to precede him into the studio.

Richmond looked round him scrutinizingly. "Nothing to distract your mind from your work, I see. That's the way my office is fitted up. I'm always suspicious of chaps surrounded by elegant fittings." And he gave Roger an approving look that was flattering, if a trifle suggestive of superiority.

"It's not wise to judge a man by any exteriors," said Roger. "What he does—that is the only safe standard."

Richmond reflected, nodded. "Yes," said he. "Yes. Is that the picture?" He pointed one brown, bony hand at the sketch on the easel.

"No," said Roger curtly, and he flung a drape over the sketch. Turning to Beatrice with rather formal friendliness, he inquired, "How is your mother?"

"Well—always well," said Beatrice. "She sent you her best. But she's cross with you for not coming to call."

Richmond grinned sardonically. "From what I've heard of Wade," said he, "he's not the kind you find nestled among the petticoats with a little cup in his hand." He smiled upon Roger. " In America, at least, you never see men who amount to anything at these social goings-on. In five years I've been to only one party in my own house, and to none in anybody else's house."

" May I help with the chocolate—Mr. Wade? " asked Beatrice.

" No. You two will sit quietly. I don't mind being watched."

While he made the closet give up the necessary utensils and concocted the chocolate with the aid of spirit-lamp stove the three talked in rambling fashion. Several times Richmond brought up the subject of the picture; every time Roger abruptly led away from it, Beatrice with increasing nervousness helping him. But Richmond was not discouraged. It became evident that he had made up his mind to see that picture and was only the more resolved because the artist had his will set against it. Finally he said:

" It's really necessary, Mr. Wade, that I see the picture. Your friend, Count d'Artois, speaks highly of your work. But I always judge everything for myself. And I must see before I decide about giving you a commission—a dozen panels for an outing-club house I and some of my friends are going to put something like half a million into."

"Why, father, you didn't tell me anything about it!" exclaimed Beatrice, flushed and agitated. And Roger understood that she, nervous about his sensibilities, was letting him know that she had not arranged this.

Her father's amused laugh confirmed Roger's impression that Beatrice was telling the truth. "No, my dear, I did forget to ask your permission," said Richmond ironically. "I apologize. Now, Wade, you see I'm not asking out of idle curiosity or merely because I'm anxious to see what you've made of this girl of mine. So, don't bother with bashfulness. Trot out the picture."

But Roger smilingly shook his head. "I couldn't undertake any work at present."

"Honestly, Chang, I didn't know a thing about this," cried the girl. Then, to her father: "He's so peculiar that he wouldn't——"

"Oh, no, I'm not such an ass as that," interrupted Roger good-naturedly. "Sugar in your chocolate, Mr. Richmond? No? When are you sailing, Miss Richmond?"

Beatrice understood—abandoned the subject. "Perhaps we shan't go," she replied.

And she went on to detail at length and with much vivacity the merits and demerits of several plans for the

155

summer she and her mother were considering. Richmond's frown deepened. After five minutes he set down his empty cup and cut squarely across her stream of lively talk.

" The panels will be a good thing—from the financial standpoint," said he, a note in his voice like a rap for undivided attention.

Beatrice glanced anxiously at Roger, said to her father: " Oh, papa, don't let's talk business. This is a party."

" *I* came on business," retorted Richmond. " And I know Wade wouldn't thank us for coming if we were here just to fool away his time."

" I usually knock off for chocolate at this hour," said Roger. " About the panels—thank you very much, but I can't do them."

" Why not? " inquired Richmond, so much irritation in his tone that it was scarcely polite.

Roger looked amused. " I haven't thought of the reason yet," said he courteously. " If I change my mind later I'll let you know."

Richmond did not conceal his disgust with what seemed to him an exhibition of youthful egotism bordering on impertinence. Beatrice, eager for her father to get a favorable impression, looked woefully depressed. " You misunderstood me, Mr. Wade," said he, resuming the Mr. to indicate his disapproval. "I did not offer you the commission."

"And I didn't accept it," said Roger, laughing. "So, there's no harm done. Let me give you some chocolate."

"Thanks—no. We are going." And the financier rose. "Come along, Beatrice."

The girl, pale and crestfallen, half rose, reseated herself, looked appealingly at Roger, who seemed not to see, then stood. "When can we see the picture?" she asked, casting desperately about for an excuse for lingering.

"We don't want to see it at all," her father put in, with a jovial, sardonic laugh that revealed unpleasantly his strong, sallow, crowded teeth. "Mr. Wade needn't bother to complete it. I'll send him a check for whatever you settled as the price——"

"Father!" gasped Beatrice despairingly. Then, to Roger, with a nervous attempt at a lively smile: "He doesn't mean it. He's simply joking."

"Your father and I understand each other," said Roger tranquilly. "The picture'll be done in a few days. I'll send it to Red Hill immediately. I always like to get a finished job out of the place. I've got a terrible habit of tinkering as long as a thing's within reach. As for the check"—he smiled pleasantly at

Richmond, who looked—and felt—small and shriveled before the large candor of the artist's expression— " your daughter is a poor business woman. She forgot to make a bargain. So it lies between your generosity and mine." Roger made a courtly bow, with enough mockery in it to take away affectation. " I'm sure mine will come nearer the value of the picture. I'll make you a present of it—with my compliments."

" Can't permit it!" said Richmond angrily.

But Roger remained suave. "I don't see how you're going to help yourself," said he. " I can send it back to you as often as you return it to me, and if you can refuse to take it in, why, so can I. You can't make me ridiculous without my making you ridiculous also. You see, you're in my power, Mr. Richmond." All this with the utmost good humor and friendliness.

Richmond could think of nothing to say but a repetition of his curt " Can't permit it!" He glanced in the direction of his daughter, jerked his head toward the door. " Come along, child. Good day, sir." Roger's expression, from the height of his tall figure, was so compelling that he put out his hand, which Roger took and shook with the cordiality of a host to whom any guest is inviolable.

Beatrice and Roger shook hands—that is, Beatrice let her hand rest lifelessly in Roger's until he dropped it. He bowed them out into the sunshine and stood in the doorway, watching them. At the edge of the forest Beatrice turned suddenly and started back. Roger saw her father wheel round—heard his sharp " Beatrice!" —saw his look of furious amazement. The girl came almost running. Roger braced himself, through his whole body a gripping sensation that might be either terror or delight.

When she stood before him, her eyes down, her cheeks pale, her bosom heaving, she said: " The other day you asked me whether I'd give up everything for you. I didn't know then. I do know now."

" Pardon me, but I did not," said Roger, calm and cold.

" However it was," she rushed on, " that question came up. And I didn't know then whether I would or would not. Well—I know now."

" Your father is impatient."

" I'm sure I would," she said, a fascinating haughty humility in her face, in her voice. And she looked so brilliantly young and ardent.

Roger's glance fled before hers. A brief electric silence, then he laughed pleasantly. " And *I'm* sure you wouldn't. And it doesn't matter whether you would or wouldn't. Good-by, Rix. Your father's look is aimed to kill."

"How cruel you are—and how blind!" she cried, eyes and cheeks aflame. And as quickly as she had come she sped away to rejoin her father.

Roger heaved a great sigh. "Now," said he aloud, "I've seen the last of her. I can resume."

VIII

"I suppose you went back to apologize for me," said her father as they started on together.

"You don't understand him," replied she miserably. "Artists—great artists—are different."

"He *is* a good deal of a man. D'Artois was right. I'll see that he does those panels." And Richmond gave the nod of a man who has money and knows that money is all-powerful.

Beatrice stopped short; her eyes opened wide. "Why," exclaimed she, "I thought you disliked him!"

"Not at all—not at all," replied her father. "He's a disagreeable chap. But all men who amount to anything are. A man who's thoroughly agreeable is invariably weak. An agreeable man's rarely worth more than twelve or fifteen a week. What this world needs is more people like this friend of yours. I saw that he had built himself up solidly from the ground. I wish I had a son like that! Your brothers are pretty poor excuses, thanks to the vicious training your mother has given them. 'Be a gentleman—make everybody comfortable—don't do anything to hurt anybody's feelings or to make yourself conspicuous.' That is, be a cipher." Richmond snorted. " A gentleman is a cipher —and ciphers count for nothing unless they're annexed after a figure that stands for something. But I suppose a successful man can't expect to have strong sons. He has to be thankful if they're not imbecile or dissipated."

Beatrice had been caught up and whirled all in a twinkling from depth to height. The way down through the woods was rough and toilsome. She flitted along as if it were smooth as a French highroad. She beamed upon her father. " What a difference between the ordinary young man—the sort we meet—and a man like Roger Wade! " cried she.

" Those tailor's dummies! " said Richmond contemptuously. " You can't compare a *man* with them."

He was on his favorite topic for private and public addresses—the topic that enabled him to express the views which had won for him the name of being the most democratic of the big financiers. Like all men of abounding mentality he was a huge talker; get him started and the only thing to do, whether one wished or no, was to listen. Usually, Beatrice, who was not fond of silence and soon reached the limit of her capacity for listening, would imperiously interrupt these monologues

162

—and both would enjoy the tussle between their wills as each tried to compel the other to listen. But this discourse—composed though it was of commonplaces he had repeated and she had heard scores of times—she drank in as if it had been the brand-new thing her soul had long thirsted to hear. Like all fluent talkers Richmond often fell victim—in conversation, never in action —to the intoxication of bubbling ideas and phrases. Before they reached the place where they had left the T cart to await their return Richmond had not merely committed himself finally and completely to the gospel of the aristocracy of achievement, he had hailed that aristocracy as the only one worthy of consideration, had ridiculed and denounced all others as utterly contemptible.

Beatrice took advantage of his pause for getting the horses under way. She gave his arm a loving squeeze. "I'm so proud of you!" she said tenderly, gazing at him with sparkling eyes and delicately flushed cheeks. "I *knew* you'd feel that way about him!"

"About whom?" said her father, whose flooding sermon had borne him swiftly far from view, or remembrance even, of the text whence it had sprung.

"About Chang."

"Chang? What Chang? Who's Chang?"

"Roger Wade."

"Oh, of course," said he indifferently. "He's a case in point."

"I knew you'd help me with him," pursued the happy girl.

"Of course I will," said Richmond. "Hasn't he been doing what you wanted about the picture?"

"I want *him*," said she, feeling close and sympathetic, completely in touch with this splendid, broad-minded father of hers.

Richmond reined in the horses so sharply that one of them reared. It took a minute or so for them to be quieted, with the groom racing round from the seat behind to steady their heads. When the cart was moving smoothly on Richmond said: "What did you say just as that brown devil began to act up?"

"I want to marry Roger Wade," replied Beatrice, too strongly under the delusion to read plain signs aright. "You see why. You've said yourself that he was one of the realest men you had seen. You can't wonder at my caring for him. All the others seem so—so puny—beside him. I'd be ashamed to show any of them as my husband. What shall I do, father? How can I get him?"

If one finds oneself pointing south when he ought to be pointing north there are two ways to act. One may veer gently and gradually, hoping that the shift will pass unobserved; or one may make the change with speed swifter than thought or sight, and may point north so stiffly that it will seem impossible that one ever was pointing, or ever could point, in any other direction. When Richmond found it necessary to flop he did not sidle—he flopped. He proceeded to flop now—with a jerk and a bang. "What are you talking about?" he said savagely. "You're going to marry Peter."

The instant prompting of instinct to Beatrice was that her father would not help, would not consent, would not tolerate. But straightway came the memory of his gallant democratic speechifyings still echoing in her ears. "You know I couldn't marry a Peter after I had seen Roger," she said gayly. "All the time you were talking—as we walked down from his studio—I knew what you really had in mind. You were giving it to me for thinking of Peter when I might have the other man. You thought I was hopelessly frivolous and snobbish like the rest of the family. But I'm like you, father. I don't want to be married to a tailor's dummy. I want a *man!*" She nodded brightly at his thunderous face. "And we'll get him—you and I!"

Richmond did not relent, not a whit. She had taken him so completely by surprise, had put him in such an absurdly false position that temper got the better of prudence. He did not view the situation calmly and proceed along lines of wisdom—using common-sense argument, appeal to material instincts and that mightiest of weapons, gentle ridicule. He hurled at her through his eyes the hot wrath of his tyrant will. "You are going to marry Peter, I tell you. I'm astounded at you. I'm disgusted with you. I'd have thought you could see straight through a cheap, lazy fortune hunter. Vanity—always vanity! He makes a few flattering speeches, and you believe he is in love with you. And you begin to make a god out of him. I'm glad you spoke to me about this. If the Vanderkiefs had any idea of it they'd drop you double-quick."

Beatrice knew her father—knew when he was in earnest. Never before had she seen or felt a deeper earnestness than this of his now. She sat dazed, staring at the restless ears of the thoroughbreds before her.

"No good ever comes of marrying out of your own class," continued he. "I thought you had more pride. I know you have. You were joking. Let's hear no more about it."

"He is not a fortune hunter," said Beatrice in a numb way.

"I tell you he is!" cried Richmond violently. "The impudent hound! No wonder he tried to work off that picture of his as a gift!" Richmond laughed with a sneer. "The impudent puppy!"

"He is a great artist," said Beatrice. " D'Artois says so."

"What of that? What's an artist? What standing has he got? But don't talk about it. I'll not be able to contain myself." He faced her sharply. "Look at me!"

The girl turned her eyes slowly, with her wounded soul's suffering revealed in them. But Richmond did not see people ever; he saw only his own purposes. "How far has this gone?"

She eyed him steadily long enough for him to get the sense of an immovable obstacle squarely across the path of his indomitable will. "It has gone so far that I'll not marry anyone else," she said, neither hot nor cold. "I couldn't."

"Don't let me hear that kind of talk!" shouted Richmond, in his rage forgetting the groom. "You are going to marry a man who can make you happy—a man in your own station—a man who has family and standing."

"But you said Roger was of the only true aristocracy," pleaded Beatrice. "You said——"

"And a fool I was, to talk to a silly, little idiot of an ignorant girl with no experience of life, with no ability to understand what I was talking about. I wasn't discussing a husband for you. I wasn't discussing the world as it is. I wasn't discussing people of our station. I wasn't discussing fortune-hunting artists. It shows how little sense you've got, that you could twist what I said into an appeal to you to marry an impudent fortune hunter!"

In his fury at her for being thus stupid he gave the off thoroughbred a sharp cut with the whip. The horse, unused to such loutish disrespect to his royal blood, leaped forward, started to run. For five minutes Richmond had to fix his undivided attention upon the horses; they gave him a bad scare before consenting to submit.

The girl, unconscious of what was going on, sat in the blinding storm of her own unhappiness.

"You and Peter are engaged?" was her father's resuming remark.

"In a fashion."

"What does that mean?"

"Not much of anything," replied his daughter indifferently.

Richmond's strong, sallow teeth looked as if they were crowded because they were pushing eagerly to the fore in competition to be first in sinking into the prey. Said he: "I want the date of the wedding fixed at once."

Silence.

"Did you hear?"

"Yes."

"Why don't you answer?"

"You didn't ask a question. You issued an order."

"And you will obey it."

Silence.

"Did you hear?"

"Yes."

"I won't tolerate sullenness. I am your father. I know life—the world—what is best for my family—for you. I don't often interfere. When I do, I expect obedience."

"It seems to me you are blustering a good deal, for one who is sure of obedience," said Beatrice, in a way that brought out all her latent resemblance to the incarnation of passionate will and willful passion who begot her.

"I've always been indulgent with all my family—with you," fumed Richmond. "But I think you know me well enough to know I'm not to be trifled with."

"Nor am I," said the girl. And again she eyed him in that unyielding way.

"Where did you and your mother pick up that vagabond, anyhow?" demanded Richmond.

"*I* picked him up. D'Artois told you——"

"D'Artois was talking about him as an artist, not as an equal."

"Equal!" cried Beatrice. And she laughed mockingly.

"Don't be impudent to me!" raged her father. "You've been brought up in a certain way. You're not fit for any other way of life. You are not to be allowed to make a fool of yourself, to muddle your life up. I'll have no scandals in my family—no scoundrels blackmailing me to release my daughter."

Beatrice's look at him was so appealing, so reminiscent of his bold talk about democracy, about the democracy of achievement, that some men, if they had been in his place, would have been ashamed and confounded. Not Daniel Richmond, however—not when his plans of social grandeur, nursed all these years in his secretest heart, were endangered.

When Rhoda was marrying the Earl of Broadstairs he had been able to keep his pose intact—had contrived to protest against one of his children's yielding to the craze for "decayed aristocrats with fly-blown titles," and to yield only because "personally, Broadstairs wasn't as bad as some," and because the girl and her mother had made it clear to him that her heart would be broken if she didn't get the man she loved— at the price such luxuries cost. He had assumed that Beatrice had been equally well brought up—to love where she should, to do as well in the American upper

class as her sister had done in the foreign upper class.
This revelation of her waywardness, the waywardness
of the child who was his especial pride, for whom he had
dreamed the most dazzling splendors of social gran-
deurs in New York—this astounding revelation put
him in the rage of his life. His face was a study in
hatefulness. Beatrice shivered as she looked at it—
but not with fear.

"Yes," said she calmly, after a pause. "I've been
brought up in a certain way. But I was born to insist
on having what I want. I want Roger. And, father,
I'm going to have him—in spite of you both."

After a pause, in a voice of dreadful calm Richmond said: "You are going to marry Peter Vanderkief within six weeks or two months—or you are going
to get the shock of your willful life."

"No," replied she, in a voice of calm equally dreadful. "I have already had that shock. I thought
mother was the snob. I thought women were the snobs.
But I see it's the men—worse than the women—you
worse than mother. Oh, father," she said, changing
suddenly to passionate pleading, "how can *you* be like
this! *You*—of all men!"

"Never mind me, young lady," snapped her father,
flying to the safe refuge of rage. "I'm going to save
you from this blackmailing fortune hunter." And the

unpleasantly crowded teeth showed savagely through the ragged gray mustache.

" I have asked him to marry me, and——"

" What! " shouted Richmond, again forgetting the groom. " Are you *crazy?* "

" I am," said Beatrice simply. " I love him. I'm crazy—permanently crazy."

" Your mother will take you to New York this very day. You'll sail day after to-morrow morning."

" I shall do nothing of the kind," said the girl.

The sound Richmond made was in the guise of laughter—of mockery. But no snarl or roar could have been so fraught with menace. "We'll see about this, miss," said he. " I'll show you who is master in my family. I'll show you you can't go on degrading yourself with this low intrigue. That hound! So he thought he could fasten himself on me—did he? I'll teach him! "

" I have proposed to him. He has refused me. I've made love to him. He has repulsed me."

Richmond's cruel mouth under his ragged mustache was horrible to see. " You shameless girl! " he cried. " It'll be one of the servants next. I must get you safely married at once. If your mother wasn't absolutely incompetent she'd have had you settled long ago."

"I shall marry no one but Roger Wade," came from the quiet figure beside him in a quiet voice.

"Have you got no sense at all? You say the puppy refused you. Don't you know why?"

"I know the reason you'd give."

"And that's the real reason. He has heard about *me!* He's got brains enough to understand that his best game is to———"

"Don't you say another word against him!" cried Beatrice, at the end of her forbearance. "You talk of my being a fool. What do you think of yourself? You don't want me to marry this man. How do you go about preventing it? Why, you show me that you are not the father who, I thought, loved me, but that you couldn't love anybody. You show me that you are not the kind of man I thought, but a snob, a hypocritical snob—yes, a hypocritical snob, who has been pulling wires behind mother—you all the time railing at her and at me and at Rhoda as snobs. And then, when you've shown me the truth about my surroundings, you go on to attack the man I love—to say about him things I know to be false. Is *that* what you call clever?"

"I'm glad you're letting me see you in your true colors," said the father, so exhausted by his passions that his voice came as little more than a hoarse whisper. " As for that—that fortune-hunter who has been making a fool of you—don't ever mention his name to me again ! "

" Do you want me to jump out of this cart? " cried the daughter, quivering with fury.

Richmond pushed the horses into their swiftest trot. He did not speak again until he reined in at the entrance to the gray chateau. Then he said viciously, " Go to your rooms and get ready to leave for New York and Europe. You have two hours and a half."

IX

RICHMOND, shrewd student of human nature and well versed in his favorite child's peculiarities of will and temper, did not underestimate what she had revealed to him—neither that which she had revealed consciously nor the no less important things she had unconsciously implied. Also, he had seen the man for whom she confessed infatuation, had measured his physical attractions and had got a fair notion of the inner charms which made the physical charms so potent. It was a time for swift and summary action; this adventurer must be got rid of before he could use the foolish child's infatuation to put himself in a position where he might cause scandal and, if he chose, could exact heavy blackmail. Theoretically, Richmond regarded his daughter as lovely and fascinating enough to bring any man in the world to her feet. Practically, he believed feeling for her had no part in the doings of " that fortune-hunting hound." He had been young and now was not far from old, yet he had not seen any exception to the rule he held axiomatic—

that wherever money is involved at all it is the only
real factor.

Yes, it was a time for action, instant and drastic.
As he drove back toward Wade's studio he strove with
his rage, trying to calm it so that his sly brain might
plot one of those subtle tricks which had got him his
vast fortune and had made him about the most admired,
most hated and most denounced man in American
finance. But every time he thought of his child's weak-
minded lack of self-respect or of the brazen impudence
of the penniless artist he fell to grinding his teeth again
and to cursing his inability to lock her up until she
recovered her senses, and to horsewhip the artist out
of the neighborhood. Richmond had been so long used
to having his will of any and every human being he
happened to need that he latterly had become really
insane when opposed. It was enough for a man to
appear in his pathway; at once he began to take the
worst possible view of that man's character, a method
which greatly assisted him in stifling the voice of conscience. Time was when he, like all men who have built
themselves up from small beginnings, had his temper
well under control, a bloodhound to be released only
when it was prudent and advantageous to do so. But
the habit of power had wrought as destructively in him
as it has in almost all those who have become rulers.

176

His temper was fast becoming a dangerous weakness—
that traitor within who overthrows where foes without
could never prevail.

When he arrived in sight of the studio there sat
" the hound " on the doorsill, smoking a pipe. Roger
did not move until Richmond was within, perhaps,
twenty yards—reasonable speaking distance; then he
rose and waited in large tranquillity. Richmond advanced until he was about ten feet away. There he
halted. To have gone nearer would have been to put
himself, the small of stature and the spare of build,
absurdly in contrast to the towering Roger—like a
meager little bush at the base of a tree. Across the
space between them he hurled at Roger one of those
glances which Roger himself had described as " aimed
to kill."

" What can I do for you, sir? " inquired the young
man at length. He showed not a hint that he was
aware of the wrath storming in the small man.

" You—you damn scoundrel! " ejaculated Richmond between his teeth—for the feeling of futility
acted on his rage like oil on fire.

Richmond's mien had prepared Roger for something like this, so he bore the shock with infuriating
composure. He eyed his insulter without moving
a muscle of his face, then turned and crossed the

threshold of his studio, reaching for the door to close it.

"Hold on there!" cried Richmond. "I've got something to say to you."

Roger went on in and closed the door. Richmond stared at it with mouth ajar. What sort of a scheme was this? What did the fellow calculate to gain toward his ends by making such a move? Richmond could not but admire its audacity. "No wonder he has succeeded in convincing the little fool that he is sincere." He advanced and opened the door. He entered the big, bare room; Roger, crayon in hand, was standing before the sketch that had been upon the easel when they left. He did not glance toward Richmond; he did not pause in his work. Richmond had not entered without having thought out a plan of procedure. Plain talk was the thing—not insulting, but plain. He must frankly assume that the artist was a detected and baffled plotter of a marriage for money.

"My daughter has confessed to me," said Richmond in a tone that was at least not insulting. "I have talked with her, and she is already ashamed of herself. So I have come from her to inform you that it will be useless for you to pursue your projects further."

The big, young man stood back from his sketch,

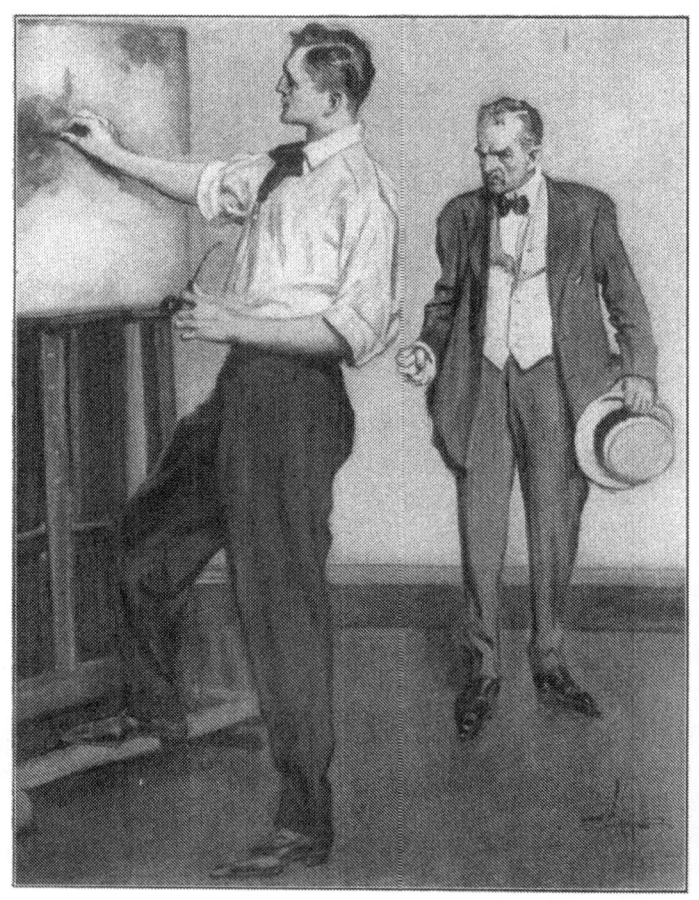

"'There ought to be a law that could reach fellows like you.'"

eyed it critically. A thin stream of smoke curled from the pipe in the corner of his mouth. He went on drawing as if he were alone in the room.

" I wish you clearly to understand," pursued Richmond, " that your attentions are distasteful to her and to her family. Acquaintance with her must cease."

Roger sketched on.

As physical violence was out of the question, Richmond did not know what to do—how to extricate himself from the absurd position into which his wrath had hurried him. He glowered at the big artist. The sense of impotence set his rage to steaming. " And I must tell you that if you had not had the cleverness to hold off—if you had lured that foolish child into marriage—you'd never have got a cent—not a cent! I'd cast off a child of mine who so disgraced her family. I'd forget she existed. But now that she realizes how she was trapped—what a slick citizen you are—she's ashamed of herself—ashamed of herself. There ought to be a law that could reach fellows like you."

While he was talking Roger was pushing his easel into the huge closet. He now closed and locked it, threw his coat over his arm and strode calmly past Richmond and out at the door. Not a word, not a glance, not a sign. Richmond followed him slowly. Roger marched at a long, swinging gait down the hill

179

toward the east and disappeared into the woods. Richmond stared after him. When the undergrowth hid him from view Richmond took out his handkerchief and mopped his face. In a long life dotted with many an unusual scene between him and sundry of his fellow-men he had never experienced the like of this.

"The scoundrel!" he said, a look of reluctant respect in his wrathful eyes. "The best game I ever ran up against."

He must hurry his girl out of the country—and not give her an unwatched moment until the steamer was clear of the dock.

Meanwhile, Beatrice had gone to her mother.

Mrs. Richmond was taking advantage of a lull in the entertaining to give herself a thorough physical overhauling. The lower part of the west wing was fitted up as a complete gymnasium, with a swimming pool underneath. She had played basket ball with her secretary and companion, Miss Cleets, had fenced ten minutes, had swum twenty, and was now lying on a lounge in her boudoir, preparing to go off into a delicious sleep. In came Beatrice.

"Well, mamma," said she, "the fat's in the fire."

Mrs. Richmond opened her drowsy eyes. "You've told your father?"

Beatrice nodded. " And he promptly blew up."

" I was sure he would."

Beatrice's expression—strange, satirical, sad, bitterly sad—could not but have impressed her mother had she not been more than half asleep. " You knew him better than I did," said the girl. " Still—no matter."

" We'll talk about it after I've had my nap."

" Oh, there's nothing to talk about."

" That's true," said her mother comfortably, as she slid luxuriously down the descent into unconsciousness —or is it an ascent? " You know there's nothing to do but to obey your father. And he's right. You'll be better satisfied with Peter." And Mrs. Richmond was asleep.

Beatrice stood looking at her mother. Her expression of somewhat undaughterly pity vanished and there was a rush of tears to her eyes, an uncontrollable tremor of the fresh, young lips usually curved in response to emotions in which tenderness had little part. " Dear mother," she murmured. She understood her mother's lot now, and sympathized in a way which Daniel Richmond's wife, unconscious what havoc those years of gradually deepened slavery had wrought in her mind, her heart, her whole life, would have regarded as hysterical and silly. Love had lifted Beatrice above

181

the narrow environment in which she had been bred and had quickened her to a sense of values she could hardly have got otherwise. She saw her mother as she was, as her mother could no more have seen herself than the lifelong drunkard, happy in his squalid sottishness, could reconstruct and regret the innocence from which he has dropped into the depths by a gradient so easy that it was unnoted. The girl realized that her mother's chief substantial happiness was inability to comprehend her own fate. "Thank God," said she to herself, "I had my eyes opened in time." And one by one before her passed faces of fashionable matrons, young and old, whom she knew well—hard or hardening features, like landscapes upon which only bleak winds blow and only meager light from cold, gray skies falls; eyes from which looked shriveled souls, souls in which all human sympathy, save the condescending charity that is vanity rather than sympathy, had dried up; lives filled with shams and pretenses; trim and showy gardens in which no flower had perfume, no fruit had taste, and where shone not one of the free, beautiful blossoms of genuine love. Not hard hearts really, but shriveled; not unhappy lives, but stunted and sunless, like plants grown in the luxury of a rich loam—in a dark cellar. The shock of disillusionment as to her father completed for Beatrice the

transformation that had been started by the under-
mining effect of Roger upon her conventional ideas—
as a thunderbolt crashes down a weakened dam and
releases its floods.

Beatrice passed a light and caressing hand over her
mother's beautifully arranged hair, bent and kissed her.
Then she stole from the room—with a lingering glance
of tenderest sweetness back from the threshold.

An hour and a quarter ticked away in that splendid room, with its wall coverings and upholsteries of
dark-red brocaded silk.   In stepped Richmond, brisk
and bristling.   He frowned at his sleeping wife, tapping his foot impatiently upon the floor.   "Lucy!"
he called sharply.

Mrs. Richmond's eyes opened, saw him.   Over her
face flitted an expression as primeval and as moving as
that of a weary slave awakened from delightful sleep
to resume the hated toil.   "Why did you wake me?"
she cried peevishly.

"Where's Beatrice?"

Mrs. Richmond resumed her normal expression of
haughty discontent.   "She was in here a while ago,"
replied she.   "In her rooms, probably."

"Did she tell you?" asked he.

"About Wade?"

"Yes," snapped her husband.   "What else is

there, pray? Has she been up to something else disgraceful?"

"Why, Dan, she's done nothing disgraceful," cried
the mother. "Every girl has those passing fancies.
But she'll not oppose you. Anyhow, her own good
sense——"

Richmond gave an impatient snort. "She's a fool
—an impetuous fool."

His wife ventured a sly, catlike look from the corner of her eye into his back. "You always say she's
the most like you of any of——"

"She takes her impetuosity from me. I hardly
need say from whom she inherits her folly."

"I can see nothing to get excited about." And
Mrs. Richmond stretched herself in preparation for a
leisurely sitting up.

Richmond regarded his wife with his habitual expression of disdain for her uselessness. He said per-
emptorily: "You are going to town this evening with
her, and you take her abroad day after to-morrow."

Mrs. Richmond sat up as if she had been prodded
with a spike. "I can't do it!" she cried. "I can't
get ready. And we've got invitations out for——"

"I'm going to send my own secretary—Lawton—
along with you, to watch her and report to me," said
Richmond. "You have shown that you are unable to

take care of her. Excited? Indeed I am excited. To find that a wretched fortune hunter has just about foisted himself on me. And what of our plans for the girl's future? Have bridge and these masseuses and hair women and all the rest of the fiddle-faddle that you fuddle about with taken from you the last glimmerings of sense?" He was storming up and down the room. "Good Heaven! Have I got to take one eye off my business to keep guard over my family? Are you good for *nothing*, Lucy?"

"I hope you were careful what you said to her," exclaimed Mrs. Richmond, alarmed by his complete lack of self-control. There had been many bitter scenes between them since their love waned as their · wealth waxed. But theretofore he had attacked her with irony and sarcasm, with sneer and jeer. Never before had he used straight denunciation, made coarse and brutal by a manner he had hitherto reserved for the office. "You can't treat her as you treat the rest of us," she warned him.

"And why not, pray?" demanded he. As she was silent, he repeated. "Why not? I said!" he cried in a tone so menacing, so near a blow, that she flushed a deep and angry red.

"Because you have made her independent," the wife was stung into replying.

"What imbecility!" scoffed he, enraged by this home truth that had been tormenting him for several hours. "She's got less than any of the rest of you. I've purposely kept her where she'd have to behave herself and love me. Your mind never was strong, Lucy. It has become flabby."

Mrs. Richmond was completely possessed by her anger. A cowed creature is hardest to provoke, cannot be roused until it is literally crazed; then it is like any other lunatic. She laughed in the face of her tyrant. "Love!" she jeered. "Love you! You haven't the least sense of humor, Dan, or you couldn't say that."

Richmond quailed.

"It's true, Beatrice has less than the rest of us. But Rhoda and I need more than she does. Anyway, my life's practically over. I've got no future—no hope elsewhere, or "—she sprang up and her eyes glittered insanely at him—" or do you suppose I'd stay on with you—you who have become nothing but a slave driver? Then there's Rhoda. She and her husband need quantities of money. The little you've given her is nothing to what she wants and fawns on you to get. As for the boys, they're too fond of being rich and showing off to dare do anything but cringe——"

"A nice brood you've brought up, haven't you?" frothed her husband.

186

"They're *your* children at heart—all of them. You've ruined them. Yes, you—not I, but you!"

He turned his back on her. "You go to Europe day after to-morrow, all the same," he cried.

"I'll do nothing of the sort!" retorted she.

"You will spend the money I allow you in the way I direct, or you will not get it," rejoined he. "Ring for your secretary and your maid and the housekeeper. Set this swarm of idlers in motion. There's no time to be lost."

"I'll not go!"

"Do you want me to give the orders? Do you want the servants to——"

"Oh, you—*devil!*" she screamed. Then she burst into hysterical tears. "And I've got no will. I'm a weak, degraded nothing. If I were a dozen years younger! Oh—oh—oh!"

Richmond rang the bell. "I've rung for your maid," said he. "Stop that slopping—and get busy." His tone indicated that he was not wholly pleased with himself.

His wife hastily dried her tears and hurried into her dressing room to remove the traces and to hearten herself with a stiff drink of brandy. Richmond continued to pace the boudoir. Marthe, the suave and ladylike, appeared with a note on her tray. She courtesied to Richmond and moved toward the dressing-room door. " What have you got there? " demanded Richmond.

" A note for madame—from mademoiselle."

Richmond snatched it from the little, silver tray, tore it open. His hand shook as he read. " Where did you get this? " he asked, in a voice from which all the passion had died.

" Mademoiselle gave it to Fillet as she was driving away."

" Go! " said Richmond; and as she went into the hall he entered the dressing room. His wife was before the dressing-table mirror powdering her nose. He flung the note down before her. " Read that," he cried.

Mrs. Richmond read:

Dearest Mother:

This is to say good-by—for the present. I've gone to New York to stop with Allie Kinnear and look about. I've no plans except not to come under father's roof again. I thought he loved me. I've found that he hasn't any heart to love anybody. He can't bribe me into putting up with his tyranny. I'm afraid he'll be cowardly enough to vent on you the rage for what's all his own fault. But he'd do that if I stayed on. So, I don't make it worse for you by going. Forgive me,

mamma. I love you better than I ever did in my life.
I'm so sorry to go—yet glad, too.

BEATRICE.

Mrs. Richmond laid the note calmly aside and resumed powdering her nose. She turned her head this
way and that, to study effects from different lights.
Apparently the note had made upon her no stronger impression than would have been made by the swift passage
of a fly between her and the mirror.

" She's gone," said Richmond, in a dazed way.

" And I doubt if she'll come back," said his wife.

." You must bring her back."

Mrs. Richmond was searching in the drawer for
some toilet article. " I can do nothing with her," said
she absently. " You know that. *Where* has Marthe
put——"

" You act as if you did not care," snarled he.

" And I don't," replied the wife indifferently.
" She's better off. I hope she'll marry Wade."

" *Marry?* " sneered Richmond. " Do you suppose
he'd marry her when he finds out that she has cut herself off? "

" Maybe so," replied Mrs. Richmond, with intent
to infuriate.

Richmond, with the wounds to his vanity inflicted
by Roger open again and burning and bleeding, gave

189

a kind of howl of rage. "Don't be a fool!" he shouted. "I say he will not marry her!"

"Then you ought to be satisfied," said his wife pleasantly.

"Satisfied?" Richmond, white with rage, shook his hand in her very face. "Satisfied? With the only one of my family that was worth while gone—you talk about my being *satisfied!*"

"Then why did you drive her out?" inquired she coldly.

Richmond flung out his arms in a vague, wild gesture, and rushed to the open window.

"You might go to Kinnear's and talk with her," suggested his wife.

"Say what?" demanded Richmond over his shoulder.

"How should I know?"

He wheeled round. "Are you on her side or on mine?"

"Oh, I'm just a fool," said Lucy.

Richmond's scowl at her changed to a scowl into vacancy. The scowl faded into a mere stare. Suddenly he burst out in a voice from which grief had washed every trace of anger: "I've got to have her back! I've got to have her back."

Mrs. Richmond's expression of amazement slowly

yielded to one of sullen jealousy. " That's right," sneered she. " Go and apologize to her. Knuckle down to her."

The husband, a wholly different figure from the bristling, bustling, self-assured tyrant of a few minutes before, went out without another word. The wife looked after him. The humiliation of having her daughter exalted while she herself was in the dust under his contemptuous foot had one consolation—the tyrant had met his match and might himself soon be abased.

X

In any city but New York, and even there in any
set but the one to which they belonged, the Kinnears
would have been regarded as rich. But in the company
they kept, their strainings and strugglings to hold the
pace were the subject of many a jest and gibe. Had
they not been of such superior birth—not merely Colo-
nial but Tory and forced to do exceeding shrewd and
heavy bribing to get back the estates forfeited to low-
born Patriots—they would have ranked almost as
hangers-on. Another generation, another dividing up
of those meager millions, and the Kinnears would cease
to make any part of the blaze of plutocracy's high society, would shine as modest satellites, by reflected light.
Thus, it was necessary that lovely Alicia Kinnear marry
money—big money. Beatrice Richmond's brother Hector was about as good a catch as there was going; so,
Beatrice and Allie became friends at school—Alicia,
being a sensible girl sensibly trained from the cradle,
needed no specific instruction from her mother in the
noble and useful art of choosing friends. The friend-

192

ship grew into intimacy, and Alicia saw to it that nothing occurred to produce even temporary coolings—this, with not the least show of sycophantry, which would immediately have disgusted Beatrice; on the contrary, what Beatrice most admired in dear Alicia was her independence, her absolute freedom from the faintest taint of snobbishness. If Beatrice had been more experienced she might perhaps have become suspicious of this unalloyed virtue. There is always good ground for suspicion when we find a human being apparently entirely without a touch of any universal human failing; Nature has so arranged it that each of us has a little of everything in his composition, and the elements that show in a character are rarely so important as those deep out of sight. However, Alicia was a sweet and generous girl, and gave a very pleasant and praiseworthy quality of liking where she felt that her station and circumstances permitted her to like—and how many of us can make a better showing?

When Beatrice, with Valentine, her maid, and two trunks, entered the big, old house in Park Avenue where the Kinnears maintained upper-class estate, Alicia was waiting with open arms. "Your telegram only just came," said she, hugging and kissing Beatrice delightedly. "But the rooms are ready—your rooms—and we've got Peter coming to dinner to-night."

"Peter!" Beatrice made a face. "Give me any-one else—*any*one else."

Alicia's blue eyes—beautiful eyes they were, so clear, so soft, so delicately shaded—opened wide. "Why, Trixy, I thought——"

"So it was," cut in Beatrice. "But that's off. Close the door"—they had just entered the sitting room of the charming suite set aside for "darling Bea-trice"—"and I'll tell you all about it—that is, all I can tell just now."

"Oh, you and Hanky will make it up——"

"Never! Whoever I may marry, it'll not be he."

Alicia looked shocked, grieved. And she was shocked and grieved. But underneath this propriety of friendly emotion she had already begun to consider that, if this were really true, Peter would return to the ranks of the eligibles—and he was through Harvard, while Heck Richmond was a junior and only a few months older than herself. An inexcusable duplicity— that is, inexcusable in any but a human being circum-stanced as was Alicia.

Beatrice laughed at her bosom friend's mournful ex-pression. "Oh, drop it," cried she. "You know Peter is no real loss. He's all right, of course—a clean, de-cent fellow, with a talent for dressing himself well. But no one would ever get excited about him."

"Does anybody get excited about anybody, nowadays?" laughed Alicia.

Beatrice nodded; into her eyes and out again flashed a look that could not but put so shrewd and sympathetic a friend as Allie into possession of her secret.

"Who?" said Allie breathlessly. "The Count? Oh, Trixy, you're not going to marry away off——"

"Not the Count," was Beatrice's quick, disdainful interruption. "What do you take me for? He's shorter than I and horribly old—over forty."

"I don't think age matters in a *man*," observed the charitable Alicia.

"I do," retorted Beatrice. "Not, of course, if one's marrying for—for other things than love. But I couldn't love an elderly man."

"Is forty elderly?"

"Isn't it?" replied Beatrice.

"But who is he?" implored Allie, all aquiver with curiosity.

Beatrice permitted a beatific expression bordering on fatuous folly to overspread her fair, young face. "Do you remember—down at Red Hill—the last time you were there—the biggest, grandest, handsomest man you ever saw——"

"The artist!" cried Allie in dismay. "Oh, dearest, I thought you were just flirting. And you are.

195

You wouldn't— Your mother'd never—never—consent. Isn't he—poor?"

"How can you talk like that?" exclaimed Beatrice, with all the new convert's energy in indignation.

"Well—one has got to live, you know," urged Allie. "And if he's poor—and your father doesn't consent——"

Beatrice laughed curtly—she had many mannerisms that reminded one of her father. "I'm not married yet —nor engaged."

"Have you talked with your father and mother?" inquired her worldly wise friend.

Miss Richmond again gave a sweetened and feminine version of her father's sardonic laugh. "That's why I'm here. I've broken with father."

"Oh, Trixy!" exclaimed Allie in terror. "You *can't* do that!"

"Oh, yes, I can. I have." She beamed on her friend. "And I've come to ask you to give me shelter for a few days—till I can look about. Father wanted me to marry Peter. I refused. He insulted me. Here I am."

Alicia kissed her with enthusiasm. "What a *strong* dear you are!" cried she. This remark seemed to her a wise and friendly—and discreet—compromise. It did not approve unfilial conduct. It did not encourage

196

Beatrice to weaken her opposition to Hanky Vanderkief. It did not commit the Kinnears to anything what-
soever. "But you must dress for dinner. Of course
I'll give you another man. I'll change my man to you
and take Peter. It's good to have you here. I *must*
rush away to dress."

But Miss Kinnear was not in such mad haste that
she could not look in on her mother, who was being
hooked up by her maid. "I'll finish mamma, Germaine," said Alicia. "I want to say something to her."
And the instant they were alone she came out with it:
"Beatrice has broken with her father because she
doesn't want to marry Peter. And she has come to stay
with us."

Alicia hooked; her mother stood patiently, apparently studying in the long mirror the way Germaine
had done her soft, gray hair. Of all the women in New
York who led the fashionable life, not one was able to
invest the despicable arts of prudence and calculation
with so much real grace and virtue as Mrs. John Kinnear.

"What shall I do, mother?" Alicia finally asked.

"Nothing," replied Mrs. Kinnear, in the tone of
one who has deliberated and decided. "We'll wait and
see. Certainly, that dreadful, dangerous devil of a
father of hers can't object to us giving his daughter

shelter—while we wait for him to try and get her back.
. . . Beatrice is very obstinate.”

“ Like iron—like steel. She says she’s in love with
an artist. He is terribly handsome, but not the sort of
man one would marry.”

“ Foreigner? ”

“ No, American. I never heard of him. I can’t remember his name.”

“ Good Lord, the girl’s crazy,” said Mrs. Kinnear.
“ Why did Mrs. Richmond let a man of that sort have
a chance to get well acquainted with her daughter?
Still, who’d have thought it of Beatrice? I’d as soon
have expected *you* to do it.”

“ Beatrice has got a queer streak in her,” explained
Alicia. “ You know, her father is—or was—very ordinary.”

“ No, that’s not it,” replied Mrs. Kinnear reflectively. “ Those things aren’t matters of birth and
breeding. I’ve seen the lowest kind of tastes in people
of excellent blood.”

“ How sweet you look! . . . I must dress. You advise me to do nothing? She didn’t want Peter at dinner. So—I’ll take him.”

That little rest between the “ so ” and the “ I’ll ”
was an excellent instance of the way mother and daughter had of conveying to each other those things impos-

sible of speech—the things that sound vulgar or shocking or basely contriving if put into words. And in no respect does the difference between the well bred and the common display itself so signally as in these small-large matters of what to say and what to imply. By this significance of silences mother and daughter were in the position—the happy position—of being able most sincerely and most virtuously, to deny even to themselves any and all intent of subtle or snobbish or intriguing thought. To impute such thoughts to such people is to excite their just indignation. As Allie departed to dress, her mother sent after her a glance of admiring love. She had brought her daughter up not as daughter, but as bosom friend, and she was reaping the rich reward; for Allie Kinnear, caring so little about everyone else that at bottom she neither strongly liked nor strongly disliked anybody, reserved and poured upon her mother all the love of her heart.

When the five women at the dinner were in the drawing-room afterwards waiting for the men, Mrs. Kinnear found an opportunity to say to Allie: " Richmond telephoned just before I came down. He is delighted that Beatrice is with us—wants us to keep her until he comes."

" She says she won't see him," said Alicia.

" I think I can persuade her."

Mrs. Kinnear was right. When Richmond called the following afternoon and Beatrice reiterated her refusal, Mrs. Kinnear said in her inimitable way, sweet, sensible, friendly: " My dear, don't you see that you are putting yourself in the wrong? "

" Why quarrel with him? " objected Beatrice. " Why stupidly repeat again and again that I will not marry Peter? My mind is made up. I shall not change, and he knows it."

Mrs. Kinnear had already debated—without letting herself know what she was about—whether or not to do all in her power to maintain the strained relations of father and daughter, " and help save poor Beatrice from the misery of marriage with a man she hates—a man who deserves a good wife." She had decided against siding with the girl because of the dangers in incurring the relentless wrath of powerful Richmond. So, her reply now was: " Dear Beatrice, you needn't be *afraid* of your father."

She had calculated well. Beatrice reared proudly. " Perhaps it does look as if I were afraid to face him," said she, all unconscious that Mrs. Kinnear was bending her to her will as easily as a basket maker bends an osier withe. " Yes—I'll go down."

And down she swept, to pause in statuelike coldness upon the threshold of the drawing-room, where her small, wiry father was pacing agitatedly. "Well, father?" said she.

They looked at each other in silence—measuring each other—or, rather, daughter submitting calmly to her father's keen, measuring eyes, while she wondered how a man so strong and daring as he could have such a pitiful weakness as snobbishness. At last Richmond said pleasantly: "Beatrice, I've come to take you back home."

She advanced to a chair, into which she dropped with graceful deliberation. "I thought you had come to apologize." Her tone was a subtle provocation.

He flushed a little—a faint glow upon his dry, wrinkled face with its huge forehead, its huge nose and its dwindling and wily little chin. "That, too," said he with astonishing self-restraint. "I was so mad yesterday that I lost my head. My digestion isn't what it once was. My nerves are frayed out."

"You admit you wronged Roger Wade?"

Richmond winced, but held to the game he had decided upon. "I admit I know nothing about him—except, of course, what D'Artois said. But I can't honestly say I believe in him. I still feel he is a fortune hunter."

"I can understand that," said Beatrice, unbending a little. "I suspected him, myself."

14   201

"Trust to your intuition, Beatrice," cried Richmond cordially. "It always guides right."

"I'm glad to hear you say that," observed his daughter. "For my intuition was that he was simple as a baby about money matters. The nasty suspicion came afterwards—when I was piqued because he had refused me."

Richmond made a large, generous gesture, strove—not unsuccessfully—to accompany it with a large, generous expression. "Well—that's all past and gone. Are you ready to go home?"

"I am not going home, father," said Beatrice in an ominously quiet tone.

Richmond ignored. "Oh, you want to stay with Allie a few days? Why not take her down with you? . . . The fact is"—Richmond cleared his throat—"the place seems lonely without you."

Beatrice's glance fell. Her sensitive, upper lip moved nervously—the faintest tremor quickly controlled.

"My car's at the door," he went on, an old man's fear-laden eagerness in his voice. "It'll take us straight to the station." He glanced at his watch. "We'll be in time for that first express."

Beatrice did not dare look at him. She said insistently: "You will say nothing more about my marrying Peter? You leave me free to marry whom I please? "

Richmond drew down his brows. Temper began to tug at the corners of his cruel mouth. Really, this insurgent child of his was exceeding the outermost limits of fond, paternal forbearance. " You've had time to think things over," said he in a voice of restraint. " You're a sensible girl at bottom. And I know you have decided to act sensibly."

Beatrice rose. " Yes, I have," said she.

" Then—come on," said Richmond, though he knew perfectly well that was not what she meant.

" You read my note to mother? "

" I pay no attention to hysteria. I waited for your good sense to get a hearing."

" I shall stay in New York," she said gently. " I am of age. I intend to be free."

" What nonsense! " cried he, with an attempt at good humor. " Where'll you stay? "

" Here for the present."

" Do you think the Kinnears will harbor you? "

" I'm always welcome here."

" As my daughter. But just as soon as they—any of the people you know, for that matter—find out that I regard anyone who's receiving you as abetting you in your folly and disobedience———"

"The Kinnears are *my* friends," said Beatrice coldly. "You exaggerate yourself, papa—or, rather, your money."

Richmond laughed—a vain, imperious, ugly laugh. "I can make the old woman upstairs put you out of the house in two minutes—and Allie will be afraid to speak to you."

Beatrice gave a disdainful smile.

"These Kinnears—and about everyone you know—have large investments in the things I control." And his tone and the twinkle in his eyes made the words conjure dire visions of possible catastrophe.

"Oh!" exclaimed Beatrice, paling. She looked at him with startled eyes. "I see . . . I see." She was calm and self-contained again. "I must not get my friends into trouble. Yes—I'll leave at once. I'll go to a hotel."

At this he lost patience. "You force me to be severe with you," said he, coming close to her and shaking his fist in her face. "Now listen, young lady. You are going home with me. And you are going to marry Vanderkief within six weeks."

Beatrice's expression was, in its way, quite as unpleasant as her father's. "You can't ruin *me*, father," said she with an ugly little laugh. "What you gave me is invested in Governments."

Richmond ground his teeth. "Don't remind me of my infernal folly. But I've had a valuable lesson. Not another cent do I give away till I'm dead."

"As soon as I can support myself," said Beatrice, "you'll get back what you gave me."

"Support yourself!" Richmond laughed—with real heartiness. He was surveying her standing there, in a fashionable carriage dress and looking engagingly fine and useless. "What could *you* do?"

"That remains to be seen," said Beatrice, flushing with mortification.

"Enough of this!" cried Richmond. "You certainly can't think me so weak and meek that I'd let you marry that fortune-hunting painter chap. I'll explain."

"Not to me," said Beatrice, walking calmly to the door. "Good-by, father."

"If you don't do as I say," exclaimed Richmond, "I'll ruin him."

Beatrice stopped short. She did not turn round, but from the crown of her head to the sweep of her skirt her whole figure expressed attention.

"He has a small competence—left him by an aunt," pursued Richmond, tranquil now. "I'll wipe it out. I'll make him a beggar, and then I'll see that he is driven from the country."

Beatrice turned round. " You—would do—*that!* " she said slowly.

" Just that—and probably more," her father assured her genially. " I think I have a little power—despite the belief of certain members of my family to the contrary."

" But he has done nothing ! " cried she. " I've told you he refused me—again and again. He has done everything to discourage me. He has wounded my pride. He has trampled on my vanity. He has told me plainly that in no circumstances would he burden himself with me."

" Then why do you persist? " said her father shrewdly.

She did not answer. Her head drooped.

Richmond laughed. " You see, your story doesn't hold together. This is Rhoda and Broadstairs over again. They conspired together to bleed me out of more than he had asked in the first place. I let them do it. But I knew what they were about. This is a different case." White and shaking, he waved outstretched arms at her. " You and your vagabond will never get a cent out of me, living or dead. And he knows it. I told him."

" You saw him? " said Beatrice eagerly. " What did he say? "

Richmond grew fiery red at the recollection of that interview, thus brought vividly back to him. "No matter," said he roughly. "You'll find that he wants nothing more to do with you. And when I get through with him he'll be glad to hide himself in some dark, cheap corner of Paris. He'll have to beg his passage money."

"Father, I told you the truth," said the girl with passionate earnestness. "He has never sought me. I have no hope of marrying him. I persisted—persist—because "—she drew her figure up proudly—"I love him!"

"A lot of pride *you've* got," sneered her father.

"Yes, I have," replied she. "I love him so much that I'd not be ashamed for the whole world to know it. I'm not one of those milk-and-water, cowardly women who have to wait till they're loved before they begin to give what they call love. I love him because he is the best all-round man I ever saw—becaues he is big and broad and simple—because he's honest and sincere—because he—because I *love* him!"

Richmond was silenced. She looked fine as she said this—the sort of woman an intelligent, appreciative man is mighty proud to have as a daughter. He was moved so powerfully that he could not altogether conceal it. But that was an impulse from a part of his nature deeply sepulchered and almost dead—quite dead so far as influence upon action or practical life was concerned. " You're stark mad, Beatrice! " he cried. " This has got to be cured at once. Come home with me! "

" Father," she pleaded, " you never denied me anything in my life. And this I want more than all——"

" I thought you said you had no hope," cried her father, encouraged to see weakness in the feminine pathos of her tones. " Now, drop this nonsense! Come with me and marry Vanderkief or I'll beggar that artist and drive him out in disgrace. Take your choice. And be quick about it. I'll not make this offer again, and I'll not stop the wheels once I set them in motion. In two days I can have him made penniless."

Beatrice looked at her father; her father looked at her. She laughed—a quiet, cold laugh. " You win," said she. " I'll go."

And five minutes later she, having passively submitted to Allie's and Mrs. Kinnear's farewell embraces, descended to enter her father's automobile. Richmond took the seat beside her with an expression of mere tranquillity upon his shrewd, dangerous face.

He had accomplished only what he felt assured in advance he would accomplish. Whenever he played trumps they won.

XI

PETER VISITS THE PRISON

WE may hesitate, back and fill, creep forward with trembling caution, in matters affecting our own affairs. But we show no such nervousness when it comes to interfering in the affairs of another. There we are swift and sure. We give advice freely; we say "ought" in authoritative tones; we even enforce judgment if we have the power. Why not? If matters do not turn out well the fault will lie not upon our advice, but upon the blundering way our advice was executed. Besides, we shall not be called on to pay the bill; destiny never settles its accounts in consequences vicariously. Richmond had given far less thought to his daughter's affairs than he habitually bestowed upon the small details of a small business deal. He felt he did not need to think about them; he knew what was good for her. Was he not her father?—and was it not a father's duty and privilege to know what was best for a daughter? So, the obstacle to the fulfillment of the destiny he had ordained for her must be swept away.

He was a man who looked at ends, not at means.

Taking all the circumstances into account, he was rather inclined to believe that his daughter was right about Roger Wade's not wishing to marry her; that for some mysterious reason the poor artist was firmly set against marrying her—perhaps was in love with some other woman, perhaps had a wife hidden away somewhere. But Roger's innocence or guilt was aside from the point—the said point being that his daughter must marry Vanderkief and so contribute her share toward broad and solid foundations for the family he was building. Thus, guilty or innocent, this artist who had had the misfortune to cross his path must be sacrificed if necessary.

He felt neither pity nor hatred for Roger Wade as he contemplated the possibility of having to ruin him. Richmond was as impersonal as are all the large forces of destiny, self-appointed or impressed—cholera germs or conquerors, cyclones or captains of industry. When he raised or lowered the price of a stock or of a necessity of life, destroyed an industry or annexed a railway, he looked on it as a destiny-ordained transaction; effects upon the happiness or misery of unknown fellow-beings did not enter his head. The suicides that followed his wrecking and looting of the M. M. & G. made no impression on him. If a man of action paused for such refinements of sensibility as in-

cidental evil effects from his great designs there would
be no action. If the Almighty were a sentimentalist
how long would chaos be postponed? " The larger
good " was Richmond's motto, and those who attacked
his right to set himself up as judge in so high and
difficult a matter were silenced by his pointing to his
triumphant success in establishing and maintaining
himself in destiny's American board of directors.

Beatrice, observing this relentlessness of his in a
romantic, impersonal way, and thinking only about his
exhibition of power and about the glories of victory,
had often admired, had been filled with pride. But now
that she had personal illustration of the meaning of
that sonorous word, relentless, she was feeling rather
differently. And hand in hand with horror of her
father there entered her heart a great fear of him.
She had fancied herself free! She had gone haughtily
away, had stepped proudly about, had admired herself
for superior strength and courage. Here she was,
back at Red Hill, as much in chains as her mother and
her brothers and Rhoda, Countess of Broadstairs.
Through and through she was afraid of this man who
would stop at nothing—and whom nothing could stop.
Bitterly and vividly and in self-scorn she was realizing
the truth so compactly presented by Montaigne where
he reminds us that the pedestal is not part of the bust.

But, although she could not lie to herself about her fear, she resolutely hid it. Her front was calm and undaunted. She accepted her check like her father's own daughter—with neither whimper nor frown. She was chattering gayly all the way down on the train. She greeted her mother as if she had merely been away for a day's shopping. She was the life of the dinner table, played bridge afterwards with her old-time skill —and that meant undivided attention upon the game.

Her father was puzzled. Did this cheerfulness indicate a plot to escape? Or, was Beatrice secretly delighted at being able to extricate herself from a situation extremely distasteful to her sober sense, without being forced to the mortification of having to confess her folly? Or, was it simply the natural and incurable frivolity of womankind? Richmond hoped and half believed that the last two guesses contained the truth; but he did not on that account relax his vigilance. It was his fixed policy to leave no point in his line uncovered, and to cover with the greatest care those points where danger seemed least likely. Thenceforth Beatrice should make no move without his knowledge. She was never alone except when shut up in her own apartment—and he had the telephone there disconnected. He was careful not to make his espionage irritating; it would not definitely disclose itself to her unless she tried to do something out of the ordinary. So far as he could judge, she did not realize that it existed.

A few days and Peter came down, to be received by her with a friendliness that delighted him, and Richmond no less.

Perhaps had Peter been born to make his own way in the world he would have developed a good mind and enough character to have enabled him to acquit himself creditably. As it was, however, his thinking had always been hired out and his character had remained almost rudimentary, except that he had been taught to resist any and all attempts to get money out of him—had been taught in much the same way that Nature teaches the oyster to close its shell when anything disagreeable tries to enter, teaches the worm to squirm out of the way when it feels a touch.

Unlike his mind and most of the rest of his character, Peter's vanity was far from rudimentary. Those born to wealth or position get a quaintly false notion of their own intrinsic importance—just as a prize milcher probably mistakes the reason for the assiduous attention of which she is the subject—the care with which she is washed and curried and fed, humored and petted, ever spoken to caressingly and considerately. Peter's vanity was as highly sensitized as the sole of the foot. He was constantly alternating between ecstasy and torment, according as he interpreted the actions of those about him—for he assumed that everyone was thinking of him all the time, that whatever was said was a compliment for him or an envious fling at him. Otherwise, one might travel far and search diligently without finding so amiable, so kindly a fellow as he. His extreme caution with money—except in self-indulgence, of course—did not produce any disagreeable effect upon his associates; they either were rich, young men, trained like himself to suspect everyone of trying to " trim " them, or were parasites upon the rich, accustomed to the penurious ways of the rich and rather admiring stinginess as evidence of strength of character. And it certainly was evidence of admirable prudence; for the merely rich man shorn of his riches is in much the same plight as a dog with its tail cut off close behind its ears.

When Peter and Beatrice went for a walk, Peter after a while noted the retainer of Richmond's personal staff lingering with unobtrusive persistence in the offing. " Why's that fellow skulking after us? " inquired he.

Beatrice laughed. " Oh, father's nerves."

" About cranks and anarchists and socialists—eh? Well, I don't wonder. The lower classes are getting damned impertinent in this country. I'm strongly tempted to go to England to live. There's the only place on earth where a gentleman can count on being treated like one all the time."

"Yes, it is comfortable," said the girl. "Except the climate!"

"That is rotten—isn't it? . . . I wish the fellow would drop us." Peter halted, frowning at the distant figure. "I think I'll call out to him."

"Oh, don't bother," said Beatrice. "He's doing no harm."

"But I feel as if we were being spied on."

"What of it?" cried she with a radiant smile. "We're not going to do anything that anybody mightn't see."

"But I've got some things to say to you—came down especially to say 'em."

"Are they things that have to be shouted?"

"No—but—he makes me uneasy—and there's you. You've got a way of looking and talking—as if you weren't taking anything seriously."

She was smiling as he spoke. But if he had been a close observer he might have seen an expression of a quite different character veiled by the laughter of lips and eyes.

"I came down to say some pretty sharp things to

you," he went on. " But, now that I'm with you, I don't seem able to get them out. But they're there all the same, Beatrice, and I'll act on 'em when I get away. I'm sure I will."

" Well? " said she. An expert in woman's ways would have gathered from the accent she put into the word and from her accompanying manner that this young woman had decided the time had come to make it easy for Hanky to unburden himself.

" You're not treating me right," he burst out. " You don't give me the—the respect that everybody else does; the—the consideration that I've been used to."

" For instance? "

Peter walked in silence beside her for some distance; these matters of which his sense of personal dignity was compelling him to complain were difficult to put into words that would not sound priggish and conceited. Finally, he made a beginning: " Of course, you're a splendid girl—the best I know—and that's the reason I want you. There isn't anybody else who combines all the advantages as you do. But—honestly, Beatrice, isn't the same thing true of me? "

He looked at her, with his mind and his face ready to resent evidences of her familiar mockery. But she was gazing ahead, eyes serious and sweet mouth free from any hint of a smile. "Go on, Hanky," said she encouragingly.

Peter felt that at last he was coming into his own. With a great deal more confidence he proceeded: "You make me feel as if—as if I were cheapening myself—hanging after you this way, taking things off you I wouldn't take off anybody else on earth."

"For instance?"

"Why, this engagement. There's hardly a girl in New York—in our set—who wouldn't jump at the chance. That isn't conceit. It's fact."

"It's both, Hanky," conceded the girl, without reserve. She looked at him, asked gravely: "Do you really want to marry me?"

"Haven't I told you?"

"When I don't love you?"

"I've been thinking about that," said Peter, with a notable air of experienced man of the world. "And it seems to me you're only showing what a fine girl you are. I'd be inclined to shy off from a girl who loved me before we were married. I like delicacy—and—and reserve—and purity—in a—a *lady*. By Jove, it seems to me there's something kind of—of brazen and forward in a girl's giving way to her feelings—when—when—she's not supposed to know about that kind of thing. It's—it's—well, it smacks of the lower

15   217

classes. They go in for that sort of thing—they and the sort of women one doesn't talk about."

A long silence followed this outburst of upper-class philosophy. Peter was revolving what he had said, with increasing admiration for his own acumen. As for Beatrice, after a fleeting smile of derision which he did not see, she resumed her own distinct line of thought. She looked at him several times—a scrutinizing look—a look of appeal—a look of doubt. Finally she said with some effort: "Peter—suppose I told you I loved another man?"

He shook his head incredulously. "You wouldn't love any man till you had the right to. Besides, where is there another man who's so exactly what you want in every way? You know we're exactly suited to each other, Beatrice. It's—it's like predestination. You'd hate to give me up as much as I'd hate to give you up."

Centered though her mind was on whether she could venture to make a confidant of him, she began to wonder at him. True, she had permitted him to speak frankly. True, their intimate acquaintance from childhood made him feel free to exhibit his innermost self without any especial nervousness or reserve. But there still remained something unaccounted for. Where had he got the courage to face her thus aggressively? How came he to be infatuated with himself so far beyond the loftiest soarings of his most self-satisfied mood theretofore? It was not long before her feminine shrewdness pointed her to the cause. "Some woman's been at him—been trying to get him away from me." In ordinary circumstances this would have pleased her no better than it would please the next woman. But just then she sincerely hoped her underminer had been successful.

"Peter," said she thoughtfully, "have you been considering giving me up?"

Peter looked flustered. But he did not hem and haw; he came straight back at her. "I haven't liked the way you've kept me on the string," confessed he.

"Is there some other girl?" inquired she eagerly.

"I've seen quite a lot of Allie lately," admitted Peter, and his manner let her know that he had been giving a large amount of thought to the advantages of making her jealous. "And I'm sure if I'd been to Allie what I've been to you she'd not treat me as you have."

Allie! Then it was all right. "*Dear* Allie" had been working in the interests of her friend. Beatrice sent a loving thought to her.

"And you must admit Allie has a lot of good points," pursued Peter, calculating that his judicial manner would set the jealous flame to spreading and mounting.

"She's much nearer your ideal of what a girl should be than I am," said Beatrice with discouraging enthusiasm. "She's fond of the same kind of life that you are. Peter—why don't you love her?"

Peter stared gloomily at the ground, then fell to switching off leaves with his stick. Was Beatrice jealous and taking this method of hiding it? Or was she really indifferent to the danger of losing one of the few first-class catches in America? The fear that the latter might be the case made him so miserable that he could not keep up the pretense about Allie.

Beatrice, desperate, hesitated no longer. "But first, Hanky, I want you to do me a favor. I want you to pretend that we are to be married and that it's to be in—say—in three months. Allie will understand. I'll explain it all to her."

Peter began to bristle. "Pretend to whom?" said he sourly.

"To father. And you must say you simply can't marry for three months. I must have time to— No matter. I hope—in fact I'm sure that I'll be able to let you off in a month."

"And have everybody say you chucked me? I like that—I do!"

"You know, Hanky, no one would believe for a minute that any girl would chuck *you.*"

"But—but you'd be doing it, just the same," he exploded. "And—I *want* to marry you."

"Now, Peter, you know perfectly well you like Allie better."

"Yes, I do *like* her better. Sometimes I don't like *you* at all. But I always *love* you."

"Habit—simply habit," Beatrice assured him airily. "You'll do it, won't you?"

"No!" cried Peter, stopping short. "No, I'll not do it. I've made up my mind to marry you. And I will."

"Aren't you ashamed of yourself, Hanky Vanderkief?" cried Beatrice. "Why, I always thought you were a gentleman."

"Oh, when we're married you'll be all right—mighty glad you did. A girl doesn't know her own mind."

"Shame on you! Trying to take advantage of the fact that my father's got me in his power."

This admission delighted Peter. "He's set on your marrying me?" he inquired.

"That's why I want you to help me."

"Then that settles it!" exclaimed Peter triumphantly. "We'll be married."

"You—side with him—against *me!*" Beatrice's scorn was superb. "Oh, I wish I could marry you—just to punish you for that!"

Peter looked uncomfortable but dogged. " I'd not dare offend your father, anyhow. It'd cost me a pot of money. He's got me up to my eyes in a lot of his deals. And if he turned against me—gad, I'd look like a sheep just after shearing. Beatrice, don't you see it? There's no escape for us. We ought to marry. We want to marry. We've *got* to marry."

Beatrice's answer was a glance of contempt. " I understand now," said she bitterly. " You'd marry Allie Kinnear, if you dared. But you don't dare because you're afraid it'd cost you a little money."

" A little! " cried Peter. " About a third of all I've got."

" And you've got about five times as much as you could possibly spend. Oh, I had no idea you were so contemptible. You'd marry me against my will—against your own heart—for fear and for money."

" I say, now! " protested Vanderkief. " That ain't fair, Beatrice."

" *Will* you help me? " demanded she.

" I can't—and I won't," replied he unhesitatingly. " And, furthermore, I'm going to put it up to you and your father that if you don't marry me next month I'll not marry you at all." And Peter drew himself to his full height and swelled himself to his excellent full figure and looked fiercely resolved.

Beatrice stood motionless, her gaze fixed upon a worn place in the grass just across the lake and not far from the cascade.

"What do you say, Beatrice?" he asked rather uneasily.

"You meant that?"

He nodded emphatically. "I did. I do."

"You'd speak to father?"

His eyes shifted. "If you compelled me to."

"Look at me, Peter."

With considerable difficulty he forced his eyes to meet hers. All the latent selfishness and pettiness in his nature seemed to her to be flaunting from them. "I'm doing what's best for *you*," said he sullenly.

She gave that short, nasty Dan Richmond laugh of hers—and his own face certainly did not suggest the sunny and generous side of his character. "Very well, dear Peter," said she. "We're engaged."

"And the marriage is next month, remember," he insisted. "We want to get to London before the end of the season."

"The thirty-first of next month." She was still looking at him with eyes full of sardonic—one might say, satanic—mirth. "Poor Peter!" she said.

"I can take care of myself," retorted he jauntily. "And of you, too. Your father understands you.

He'll see to it that you don't have the chance to make a fool of yourself and spoil your life after you're married."

Beatrice burst into a laugh full of pure mirth. "You *are* a joke!" she cried. "Poor Peter!"

"Let's go back to the house," said he angrily.

"Yes—to tell the glad news."

"Now, don't put on with me, Beatrice. Do you think I haven't got good sense? I know that in reality you are delighted. You seem to have a prejudice against doing anything in the ordinary way. You want to make me feel in the wrong—to get an advantage over me from the start. But I'm on to you. So —come along!"

Beatrice laughed again. And again she said, "Poor Peter!"

XII

UNDER COVER OF NIGHT

BACK at the house Beatrice and Peter went into the east drawing-room, where Mrs. Richmond was giving tea to her half dozen guests. As they entered from the hall Richmond appeared in the opposite doorway of the billiard room. He swept Peter's face with one of his keen glances. As soon as the agitations and read-justments incident to new arrivals were over, he took his daughter aside.

" Been quarreling with Peter? " said he.

She turned her head, called out: " Hanky—just a minute. You'll excuse him, Mrs. Martini? " And when Peter, red and ill at ease, was with them in the deep window, she said: " Tell him."

" Your daughter has—has consented," said Peter.

Richmond beamed and wrung his hand.

" And as we want to get to London for the end of the season," continued Peter, " we'd like to be married the last of next month."

" No objection—none whatever," said Richmond.

"I'm not sure," said Beatrice, all this time inscrutably calm. "I'll have to talk with mother first. It's not easy to get together the clothes in such a little time."

"Nonsense," cried Richmond. "There's the cable."

"And you'll want most of the things sent to you in London," suggested Peter.

Beatrice shrugged her shoulders. "Just as mamma says." And she strolled over to the tea table and cut herself a slice of layer cake, which she proceeded to eat with much deliberation and enjoyment.

The two men stood together observing her. Up came Mrs. Martini, slim and willowy and dressed in the extreme of the skin-tight fashions of that year. "What are you two looking so gloomy about?" inquired she.

Richmond scowled. "Gloomy?" said he, with a disagreeable laugh. "We feel anything but gloomy. That is—er—of course my feelings are somewhat confused. I've just learned that Peter's going to take Beatrice away from me the end of next month."

Peter's smile in response to Mrs. Martini's effusive congratulations was sickly, was with difficulty kept alive long enough to meet the requirements of conventionality.

Beatrice had not shown the faintest sign that she was conscious of imprisonment. So far as Richmond observed, not once had she made any attempt to break through or even to explore the limits assigned her. Had it not been for the discontent plain to see upon Peter's florid, vigorously healthy countenance throughout the four days he lingered at Red Hill, Richmond would have assumed that his daughter had regained her reason as he had felt confident she would. Beatrice did make an effort in public to treat Peter as her fiancé; but she had to give it up. Her nerves refused to assist her in her game of hypocrisy beyond a certain point —and Peter had become physically repulsive to her. She did not regard this defect in her otherwise perfect pose as serious. She knew that her father was not one to relax vigilance because he had won. So, what advantage would there be in striving, and probably failing, to remove his last suspicion?

Without betraying herself she had thoroughly examined all the metes and bounds of her prison. She found it everywhere worthy of her father's minute ingenuity. By means of his pretext of alarm about cranks and kidnapers she was being thoroughly spied upon without the spies suspecting what they were really about. By day there were the personal guards, to inform him if she tried to communicate with Roger either personally or by message. By night there were the watchman within and the three patrolmen without, and a system of burglar alarms that made it impossible for anyone either to leave or to enter without flooding the whole house with light and starting up a clamor of bells from attics to cellars.

Apparently she was as free as air—free to roam anywhere in the vast wilderness surrounding the gardens and terraces and lawns from the midst of which the big chateau rose. Really, she could not move a step in secret—and to give Roger the warning she must see him face to face without her father's knowledge. For, if her father purposed to keep faith with her, it would be folly to give him reason to feel he would do well to ruin Roger anyhow; and, if he did not purpose to keep the agreement under which she had returned and had accepted Peter, it would be madness to provoke him to attack Roger immediately. She must see Roger secretly.

But how?

If chance there was, that chance must be under cover of night—night, when she was at least free from the espionage of human eyes. How could she get out of the house undetected and get back into it unsuspected? And if she could accomplish this well-nigh impossible feat, how arrange to meet Roger—when she could not communicate with him, when she did not even know where he lived?

Every system of human devising has its weak point. By observing and thinking Beatrice discovered the weak point in this system of her father's. As soon as she formed her plan she got ready this note:

Chang:

It is absolutely necessary that I see you for a few minutes. My only chance is at night. So, come down to the cascade at one o'clock the morning after you get this. Don't fail me. Don't think me hysterical or sentimental. I might almost say this is a matter of life and death.

R<small>IX</small>.

The burglar alarms were switched on every night by Conrad Pinney, the superintendent, just after the house was closed. They were switched off at five in the morning by Tom, the indoors watchman, when the lowest rank of menials in the service of the establishment descended from their little rooms under the eaves of the west wing to make ready the first-floor rooms for the day. The house was closed as soon as the last member of the family went up to his or her rooms. To escape, she must choose the moment or so between the ascending of the last member of the family and the switching on of the alarms—and it must be on a night when some one member of the family stayed down long enough after the going of the rest to make it certain there would be no accidental glancing into her rooms to see that all was well. To get back into the house she must wait until it was opened at five o'clock and slip in unseen by the menial sweepers and cleaners and polishers.

On Tuesdays and Thursdays her father brought from town a bundle of papers which he usually sat up with until midnight or even one o'clock. Then he and Pinney often walked up and down the terrace before the main entrance and smoked for twenty minutes. Peter went away on a Monday. On Tuesday night there were no guests. At dinner were only the family—her mother, her father and herself, her mother's secretary, Miss Cleets, Mrs. Lambert, the housekeeper, and Pinney. As they sat at table Beatrice revolved her project, decided she would risk a slight change in it that would spare her a night outdoors and the danger of being seen as she entered in the early morning. After dinner she and her mother and the housekeeper and Pinney played bridge until half past ten. By eleven o'clock everyone was gone from downstairs but her father, Pinney, and two servants. In her room in the dark she waited until half past eleven, then changed to outing dress, descended and slipped into the gray

salon. Its windows had been locked for the night.
She unlocked one, opened it, went out upon the broad,
stone veranda, closed the window behind her. The sky
was fortunately overcast, or she would have been in
full view, as the moon was on that side of the house.

She crept along in the shadow of wall and shrubbery until she was in the woods. There she struck into
a path and fled down the hill toward the boathouse.
When she was about half way she remembered the outside watchmen—remembered that the boathouse was
one of their stations. It would be folly to risk running into them; she must make the trip to the studio
on foot by rounding the end of the lake—full five miles
instead of less than three. At the shortest she would
be gone, not about two hours, but more than three. So,
it was useless to think of getting in before her father
went to bed and the alarms were switched on. Instead
of hurry there was time to waste—all the time before
five in the morning. She strolled along, taking the
longest way and keeping entirely clear of the watchmen's routes among the several groups of widely separated outbuildings—the stables and garage, the
water, lighting and laundry plants, the kennels, the
hothouses, the farm and dairy buildings.

A fine, soft rain fell, but it did not trouble her as
the foliage was now—early May—so thick that it was

almost a roof. When she came out of the woods near the studio the rain had ceased and the moon, never so thickly veiled that it did not give her light, sailed in a clear path among the separating clouds. She looked at the watch on her wrist; it was nearly one o'clock. " I came too quickly," she said. " I must do better going back."

She found the studio door open, as she expected; there were no tramps in that region, and Red Hill was guarded only because New York thieves might plan an expedition expressly to plunder it. She dropped the hasp from the staple, pushed the big door open.

The room within was in the full pour of the moon now straight above the huge skylight. She looked round, her heart beating wildly—not with fear, not with expectation, but with memory. From that bench there she had first seen him. There she had watched him making chocolate. There they had sat drinking it, she admiring the swift, vivid play of emotion upon his handsome face—and what interesting emotion!—so free —so simple—so strong—so genuine! She went to the bench, seated herself, stretched herself at full length— and sobbed. " Oh, if you only knew ! " she cried. " I'm so different now ! I've learned so much—and I love you —love you, Chang ! " It thrilled and comforted her to speak out her heart without reserve in that place.

She searched the room for some memento of him. In one of the wide chinks in the masonry of the chimney she found a pipe—an old, evil-smelling thing, its mouthpiece almost bitten through. She laughed and cried over it, touching it caressingly, making a face at its really fearful odor, but loving it none the less. She tore up an old newspaper, wrapped the pipe carefully to shut in that odor if possible.

She sat on one of the rough, uncomfortable chairs and proceeded to live over every moment of her acquaintance with him—to recall all he had said and done and looked, all his little peculiarities of gesture and accent; to analyze his fascination for her—why she loved him—the thousand and one reasons in addition to the real reason—which, of course, was that he was Chang, the biggest and straightest and honestest man she had ever known, not even self-conscious enough to be modest. The moon crossed the skylight; the room faded into half darkness; the moon reappeared at the west window, high up in the wall. She dreamed on and on —the dreams with which she filled most of her waking moments when she was alone. When she remembered to look at her watch it was five minutes after three!

She sprang up, took the note from her bosom, thrust it three quarters through the crack between the closet door and its frame, just above the lock. Would

16   233

he get it that morning? Or, would it be several days before he came there? " I'll go to the cascade two nights," said she. " Then, if he doesn't come, I'll try some other way."

When she reached the top of Red Hill it was day, though the sun was not yet above the horizon. She circled round until she was opposite the main entrance, but well concealed. She had come down early so often that she knew the routine through which the servants would go. Just as the first rays of the sun lit upon the topmost of the pointed roofs, Tom, the indoors watchman, appeared in the main entrance. The alarms were off. She circled back to the west and, by way of the dense shrubbery that would hide her from any chance gazer from windows, she gained the veranda—the unlocked window of the gray salon. Her heart stood still while she was raising that window. When no sound of bells banging and clanging came she drew a long breath, stepped weakly through, lowered and locked the window. The rest of the journey was comparatively free from danger.

When her maid came in at nine o'clock she was sleeping soundly; and all traces of her expedition had been removed by her own unaccustomed hands from skirt and leggings and shoes. The old pipe in its newspaper wrappings was hidden deep in a drawer of lingerie odorous of delicate sachet—a drawer of which she had the only key.

Getting away from the house the next night was not so easy.

Several guests came from town in the afternoon. She was obliged to stay down until the last, had difficulty in preventing Josephine Burroughs from following her into her room to chatter for an hour or longer. All evening, as her father lingered in the drawing-room, she had forced herself to act in her gayest, most unconcerned manner. Her nerves were on edge and she had a fever. She knew the servants were closing the house in mad haste. There was no time to change dress or even shoes; there was just time to send her maid away, to catch up a long wrap, turn out her lights and dart downstairs. Probably no one was yet in bed, but she must take the chance of some accidental late call upon her. As she raised the window in the gray salon she confidently expected to hear the bells, to be dazzled by sudden flash of lights. She did not breathe until she had it lowered.

It was after midnight. She congratulated herself on having fixed one o'clock as the hour for the meeting. She would have just time to reach the little cataract. She had not gone far before her slippers were in a dreadful state and her legs wet to the knees. " The excitement's the only thing that can save me from the cold of my life," thought she. Colds were serious matters with her—disfiguring, desperately uncomfortable, slow to take leave. Long before she reached the lower end of the lake she could feel that her dress was a bedraggled wreck, high though she had held it. As she went along the rough shore path she glanced from time to time at the meeting place on the opposite side. The moon made everything distinct; he was not there. Had it taken her longer to come than she thought, and had he gone? Or had he disregarded her note? Or had he not yet got it? " I don't believe I'll dare come again," she said to herself despondently. But she knew that she would.

She crossed the brook on the stones that fretted it. She reached the place where she could see the grass worn by his working at his easel, the mud of the lake's brim creased by the keel of her canoe. She looked all round, straining her eyes into the dimness under the trees.

" Chang! " she called.

She gazed, listened, waited. " Chang! " she called again, a sob in her voice.

From the deep shadow of the maple tree immediately in front of her came Roger's voice: " Some one is coming toward us in a boat."

"'Chang!' she called again, a sob in her voice."

"Don't move!" she exclaimed in an undertone.
"No matter what happens, don't show yourself. I
must speak quickly," she hurried on. "That money
you said you had—you must sell out whatever it's invested in and put it in Government bonds—right away.
Will you? Promise me!"

"I can't," replied he. "It's in bonds of the Wauchong Railroad, that's just gone into the hands of a receiver."

Beatrice gasped. "Oh!" she cried. But she must
not delay. "My father did it," she hurried on, "because he wants to ruin you and drive you out of the
country."

Roger laughed quietly. "Don't worry, Rix. I'm
all right."

"I've got so much to say. I must see you
again——"

"No. This is good-by. I read about your engagement, and I was glad you had made up your mind to do
the sensible thing. I hope you'll be happy—and you
will be. I'll send you the picture as a wedding present."

"Chang—don't believe that," cried she imploringly.
"I *must* see you. As soon as I can I'll let you know.
I'm watched. But I'll give them the slip and——"

"You'll do nothing stealthy—not with my help,"
answered he. "I'll not come again——"

237

The clash of oar in lock struck both silent. A row-boat glided from the shadows, thrust its nose far up the muddy shore. Beatrice immediately recognized her father the only occupant. He stood up, looking round. He said in a voice of suspiciously pleasant intonation, " I see Wade hasn't come yet. Well, I'll wait and take you back. The walking's bad—especially in that kind of dress."

Each could see the other's face plainly in that bright moonlight. She showed no more sign of agitation than he, and he was suave. Beatrice spoke. " Yes, I've ruined my dress. And the slippers—they're pulp." She glanced round. " What time is it? "

" Half past one," he announced, as the result of a look at his watch.

" It's later than I thought. I'm ready to go home now."

" I've plenty of time," protested Richmond.

" No. Let's go. There's nothing to stay for."

And she stepped into the boat, steadying herself with a hand on his shoulder as she passed him on her way to sit in the stern. It had been almost necessary that she steady herself somehow in passing him in that rather narrow rowboat. She was hardly conscious that she had touched him; he was touching her as a matter of course, and also his own guiding and steadying hand was on her arm. Yet the incident, apparently trifling, was in fact most significant in itself and fraught with highly important consequences. In the first place it showed that, though father and daughter fancied they were hating each other to the uttermost, they in reality were still father and daughter, with at least one strong, uncleft bond of sympathy through the recognition by each in the other of qualities both intensely admired— for two people who deeply hate do not touch each other except in anger. Also, it altered their immediate relationship; it softened the animosities that were raging for utterance in each, and made it impossible for the quarrel that was bound to come to be of exactly the same complexion—of the same peculiar character it would have taken had they not touched each other.

When she was seated he pushed off and disposed himself at the oars. He kept to the middle of the lake, where the light was clear and strong. They had not gone many yards on that water journey of three miles before her father said:

" You wanted to tell him what I warned you I would do? "

" Yes."

" And then you intended to break your promise to me? "

" No. I made no promise—not in so many words.

But I was going to stand by the engagement. Peter has become repulsive to me, but—any man would be equally so. And I might as well marry and have done with."

"A few years from now," said her father, "you will thank me for having saved you from your folly."

She dropped her hand into the water. The moonbeams glistened on her yellow hair, on her smooth, young face and neck.

"You ought to have known," pursued her father, "that I would not have told you I would ruin Wade unless it was impossible for him to escape. I have put his investments in such a position that I can wipe them out or not. What I'll do will depend on whether you are foolish or sensible."

She glanced up for an instant. Then he was not so guilty as she had thought—that is, *perhaps* he was not.

"You say you didn't intend to break the engagement," he went on. "Why, then, did you come here to-night?"

"Because you had made it impossible for me to let him know in any other way."

"You could have written," rejoined he; the familiar note of suspicion, of the keen mind on the scent for the hidden truth was strong in his voice. "I've no control over the mails."

"I didn't want to put on paper—such a thing—about—my father."

Richmond rowed in silence perhaps ten minutes. Then he said, and the note of affection was fully as strong in his voice as the note of suspicion had been before:

"Was that your only reason?"

"I thought so," replied she. "I realize now that I also wanted to see him—to see if there was any hope."

"You'd feel fine—wouldn't you—if you made a fool of yourself with this man and then found out that he was already married?"

The change in her expression was apparent even in that misleading light. During the long silence he saw that she was revolving his sinister suggestion. He took his time before going on in a calm, deliberate tone: "We know nothing about him—except that he is a man you, in your right senses, would never think of marrying."

"That is true," replied she, "if you mean by right senses the sort of girl I was brought up to be."

"The sort of girl you *are*," said he with gentle emphasis. The Daniel Richmond of rage and threat was engulfed in the wise and skillful man of affairs.

She looked at him with her old-time, gay mockery. "You've decided to take a different tack with me, I see."

241

Richmond met smile with smile—and it was from him that she had got the peculiar charm of her smile. " I admit I've been blundering," said he. " My eagerness to have you do what was best for you blinded my judgment. And it was very exasperating to see you rushing headlong into a folly you'd repent all your life. It's hard for an older person to remember how inexperienced youth is, and to be patient. But I'll try to do better. . . . I sent your mother to see whether you were in your room. I don't know why I did it. I've got instincts that have saved me in tight places many a time. She went, came back—said you were there. But she can't deceive me face to face. She has learned that I scent a lie like a terrier a rat. So, I went myself. When I saw you were gone it sobered me." He said these things in a thoroughly human way, sincerely, simply— himself as he was for the daughter he loved.

" I'd like to be able to—to do as you wish, father," said she with gentleness. " But when I told you——"

" Let's not discuss that now," he interrupted. " Tomorrow, perhaps. Not now."

Another silence, with the girl rapidly softening toward her father—her always indulgent father, and she, the recently worldly, could appreciate his point of view —why, at times, her own new point of view seemed an aberration in a dream.

She said: " Have you reason to think he is—is married? "

" So have you."

" He never told me—never hinted such a thing."

" Did he ever tell you he was not married? "

" Certainly not." Beatrice laughed aloud. " I never told him I was not married."

" You say you asked him to marry you? "

" Yes—I did."

" And you say he refused? "

" He refused absolutely. He laughed at the idea that I really cared for him. If you could have heard, father! That's why it'd be unjust for you to blame him. It was every bit my fault."

" Why did he refuse to marry you? " her father asked calmly.

" Because he did not care, I suppose—care enough."

" What reason did he give? "

" He didn't think it would be good for his career. He— Oh, he had a lot of reasons. They didn't seem to me to amount to much, for, of course, everybody wants to get married, and expects to, some time. That was why I—hoped."

" Don't you think he may have been evading— didn't want to tell you the real reason? "

Her father's calm, searching insistence, free from

anger or malice, friendly toward her, not unjust to Roger—it began to agitate her, to fill her with vague doubts and fears. " But if he had that reason," urged she, " he could have ended everything at once by telling me."

" Unless he had a reason for silence," replied Richmond. And with quiet acuteness he explained: " Maybe he's planning to get rid of his wife so that he'll be free to accept you—and the fortune he thinks goes with you."

" You're trying to prejudice me against him! " cried the girl, all in a turmoil over this subtle attack, which seemed to come as much from within as from without.

But her father was equal to this emergency. " If you intend to keep your engagement," said he, " if you have no hope of being accepted by this young man you know nothing about—you wish to be prejudiced against him—don't you, Beatrice? "

There seemed to be no effective answer to this shrewdness.

" Yes, I do want to prejudice you against him," continued Richmond. " I want you to wake up to the fact that you've been doing all these foolish, compromising things for a man about whom you know absolutely nothing."

" I'm *sure* he's not married! " exclaimed Beatrice with overemphasis.

" Maybe not," was her father's unruffled reply. " But it does look exceedingly strange—doesn't it?—that a girl like you should be refused by a poor nobody —for no reason."

" He is honest and independent," replied Beatrice strongly—but not so strongly as she wished. " He wouldn't marry me unless he loved me."

" But I should think," subtly suggested Richmond, " it would be—well, not so very hard for a man to fall in love with a girl who had so many advantages."

Beatrice's vanity lined up strongly behind her worldly common sense in conceding plausibility—and more—to this suggestion. She laughed, but she was impressed.

When they were near the house her father said good-humoredly: " Will you take me in the way you came out? I've told Pinney not to turn on the alarms until I come out of my study—where he thinks I am."

So, father and daughter reëntered Red Hill by stealth, getting a lot of fun out of the adventure—and separating at her door with a good, old-fashioned, old-time hug and kiss.

XIII

THE bill for that excursion in flimsy dress and slippers through the wet, cold woods was promptly presented; and, after the rude manner of all such bills, it had to be met on sight. As has been hinted, Beatrice did not have those refined, ladylike colds which enable heroines of fiction to continue in undiminished loveliness. She had the plain, human cold that reduces its victim to a wheezing, sneezing, snuffling hunk of misery, swollen of eyes and nose, laden with pocket handkerchiefs. She let no one but the family see her at such times—and was just as well pleased if they kept away.

Thus, she now had five days for uninterrupted reflection, in a humble, most penitential frame of mind. Her father did not disturb her, flattered her with attentions of specially selected flowers, of solicitous inquiries twice a day, not through secretary or butler or valet, but personally seeking her own maid.

The third day her mother came with glowing accounts of what he purposed doing for her in commemoration of the marriage. The chief items were mag-

246

nificent jewels and the Red Hill estate. As the jewels
would be too dear, to her who loved jewels, for her ever
to think of realizing on them, and as the Red Hill estate would call for a huge annual appropriation from
her father's bounty for maintenance, it must be said
that Richmond, resolved to keep his children dependent,
had chosen not uncannily. But Beatrice was in no
mood to tear his acts into shreds in search for the slyly
concealed motive. Since he had reversed her expectations by dealing gently with her when he caught her
at the cascade, she had almost restored him to favor
in her thoughts. Nor did the fact that gentle dealing
was absolutely the only course left open to him affect
her generous judgment. This news of the gifts, the
excited talk of her maid, on her own behalf and also
in repeating what was being said below stairs, the
journalistic comments on the approaching " alliance "
—all these things tended to put marrying Peter before
her in a less unfavorable light. And she was not seeing
Peter—nor Roger.

Abased by her cold, she took a low view of her go-
ings on with Roger. She succeeded in shaming her
skulking pride into the open, where it made earnest
efforts to reproach her for having thrown herself at a
man who had promptly and decisively repulsed her.
No matter what his reason. He had shown her that he

did not love her—and did not want her love. The older people grow, the less nervous they are about being sillily romantic; they glory in the divine follies of love. Young heart being all they have left of youth's fair, fleeting riches, they try to enjoy it to the uttermost. But young people, if at all sophisticated, shy from extravagant romance; they fear to be convicted of the horrible crime of being young and green; they dread falling victim to the humiliating swindle of loving more than they are loved, of giving more than they get. Until Beatrice met Roger she had prided herself on the control of her mind over her heart, on being "woman of the world." She now began to smile—faintly, but with attempt at mockery—upon her delirium of love. She did not regret it, did not repent it. But she thought of it as a thing of the past.

Her father dropped in on her for a little talk before dressing for dinner. He had never been so attentive—and no man could be more fascinating than Richmond, when he wished. "I've got to make a tour of the Northwest," said he. "I must start not later than the twenty-second of May—and be gone a month. I wish you'd either put off the wedding till I get back or have it before I go. When Peter comes down tomorrow you and he can talk it over. You know I'd rather you married before I go. I'm not as young as I once was, and there's an element of uncertainty in these journeys. But it shall be just as you say."

"It'll have to be put off," said Beatrice.

"Don't forget that Peter has made arrangements for you to be presented at court the tenth of June."

"I simply can't get ready."

"Your mother thinks you can," said Richmond, showing his keen disappointment, but altogether in regret, not at all in anger or reproach. "Still, do the best you can. Think it over. Talk with Peter."

"I'll do the best I can," said Beatrice. She had protested more strongly to him than she had in her own heart, for she was now sunk down into indifference. Nothing seemed to matter. The cold had left her physically below par; her mental state was therefore blackly pessimistic. Roger's lack of response seemed profoundly discouraging; she began to doubt whether she loved him—whether she ever had loved as she had fancied. We should get very much nearer to the truth about human adversities and disasters—the truth about their real causes—did we but know exactly what was the state of health of the persons chiefly concerned. Beatrice well and Beatrice ill were two absolutely different persons.

"Yes—I know you'll oblige me if it's possible," said her father.

The next day happened to be a Sunday. Richmond himself motored down to meet Peter, who was arriving in time for lunch.

As the young man descended from the train it took no skill whatever at reading faces to discover that he was out of humor—had been brooding over Beatrice's treatment of him, and in the brooding had lost nothing of the grouch he had taken away with him. A weak man never looks so weak as when he is out of humor; accordingly, Peter was showing his true character, or lack of character, with a distinctness that irritated Richmond even as he reflected how admirably it fitted in with his plans. Peter was not to blame for his weakness. He had not had the chance to become otherwise. He had been deprived of that hand-to-hand strife with life which alone makes a man strong. Usually, however, the dangerous truth as to his weakness was well hidden by the fictitious seeming of strength which obstinacy, selfishness, and the adulation of a swarm of sycophants and dependents combine to give a man of means and position. Richmond, for all his reverence for Peter's lineage and wealth nearly two centuries old, had not for an instant been deceived as to his personal character. One reason why he felt so satisfied with him as a son-in-law was his belief that Beatrice could be happy only with a man she could rule; and on this

Sunday of Peter's arrival with his weakness stripped naked to the most casual eye by his bad humor, Richmond was better pleased than ever with his selection for his high-strung daughter.

"Peter," said he sharply, when he had him in the limousine.

The young man clinched his hands in a feeble gesture of preparation for resolute resistance.

"I've got to go West the middle of the month. I want you and Beatrice to marry before I go—say, on the twentieth. You have to be in London early in the second week in June?"

"Yes," said Peter reluctantly—the yes of a man lacking the moral courage to say no.

"I'll not be in the East again before the middle of June—maybe July."

"Can't do it," said Peter with a sudden scowl at the back of the chauffeur separated from them by thick glass.

"Why not?" inquired Richmond in the animal trainer's tone and with the animal trainer's eye upon the unhappy Peter. "Why not?"

"I'm not sure I shall marry at all," said Peter, and his fright distorted his bluff at resoluteness into a sort of nervous impudence, like that of the schoolboy braving the teacher's uplifted ferule because the rest of

251

the school is waiting with ears that long to hear him howl and beg.

Richmond twisted his small, wiry body round in the seat that he might bring the various batteries in and behind his face full upon Vanderkief. " Is this a joke? " he demanded.

" I wish it were," replied Peter diplomatically. " I've made some discoveries that will compel me to— to relieve your daughter of—of the engagement which —which is so distasteful to her."

Richmond's policy in dealing with his fellow-men was to strike his heaviest blow first—that is, he blew up the intrenchments before he charged the intrenched. He laughed in that gentle, light way which is as the soft tap of the nettle leaf that instantly produces a swelling and a smarting. " So, this is why you've been sneaking round these last three days, trying to dispose of the stocks I let you in on."

Peter grew sickly pale. " I've—I've been—arranging my affairs somewhat," mumbled he.

Richmond laughed again — cheerily, genially. " This world," said he, " is peopled by fools. But the biggest fool of all is the fellow who thinks he is a little less of a fool than the others. That seems to fit you, my boy. You must think I was whelped only yesterday. Do you suppose I trust people because I take 'em in with me? Why, I'd have been in the jail or the poorhouse long ago if I had. When I let you in I locked the door behind you. I always do."

Peter's hands were trembling so that they shook the stick round which he had them clasped.

"You think you've sold out," continued Richmond. "Instead, you'll find to-morrow that you still have all you bought through me—and that you've got to buy as much more."

"But I can't do it," pleaded Vanderkief—and his voice was not much better than a whine. "I've got no ready money. I'd have to sell real estate that's been in the family from the beginning."

"I'll take it on mortgage," said Richmond reassuringly. "So, you needn't worry about that, my boy."

"But we never *mortgage!*" cried Peter. His face became shiny with sweat. "No, indeed—we *never* mortgage, Mr. Richmond. I'm much obliged, but *we* never mortgage."

"Got to begin some time," said Richmond. And seeing that his prospective son-in-law was in the proper state of flabbiness, he went back to the point. "Now —as to the trouble between you and Beatrice. Please explain it. Let's see just what it is."

"She cares nothing about me."

"Who says so?"

"She does."

"When?"

"When we became engaged."

"Yet you proposed and she accepted."

Peter squirmed. "But I didn't know she cared about—about some one else."

"Who?"

"An—an artist."

"Who?"

"I met him at your house." Peter's anger was rising, as will the anger of the worst frightened boy in the world if the whipping is kept up long enough. "I might have known," he cried. "I did suspect, the day I saw him painting her. But it seemed absurd that a girl of her position——"

"It *is* absurd," cut in Richmond. "Who told you this story?"

Peter did not reply.

"My daughter?"

"No. I'm not at all likely to——"

"Then it was Allie Kinnear," said Richmond, and Peter guiltily felt as if the information had been wrenched from him. "So, *she's* trying to marry you?"

"Mr. Richmond," said Peter with the stiffness of

an insulted man of ancient lineage, " I have the highest esteem for Miss——"

" So have I," interrupted Richmond. " She's a pretty, bright, shrewd girl. She fools everybody. But I'd have thought *you* would have been on guard."

" I assure you, sir, Miss Kinnear——"

" Oh—by the way "—Richmond broke into Peter's sentence as if a thought on another subject had happened to flash through his mind. " Bring those mortgages to my office before two o'clock to-morrow," said he carelessly. " I've an appointment at two-thirty. That gives us a clear half hour—plenty of time."

Peter seemed to wither. The internal havoc was more dire than the external; for, internally, he had shriveled.

" Miss Kinnear is pretending to love you," went on his tormentor, harking back to the matrimonial business. " I want to find out just how far you've walked into her trap."

" She has made no pretenses," protested Peter. " I'm sure if she married a man it'd be because she cared for him."

" Fudge, Peter — fudge! " laughed Richmond. " You're a man of the world. You know what she wants." Then, with gimlet eyes and with bony finger poking into the heavy muscle of Peter's arm: " If you

255

wish to know what anybody wants you don't listen to what they *say*, you look at what they *need*."

This was the kind of shrewdness that made impression upon Peter, the sensitively suspicious. He winced, looked uncomfortable and sheepish.

" There's nothing in that artist story," scoffed Richmond. " You know Beatrice. She's very proud. Take my advice, don't speak to her about it. If she got a notion that you were flirting with Allie—" Richmond made a gesture suggestive of vague, vast dangers.

" I hope, sir, you've not got the impression that I —that I—" Peter came to a full stop.

" I've got no impression at all except that you wish to marry Beatrice on the eighteenth."

" The twentieth," corrected Peter.

" The twentieth, then." Richmond had now changed his manner to the benevolent paternal. " And do be sensible, young man, and make no trouble between Beatrice and Allie."

Thus it came to pass that when Peter and Beatrice were strolling down the Italian garden after lunch, Peter lost no time in obeying Richmond's orders. Nor did he set about it with any reluctance, for Beatrice was once more herself and, in a costume that gave her every charm its best chance, was enough to turn a far steadier head than Peter's had been in several years where she was concerned. " Don't you think," said he, " that we'd better change the date to the eighteenth? "

She made no immediate reply. They walked slowly toward the arch at the farther end, he glancing at her from time to time with a notion that she had not heard. At last he asked: " Did you hear? "

She nodded, seated herself on an old stone seat from the garden of an ancient palace, where it had no doubt participated in many a fateful interview between man and woman.

" What are you thinking about? " inquired he.

" About our marriage." She gave him a steady, penetrating look—the sort of look that always made him ill at ease with her and a little afraid of what marrying her might mean. " Do you want to marry me, Peter? " she asked.

" What rot! " exclaimed he. His glance shifted.

" You know you don't," rejoined the girl. " Your good sense tells you I'm not the sort of woman a man would enjoy being tied to unless she loved him. You don't want to marry me, and I don't want to marry you."

" What's the use of this kind of talk? " he remonstrated.

" Every use. Let's refuse to marry."

Peter looked strangely alarmed, glanced round as if in mortal dread lest they were being overheard. "If your father hears of this he'll blame me," he cried. "I tell you I want to marry you. I'm determined to marry you. I've given my word and you've given yours. And we'll marry on the——"

"I ask you to release me," interrupted the girl.

"I'll not do it!" And visions of money pouring out and mortgages pouring in put a note of shrill hysteria into his usually heavy voice.

"I thought I could marry you," said Beatrice, strong, vigorously strong under a surface of sweet gentleness. "I find I can't. You'll release me."

"I will not!" exclaimed Peter, once more shiny with sweat and mopping industriously. "And I want you to tell your father that I absolutely refused to release you—that I insisted on your marrying me."

"My father?" said the girl wonderingly. "What has he got to do with it?"

Peter was winded for the moment. He recovered quickly, hastened to explain: "I—I've the highest respect for your father. I wouldn't like him to think for a minute that I was careless about my word—or that I wasn't bent and determined to marry you. I want you to understand, Beatrice. I hold you to your promise."

"As I've told you, I love another man," said Beatrice. "I thought I was getting over it. I find it was simply a fit of the blues." She smiled absently. "I ran across an old pipe of his that I had locked in a drawer—a horrid, smelly, old pipe. And—Peter, were you ever in love?"

"With you," said he, sullen and jealous—and certainly her expression, her tone, were not soothing to his vanity, fine and beautiful though they were in themselves.

She laughed. "Your grandmother!" mocked she. "That pipe—it was like one of those enchanted things in The Arabian Nights. It made me see "—her eyes grew fascinatingly tender and dreamy—" and see— and *see!* . . . Could you marry a woman who felt like that about another man?"

"Then why did you engage yourself to me?"

"Because he won't have me," confessed she, her old-time pride in her love rampant.

"I never heard such rot!" exclaimed he in disgust.

"And I know you really don't want to marry me," she went on in a voice of appeal, of confidence in his manhood, in his friendliness for her, his childhood playmate.

If Richmond had been standing behind his daughter, making menacing faces at Peter over her shoulder, that sore-beset, young man could not have felt him more curdlingly. " You don't know anything of the kind," he blustered. " Don't you dare tell your father anything like that."

She scrutinized him. " You seem to have father on the brain. . . . Peter—Hanky—*what* has he been saying to you? "

" Nothing," lied Peter shiftily. " Not a word."

" That isn't true, Hanky. Is it? "

He hung his head.

" Own up. He's been—threatening you? "

" Now, look here, Beatrice—you are trying to get me into trouble," pleaded and protested Hanky. " I haven't said a word about your father's having spoken to me of you."

" What has he been threatening? " persisted the girl, her hand on his arm. " You can trust me, Hanky. You know, I keep my mouth shut."

" I've got nothing to tell," he insisted with a kind of whining doggedness. " All I say is, I want to marry you. If you're stuck on another man and won't marry me I can't help it. But *I* want to marry *you*."

" I understand perfectly—perfectly," said Beatrice. " He's compelling each of us to marry the other. I want to marry another man. You want to marry Allie. But——"

260

"I don't want to marry Allie!" he protested with the energy of terror. "I said nothing to you about her. Anyhow, I regard her as an underhanded, designing fraud. She told me about you and Wade. Yes, she was the one that did it."

"Well, why not?" cried Beatrice. "I've no objection. She knows I want to get out of marrying you."

Peter's eyes glistened with hope. "You gave her leave to tell? You asked her to tell?"

"Practically. What of it?"

"I *am* glad to hear that!" cried he with a gusty breath of relief. "I was beginning to think women were all alike—that there wasn't any such thing as sentiment in them."

Beatrice's eyes sparkled with mischief. "Yes, Hanky, and she practically had my permission to make love to you. I'm sure she's just dying to marry you. Now, you'll release me, won't you?"

Peter lit a cigarette and inspected the horizon as if hoping to sight something in the way of aid. "I can't do it, Beatrice," he finally said, deeply apologetic. "If I could tell you what a ghastly fix I'm in, I assure you you'd not blame me."

"I don't blame you," said she. "It's just as well for me to do it alone."

"You're going to release me?" cried he eagerly.

"What would father say if he saw you now!" said she.

The eagerness whisked out of his face.

"That's better," mocked she. "But I'll not tease you, Hanky—with your soul torn between love and money. I shall take the whole responsibility. I shall refuse to marry you."

But Peter continued to look depressed. "Your father'll think it was something I said."

"My father will not think I could have been discouraged that easily—or at all—if I wished to be your wife. He'll know you are too fond of money to risk losing any. Don't be alarmed, Peter. Father will understand the instant you tell him."

"*I* tell him!" cried Peter. "You'll have to do that yourself. You're used to him. You don't realize how he gets on my nerves. If I tried to tell him I'd get permanent paralysis of the tongue before a word came."

"What a stupid you are! Don't you see that I'm letting you tell him, as a favor—to help you to escape? You go to him—complain of me—urge him to make me keep my promise. Understand?"

Peter saw it, looked humble apology.

"Put it to him as strong as you like," pursued

Beatrice. "You can't make it any worse for me, and you'll make it a lot better for yourself."

Peter looked at her so admiringly that she sent him away on the instant. She knew him—knew how easily she could get him back if she wished, and how little it would take to make him forget his resentment at her failure to appreciate him and at her father's energetic methods—and his dread of what life with so strenuous a will as hers might mean. "Tell him right away, Hanky," advised she, pointing with her sunshade to where Richmond stood in the library window observing them. "Let's get it over with."

Mrs. Richmond sat writing at a desk not far from where Richmond was standing. As Peter started up the walk toward the house Richmond said to his wife: "What a chucklehead Peter is! No wonder Beatrice felt like balking."

"Oh, I shouldn't say Peter was worth getting excited about, one way or the other," replied Mrs. Richmond.

"The young men growing up nowadays are a mighty cheap, thin lot. He's as good as any." Richmond pressed his lips together firmly. "And he's the best possible husband for her. A strong woman ought to marry a small man if there's to be peace."

Mrs. Richmond sneered—faintly and covertly—at the paper before her. She did not miss any of the possible implications of her husband's remark. For once, however, she did him an injustice. He was not hitting at her—had not meant to insinuate that a strong man ought to marry a small woman, and that Daniel Richmond had done this very thing. He was thinking only of his daughter and Peter. He would have liked to provide her with a real man; he sincerely regretted the exigencies of his game—of the game of life as it lies—that forbade it, that forced him to give her only a Peter Vanderkief.

He consoled himself by feeling that she would before many years appreciate what he had done for her —this, when she should have installed herself in the dazzling position her ability would make out of the wealth he could give her and the prestige she would get through Peter's ancient lineage. Being a man of imagination—as every man who achieves in whatever direction must be—Richmond had a strong vein of sentiment, of romance. He could not but sympathize with his daughter's heart trouble, now that her acquiescence in his plans permitted him to be fair-minded—in secret. But romance was a fleeting thing, while the things he had been planning for her were not springtime ephemerals, but the substantialities that make a human being comfortable and often happy the whole life through from youth to old age.

When Peter entered, Mrs. Richmond had finished her note and was just departing. " Will you drive with me in about an hour? " asked she, passing him in the door.

" Sorry, but I've got——"

" Oh, if Beatrice needs you," laughed she, going on and leaving the two men alone.

Peter interrupted Richmond's reverie with a bomb. " Beatrice has broken the engagement," said he nervously. " She refuses to marry me."

The small, wiry figure in the window swung round with a jerk. Gone were the sentimental reflections inspired by the lovely prospect from that window, his daughter the crown and climax of the loveliness. " Why? " he shot at the young man.

Peter shrank only a trifle. He was strong in his strong case. " Because she does not care for me and cares for some one else."

" That trash again! You refused to release her? "

" Yes, sir," said Peter, proud of his virtue.

" Well? "

" She released herself."

Richmond wheeled round, noted his daughter seated in the same place, twirling her pale-blue sunshade and looking idly about. He wheeled back, started for the door.

"Pardon me, sir," said Peter, "but I am taking the train for town. This puts me in an embarrassing —painful——"

"Wait here," ordered Richmond, and disappeared.

Peter, discreetly standing well back in the room, watched the father speeding toward the daughter and awaited in nervous suspense the crash of the collision. He marveled that she could sit placidly when she knew exactly what was coming. "She *sure* is the real thing," he muttered. "Where can you beat it? A sport —that's what I call her—a good sport."

When Richmond arrived within comfortable speaking distance of the placid girl with the sweet smile of welcome he began. "How did Vanderkief get this false impression?" said he in a flexible tone, readily convertible either to geniality or to wrathful imperiousness.

"Has he told you I am willing to marry him?" inquired she.

Richmond beamed. "I thought the numskull didn't know what he was talking about!" he exclaimed. "He says you won't marry him."

"Oh," said Beatrice with her merriest smile. "I thought you said he had a false impression."

Richmond shook his head impatiently. "Have you or have you not told him you'd not marry him?"

"Yes," replied Beatrice, eyes dancing with the pleasure of teasing him.

"Yes—what?" demanded he.

"What you said," replied she.

"Beatrice—I insist on a serious answer. Peter came to me and said——"

"Oh, papa! Surely, you're not going over that again. You said it all before."

Richmond paused to frame a question that could be answered only plainly. "Did you tell Peter you would not marry him?" he said sternly, though he had too good a sense of humor not to appreciate her childish cleverness.

"I did," laughed Beatrice, engagingly at her ease. "Can you blame me?"

Richmond seated himself on the bench beside her. "You realize the consequences of your refusal?" he said coldly.

Her face became sober. The eyes with which she met his gaze were as resolute as his own. "I realize the consequences of *not* refusing," said she. "And I'm prepared to take the consequences *of* refusing."

Richmond's baffled expression was pushed aside by one of arrogant anger. "What did Peter say to you?

I understand this affair. I'll make that young man writhe for his impudent treachery!"

" He pleaded with me to marry him. He refused to release me. He went straight to you——"

" You can't trick me!" cried her father, his expressive eyes sparkling ominously. " Before I get through with this situation I think all concerned will regret having crossed my will. That's always the way —good nature is mistaken for weakness."

" You may ruin Peter if you feel you can afford to be so contemptible," said Beatrice unmoved, " and you may ruin Roger Wade—though I doubt if he'll regard losing a little money as ruin. But you——"

" I told you I'd drive him from the country in disgrace!"

Through the youth of the girl showed her inheritance of strength of soul, to make a woman of her, a personality a match for his own. " If you bring out anything disgraceful about him that's true you'll be only doing what's right," said she calmly. " If you try to damage him with falsehood I shall myself tell who's doing it and why."

A sense of his powerlessness against her silenced him.

" You may do your worst, as I was saying," she went on. " But I shall not marry any man I do not at least respect; I shall not marry any poor, tiresome creature like Hanky. I've learned better. I've found something with which to contrast life with him. And I cannot and will not do it."

There, of course, had been a time in Daniel Richmond's career when he had made his way and gained his points by discussing and reasoning with his fellow-beings. Every leader wins leadership by persuading his fellows that he has the necessary qualifications. But that time had long passed; for many a year Richmond had been in the habit of deciding what to do at a council within his own brain and informing the outside world of his decision only by acts and orders. He now continued silent, regarding the ground; he was fighting for control of his temper, fighting for the calmness to argue with this rebel daughter. To make her reasonable he must first become so, himself.

"You have not known this artist long—have you?" he said at length in the tone of a rational being and a father.

"Long enough," replied the girl.

"Long enough for what?" inquired the father pleasantly, though his daughter's tone—she being still much ruffled internally—was teasing his temper.

"Long enough to know that I care for him."

Her father laughed agreeably. "You and I are

269

much alike, my dear," said he. "You know yourself well enough to know that the real reason for your excitement is opposition. Now, be reasonable. What could I do but oppose? Can you blame me for opposing? Can you wonder that I am afraid you will do something foolish—something you will regret your whole life? Suppose this was a case of some other father and daughter—a case you had no personal interest in. Would you be on the side of the father or of the daughter?"

There was no resisting this fairness, so fairly put. Beatrice smiled. "On the side of the father," said she promptly. "I don't expect you to understand, father. I see all your arguments. I see how foolish and headlong I seem to you. But— The fact remains that I love Roger Wade. I know I am not making a fool of myself in loving him. Oh, you'll say that in the same circumstances other girls have said the same thing, when they were simply blinded and deceived by their craze for romance. But this case is the exception. And I *know* it." She looked at him with her sweetest expression. "Let me ask you a few questions. Do you *know* Roger?"

"I understand that sort of man perfectly. It's a familiar type. Every girl with expectations has several such buzzing about her."

"'Not another word! I'll show you, miss—'"

"Is that *honest*, father? Is that really the impression you have of Roger Wade?"

The dangerous look reappeared in Richmond's face —in his eyes, round his mouth.

"Now, don't get angry, father. That would be confession, you know. One does not get angry in a discussion unless one is in the wrong."

"Who wouldn't get angry, seeing a girl like you bent on making a fool of herself."

"If you were where you were when you started, and you met such a man as Roger, you'd be———"

"Don't speak his name to me," cried Richmond, twitching and squirming. "I ask you to take time to come to your senses."

"I've tried that. When I don't see him, it's even clearer to me than when I do that I must marry him. Besides, if he *weren't* on earth now, I still couldn't marry the Hanky sort. Oh, father dear—can't you see the change in me? As you say, I'm like you. Put yourself in my place. Would *you* marry the sort of person Hanky is—the sort all the Hankies are—if you could—" She sighed. "But I can't. He won't. Father, please help me!"

There was a conflict of expressions in Richmond's face as she made this appeal movingly. It was sheer confession of fear of his own better self which loved his daughter, which respected the things she was now learning to respect—it was sheer confession when he flew into furious rage—the one mood where a human being is safe from the entreaties of heart and the counsels of higher intelligence. "You are crazy—plain crazy!" he cried in his most insulting tone. "There's no excuse for you—none! Reasoning with you is time wasted."

"If I'm crazy there's every excuse for me," answered she, with the placidity of the anger that is beyond the stage of bluster and sputter. "If I'm not crazy there's no excuse for you."

"Answer me! Are you going to be sensible? Are you ready to drop tomfoolery and make a happy and contented future for yourself?"

"If I can," replied she. "If Roger will——"

Up sprang Richmond. "Not another word! I'll show you, miss——"

"Yes, one word more," interrupted she. "I want to say just one thing more. If you do not agree to let Peter and Mr. Wade alone I shall leave your house at once—and this time it will be for good."

"*You*—threaten *me!*" he shouted, shaking with fury, for that sense of ultimate powerlessness with her had driven him quite insane.

"Do you wish me to stay or to go?" asked she, her

color gone, but every sign of steadfastness in her face, in her figure, in her attitude.

" Go!" he shrieked. " Go—and make a fool and a scandal of yourself. Go! Go! Go!"

And away he rushed, a crazy man.

XIV

PETER met her in the main entrance. " How did he take it? " he asked excitedly, his nerves obviously un- strung.

" Not very well," replied she.

" Yes—I saw him tearing away into the woods. Good Lord! How *can* you take it so quietly! "

By way of answer Beatrice shrugged her shoulders and lifted her eyebrows.

" Beatrice—honestly don't you think we'd better go ahead and do as he wants? He is a dangerous man —believe me, he is. I don't like to speak so of your father, but everyone agrees that he——"

" You can never tell a man's family any news about what he is," said Beatrice.

" He'll make life a hell for you," groaned Hanky. " And he'll make mischief for me."

" I think not," replied she. " He'll have other things besides you to occupy him. He knows it's wholly my fault."

" But, Beatrice—don't be obstinate. You must know it'd really not be so rotten bad to marry me."

"I thought I mentioned the fact that I'm in love with some one else."

"Oh—to be sure," said Peter. "I suppose that has got something to do with it. But your obstinacy——"

"That's it," mocked the girl. "Obstinacy. Well, whatever my reason is, I'm leaving here by the next train."

"But I was going by that," objected Hanky. "I must get away from here."

"Better stay on and let father see you're not at all to blame," advised she. "If we went up town together he'd be sure you were conspiring with me."

"Oh, I'll stay—I'll stay," cried Peter. "But where are you going, Beatrice?"

"Not to get any of my friends in trouble," said she. "I'll take Valentine and go to a hotel—to the Wolcott. Come and call. I'll not tell father."

"At a hotel!" Peter stared stupefied. "You don't mean you're leaving home—for good?"

"Wouldn't you—in my place?"

"No. I'd be sensible and marry the man my father wished."

Beatrice looked at him quizzically. "Hanky," said she, "you ought to fall on your knees every day of your life and give thanks that you had the good luck to escape marrying me."

275

Her mischievous smile, her mocking tone, combined with the words themselves, had an immediately tranquilizing effect upon him. Not for the first time by any means he had a chilling, queasy misgiving that there was truth in that view of a marriage between them. After a pause he said:

" But what will you do? "

" Blessed if I know," replied she, as if the matter were of not the smallest consequence.

" You'll have no friends. Nobody'll dare be friends with you."

" Have I any friends now?—any worth calling my own? "

" Then, as I understand it, you haven't got much money. About enough to pay for dresses? "

" About."

" Then—what will you do? " repeated he, a real, friendly solicitude in his voice and, better still, in his eyes.

" That's unimportant. I'm escaping worse than I could possibly be running into."

" Marry me, Beatrice," cried he. " It's not a bad bet if you lose."

She put out her hand impulsively with a grateful smile, the sweetest and friendliest he had ever had from her. " I like that, Hanky! And I like you when you show what you really are. But I'm not taking advantage of your generosity."

"I mean it, Beatrice—in dead, sober earnest—on a cold collar."

She shook her pretty head smilingly. "Good-by. Come to see me. If we run across each other when father's about scowl and look the other way."

"What do you take me for?"

"For a person with a little sense. Keep solid with father—for Allie's sake.

"But I want *you*——"

She fled, laughing as if she had not a care in the world.

She tried to make her departure unobtrusive. But her father would not have it so. Coming toward the house with the worst of his rage about steamed away he caught sight of her and her maid waiting while several trunks and packages were being loaded on the roof of a touring car. At the sight he went insane again. He rushed wildly toward them and shouted out, heedless of the servants: "Take that car back to the garage, Léry! Valentine, go into the house—report to Mrs. Richmond. And you"—he glared crazily at his daughter —"if you leave here you walk!—and you never come back!"

Beatrice took the hand bag from her maid. "Good-

277

by, Valentine," said she. There was a wonderful, quiet dignity in her bearing—a delicate correctness of attitude, neither forward nor shrinking—evident sensibility to the situation, yet no desire to aggravate it by show of superior breeding or by defiance. It was a situation savagely testing character. Beatrice responded to the test in a way that augured well for her being able to look out for herself in any circumstances. She smiled pleasantly, yet with restraint, to the agitated servants and started down the road.

Valentine hesitated, then set out in her wake. " Come back here!" shouted Richmond. " You are in my employ, not my daughter's."

Beatrice, guessing what was occurring, paused and turned. " Do as my father says," she said. " I shall not be able to keep you."

" I, too, belong to myself, mademoiselle," replied the girl with a quiet dignity equal to that of her mistress. " I cannot stay here. I'll go with you if I may. But— I'll not stay here."

Richmond, realizing that his rage of the impotent had once more whirled him into an impossible situation, disappeared in the house. Before Beatrice and Valentine reached the lodge the auto overtook them. The chauffeur, Léry, swung the car close in to the footpath beside the road, jumped from his seat, opened the door.

"Did my father send you?" asked she.

"Yes, mademoiselle."

When the two women were seated—Beatrice insisted on Valentine's sitting by her—Beatrice said: "I don't believe Léry."

Valentine gave a queer, little smile.

"But," continued Beatrice, "father will never make any inquiries."

"Léry understands," said Valentine.

"Understands—what?"

"That you will win. Your father adores you."

"You don't know," said Beatrice, shaking her head in a decided negative. "And I can't tell you."

XV

BEATRICE had selected Valentine as her maid after trying more than a score of various nationalities. She had selected her because Valentine was a lady, and she could not endure servility or veneer manners in the close relations that must exist between mistress and maid. In calling Valentine a lady Beatrice did not mean that she was a "high-toned" lady, or a fine lady, or a fashionable lady, or any of the other qualified ladies, but that she was just a lady—well mannered, with delicate instincts, intelligent, simple and sincere. Valentine acted as Beatrice liked to believe she herself would act if she had to work for her living and happened to find being lady's maid the most convenient way to do it.

At the Wolcott Beatrice registered beneath her own name that of Miss Valentine Clermont. When the two were in the little inside suite Beatrice took by way of making a beginning in the direction of the practice of economy, she said:

"For the present, at least, you are to be my companion. I can't live here alone or just with a maid.

280

So, the parlor is to be changed into a bedroom for you."

"Very well, mademoiselle," promptly acquiesced the intelligent Valentine, showing how rightly Beatrice had judged her.

"Miss Richmond," corrected Beatrice with a smile.

"Pardon—certainly," said Valentine.

"We are rather cramped here," Beatrice went on. "But I guess I'll be looking back on this as spacious luxury before long."

Miss Clermont smiled.

"Why do you smile, Miss Clermont?"

"You do not know your father, Miss Richmond."

"I assure you we have parted finally," said Beatrice. "If you have any idea that in following my fortunes you are going with a person in the position I had until two hours ago, put it out of your mind. I can pay your wages—beg pardon, salary it is now— through next month—perhaps for another month after that. Then I shall be— Well, mine is a precious small income—and will be smaller. However, I'll see that you get a place soon."

Miss Clermont smiled.

"Why do you smile, Miss Clermont? Because you don't believe me?"

"Not at all, Miss Richmond," protested Valentine.

"If you're right about your situation—then I shall stay with you until you are settled—and, possibly, I can help you. If you are wrong—then I shall stay on as your maid until you marry. After that—Monsieur Léry and I are engaged. When we marry we shall go into business together."

Beatrice paused in arranging her hair, turned and, half sitting on the low bureau, looked at her companion with the expression of one who has just given birth to a new and fascinating idea. "Why shouldn't *we* go into business—you and I?" she said. "I'll have to do something," she went on. "I simply can't content myself to live on—on what I'll have after a few days from now. I love luxury—nice surroundings—good things to eat—beautiful clothes. Why not dressmaking?"

"We should get rich at it," declared Miss Clermont.

And then it came out that she and Léry had been planning a dressmaking business. Miss Richmond was just what they needed to make it a swift and stupendous success. They had ten thousand dollars. If Miss Richmond could put in as much and would be a public partner attracting fashionable trade, giving the establishment eclat by wearing beautiful dresses in fashionable restaurants or for drives in the Avenue, and so on

—and so on. "I can put in at least ten thousand," said Beatrice. "And I have ideas about clothes."

"Indeed, yes," assented Valentine warmly. "You have a style of your own."

"Yes, I think you and I have got me up rather stunningly these last two years," said Beatrice.

The dressmaking business was as good as started before they had dinner—at which Miss Richmond had her companion sitting opposite her. Miss Clermont as a companion was a triumph. No one but a French-woman could have glided so easily from menial to equal. "But then, I knew she could," thought Beatrice, "the instant I looked at her hands, when she came to try for the place. Hands tell more than faces—and hers are the hands of a lady."

At noon the next day, while Beatrice and Valentine were out walking, Peter telephoned, leaving word that he would call at half past four. At that hour Beatrice received him in the hotel parlor. He eyed her with admiring wonder. He expected to find all sorts of signs of her altered position—would not have been surprised had she already begun to look dowdy and down at the heel. Her radiance of spirit, of body and of toilet struck him as little less than miraculous. "You certainly are a cool one," said he. "Why, you don't look a bit upset."

"Never felt so well in my life," declared Beatrice.
"I feel so—so—free!"

Peter shook his head warningly. "Wait till you
have had a full dose. Wait till you really find out what
you're up against."

"What is it?"

"Oh, you're out of your world. It's all very well
to jump into the water and swim for a few minutes—
just for the fun of the thing. But how about going in
for being a fish and *living* in the water—eh?"

"I'd no idea you could do so well, Peter," said Beatrice. "That's both wise and witty. Why didn't you
begin that sort of talk sooner?"

"Oh, I say!" protested the young man. "I'm not
such a mutt as you thought me. No one could be."

"Better and better," cried Beatrice. "First thing
you know I'll be trying to steal you back from Allie."

Peter colored consciously. He said with a foolish
attempt at the offhand: "Oh—I saw her—at lunch.
She wants to come to see you, but don't dare. Your
father's got her father right where he can put the
screws on him."

"She might have telephoned," said Beatrice, and
her tone even more than her look showed how Allie's
defection had hurt, how it was rankling.

Peter looked depressed. "Yes—I suppose she

might," conceded he. "But don't be too hard on her, Beatrice. You know how afraid we all are of your father."

"*You're* here," said Beatrice sententiously.

"Yes." Peter reddened. "Hang it, I can't fake with you. Fact is—well—while I hope I'd have come anyway, still, I'd not be so open about it, I'm afraid, if I hadn't your father's consent."

"He told you to come!"

"He hasn't given up," said Peter with the air of a peddler undoing his pack. "Asked me if I knew where you were stopping. I said yes—that you told me. He asked where. I couldn't think of any side step, so I let out the truth. Any harm in that?"

"Not the slightest. I'm not hiding from anybody."

"Then he said—just as I was leaving him on the ferry this morning: "If you wish to call on my daughter and try to bring her to her right mind I've no objection.""

"And I've no objection, either," said the girl, "unless you try to bring me to my right mind. That one subject is taboo. You understand?"

Peter nodded. "I knew you meant it yesterday. I'm going ahead with Allie. You and I are such old friends that I feel I can talk things over with you. You see, it's this way. I want to get married and settled. We all marry and settle young in our family. I can't have what I want—but I can get something mighty good. Allie's a trump. Such a comfortable sort."

"You couldn't do better," said Beatrice with more warmth than she felt. For she had her eyes open to Allie now—too recently open for her to be tolerant of what were weaknesses of the same species as Beatrice's own, if of a different genus.

"I'm not really in love with her," continued Peter. "But——"

"But that's of no consequence," said Beatrice. "You're one of the sort that thinks whatever belongs to them is the grandest ever. You'll soon be crazy about her."

"And she'll always look well, too. She's the image of her mother, and the way to test a girl's staying quality is to see how her mother holds together. Yes, Allie's good for the whole run—right into the last quarter."

Beatrice and Peter went into the restaurant and in a quiet corner sat down to the sociability of tea. "Hanky," said she, "I am going to treat you as a friend. I am going to ask you to attend to some matters for me which you must promise me never to speak of."

Hanky showed that he was as highly flattered as

the next young man would be by marks of intimacy and confidence from a pretty and superior young woman. "You can count on me—for anything I feel I've the right to do," said he. "But, whether I do it or not, I'll keep my mouth shut."

Beatrice poured the tea in reflective silence. Not until she had tasted her own cup did she venture to begin expressing the thoughts she had been arranging. "Roger Wade has about forty thousand dollars invested in the bonds of the Wauchong Railway."

Peter leaned back and gave a low whistle. He shook his head and repeated the whistle.

"I see you understand."

"I begin to," said Peter.

Looking down at her plate and speaking somewhat nervously and hurriedly the girl went on:

"I want you—through your broker or banker or however you please—I want you to buy those bonds at what their market price was before the road went into the hands of a receiver. I think it will take about fifty thousand dollars. But buy them if it costs a hundred thousand. I can't go higher than that."

Hesitatingly she lifted her eyes. Peter was sitting back in his chair regarding her with an expression it makes any human being proud to have caused in another's face.

287

A little color came into the girl's cheeks and into her eyes a look of gratitude for the compliment and of pleasure in it. She went on:

"You understand, no one must know—must have the ghost of a suspicion. Especially Roger Wade. But no one—no one."

Peter busied himself at lighting the cigarette he selected with care from the dozen in the huge gold case he carried in the inside pocket of his sack coat.

"Your agent," continued the girl, as if laying before him a carefully thought-out plan, "can say he represents some men who are getting ready to fight to get control of the road."

"I didn't know you knew anything about business," said Peter huskily, just for something to say.

"A little," said Beatrice, who, in fact, was her father's own daughter—though, of course, she was not foolish enough to have failed to use to its uttermost value the favorite feminine pretense of being hopelessly incapable when it came to matters like business. "Will you do it?"

"How much'll you have left?" said Peter.

"Plenty," Beatrice assured him. "Plenty."

"I know better."

She made an impatient gesture. "I'll have more than enough to carry out my plans."

" There's no reason on earth why you should do this," protested he. " You——"

" Drop it, Peter," said she with a touch of her old imperiousness—of her father's intolerance of objection from inferior minds. " I know what I'm about. Roger Wade is being stripped of all he has through no fault of his—through my folly. I got him into the scrape— a scrape he wanted to have nothing to do with. It's up to me to get him out."

" He had no business to come fooling round you! "

" He didn't, Peter," said the girl with convincing candor. " He— I see I've got to tell you. I proposed to him, and he refused me."

" *You* did—*that!* "

Beatrice blushed and laughed. " Oh, I made an idiot of myself. I thought he was hanging back because he was awed—because father was rich—and all that."

Peter narrowed his eyelids and screwed up his mouth in an attempt to look acute. " He's working some sly dodge. Mark my word, some sly dodge." And he wagged his head wisely.

" I wish he were! " sighed Beatrice. " Because he liked me I thought he—cared. You see, Peter, I'm telling you everything. Will you do what I ask? "

Peter settled deeper in his chair. " I'd like to—I

want to—but—" At the beginnings of disappointment and disdain in her expression he straightened, flushed. " Yes, by gad, I *will* do it! "

" Why did you hesitate? "

" I didn't."

Beatrice looked at him doubtfully; suddenly she realized. " You fear father'll find out you did it? I hadn't thought of that. No—you mustn't, Hanky. I'll get some one else."

" You've got to let me do it," insisted he. " Anyone who didn't know all the circumstances would make a mess of it. I want to do it. And it isn't much of a risk."

The event was that she yielded. Toward noon the next day he telephoned that he had the bonds—had paid forty-one thousand dollars for them — exactly. " I've got them here at my house. I can bring them to you this afternoon if you like."

" Do," said Beatrice.

And at four he came with a parcel. Her eyes brightened at sight of it. " I, too, have a package," said she.

" So I see. What is it? "

" Your forty-one thousand in Governments."

" But Governments are worth more."

The girl laughed. " Not a cent. I didn't say forty-one thousand par. I had the exact calculation made at the bank."

"What an ass I am, to forget you were Daniel Richmond's daughter."

"Give me my railway bonds."

The exchange was made, he pretending that he did not dare release his hold on his package until she had given him a hold on hers. The waiters, idle in the restaurant at that hour, grinned at the sight of so much gayety in two such superior-looking, young people. And it certainly did look like a love affair—an engagement. Nor is it surprising that Peter, full of the sense of having done her quite a favor and not without risk to himself, should have again become hopeful that this girl—"such a stunner—and so dead square, too"—might be thinking more favorably of him.

"Now that these things are straightened out, Beatrice," said he, "and as you've got over your notions about Wade—why not give *me* a chance?"

She laughed. "Allie's affianced!" mocked she.

"I've told you that——"

"But," interrupted she, "I never told you that I was—was cured—of Roger Wade."

"But you are. And he's off your conscience."

Beatrice's eyes had an expression that sent a pang —and a thrill, too—through him. "Peter—I love him," she said with quiet intensity—Dan Richmond intensity. "And I think you know now what that means with me."

He paled, stared at his cup. "I wish to God I didn't," he muttered.

"Now, Peter, you don't mean that and you know it. The only reason you keep after me is because you've always been used to having your own way and you hate to be baffled."

"That's all the reason you stick on after Wade," retorted he.

She laughed. "I'll admit that has something to do with it. But not all, Hanky. And the other part's the important part."

"You must know he's after your money," said he, looking down sourly.

"And you?" retorted she.

"Oh, I," said he with Vanderkief hauteur. "I fancy I'm above suspicion."

"Father says that the people who do the queerest tricks are the ones that're above suspicion—and take advantage of it. My, but you're red, Hanky. And while we're suspecting— Did you get those bonds for me just because you——"

"Don't say that, Beatrice!" he cried. "Honest, I didn't. I wasn't trying to collect."

" I believe you," said she. " Please don't do anything to make me doubt."

" I won't. I throw up the sponge. I'll not annoy you any more."

" You'll be friends? "

" I'd hate to lose *your* friendship," said he with his slow, heavy earnestness. " It's the thing I've got that's most worth while."

XVI

BEATRICE had carefully avoided learning anything at all about the Wauchong Railway before investing nearly half her fortune in its bonds. She wished to spare herself the temptation to hesitate; and she was too fond of money as a means, too alive to its value, too well trained in the matter of foolish investments, to trust her newly developed virtue far. But now that the thing was done she made thorough inquiry into the affairs of the railway. It did a losing passenger business; it had made its money—very satisfactory earnings—by reason of its northern terminal being in a group of rich coal mines. Her father ruined the road by so juggling traffic agreements with the coal companies that the Wauchong's whole paying freight business was at a stroke transferred to another road. The bonds were next to worthless. On the face of the facts she had spent forty-one thousand dollars for a few ounces of waste paper.

She was glad to find, on searching her heart, that she had not the faintest feeling of regret for her action.

It gave her a gratifying opinion of herself to discover that, on the contrary, she regarded her investment with satisfaction and pride. But these emotions did not clash with a strong desire to recover the lost forty-one thousand, if that could be brought about. She gave the matter anxious and intelligent thought. The only plan that came to her and seemed at all practicable was to let it leak out in Wall Street that a big block of the bonds had been taken at more than par by Daniel Richmond's daughter *after* the wiping out of the road's revenues. This news would probably boom the bonds and stocks if sent out adroitly. But Beatrice decided against the scheme; she could not forget the losses to the innocent it would involve. Perhaps the time had been—and not so very long ago, either—when this view of the affair would not have occurred to her. But since then she had experienced, had suffered, had learned. With a sigh she put the bundle of bonds away in her safety-deposit box and entered their cost to profit and loss. Her total income was now reduced to just under twenty-seven hundred a year. "And I need at least that many thousand," thought she. "Let us see what this dressmaking scheme has in it."

And she proceeded to revolve Valentine's project with a deliberate, pessimistic, flaw-seeing scrutiny that would have commanded the admiration of her father and would have increased his amazement how one so strong in the head could be so weak in the heart. She questioned and cross-questioned Valentine, who, for all her cleverness, had far too much of the optimist in her composition. Beatrice had learned from her father that hope, an invaluable ally when the struggle is on, is an enemy, the worst of enemies—a traitor and a destroyer—if admitted to the counsels when the struggle is planning. So, she took the worst possible view of every phase of the proposed enterprise, and insisted that all calculation be based upon the theory that they would lose money from the start, would lose heavily, must prepare themselves to hold out for the longest possible period against not only bad business, but also bad luck.

Meanwhile, Peter was engaged in strenuous combat with a generous impulse which seemed to him as out of place in his mind as an eaglet in the brood of a hen. But the impulse would not expel; it lingered obstinately, fascinating him as the idea of doing something unconventional sometimes seizes upon and obsesses a primly conventional woman. Finally, it fairly dragged him into a kind of rake's progress of generosity—for good has its rapid road no less than evil. It put him alone in his speediest auto and, in the teeth of his dread of being seen by Richmond or by some one who would tell Richmond, drove him along the dusty highways of Northern New Jersey until he came to Deer Spring—to a charming old farmhouse in its farthermost outskirts.

He went up the flowery lane to the old-fashioned porch, so cool, so quiet, so restful, behind its odorous veils of blooming creepers. A little exercise with the big brass dragon's head that had served as knocker for the best part of a century, and a pleasant-looking old woman came round the corner of the house, wiping her hands on her kitchen apron. Said Peter:

"Is Mr. Wade at home?"

"Not just now," replied she, her head thrown far back that she might inspect him through the spectacles on the end of her long, thin nose. "I reckon most likely he's up to the studio."

"Where is it?"

"You follow the path back of the house—through the woods and the hollow, then up the round-top hill. You'll have to walk. It's a right smart piece—about a mile and a half."

"Is there any place where I could "—Peter stopped and blushed; he had caught himself just in time to prevent the word "hide" from slipping out—"where I could put my machine?"

"There's the shed behind the house."

"Thank you." And he sprang away to get the auto tucked out of sight.

When this was accomplished his mind became somewhat easier and he set out for the studio. He got on fairly well with himself—until he stood face to face with the big artist. Wade regarded him inscrutably: Peter regarded Wade with an expression which, in a woman, would have betokened an impending fit of hysteria.

"You don't remember me, Mr. Wade?" said he.

"I remember you perfectly," Roger replied.

"I—I called on a matter of—that is, not exactly of—well—a matter."

"Will you come in?" said Roger, standing aside.

"Thank you—I'll be glad to," was Peter's eager reply.

Within, his eyes made for a covered canvas on an easel in the middle of the big room. "Is that by any chance Mr. Richmond's picture?" asked he.

"Mr. Richmond's picture?" said Roger. "I know nothing of any picture of Mr. Richmond."

"*For* Mr. Richmond."

"Neither of nor for."

"I beg your pardon," stammered Peter. "I rather hoped you'd let me have a look at it. You know, I was engaged to Miss Richmond."

298

Roger continued in his waiting attitude. Peter felt himself dwindling before this large, dark calm. He shifted uneasily from leg to leg, opened and shut his mouth several times, finally burst out: " I say, what an ass you must think me." And he gave Roger an honest, pathetic look of appeal—an ingenuous plea for mercy.

The large, dark calm was rippled by a smile—a very human smile. It made young Peter instantly feel that he was talking with a young human being just like himself.

" I did want to look at the picture," said he. " You know the one I mean—the picture of *her*."

Roger's gaze wavered a little, steadied. " I'm sorry—but it's not finished," said he.

" Oh—I see. And, naturally, you do not want anybody to look at it. Well—I'll come another time—if I may."

Roger bowed.

Peter was desperate. He puffed furiously at his cigarette, finally burst out: " Did you know that Miss Richmond and her father had quarreled? "

" Really? " said Roger politely, and so far as Peter could judge the news interested him only to the degree more discouraging than no interest at all.

" Yes—they've quarreled—and she's left home—is

299

living alone at a hotel in New York—says she's never going back."

Peter was not sure, but he thought he saw a something or other flash across the artist's face, like a huge, swift-swimming fish near the surface of opaque water. He felt encouraged to go on.

"I think I ought to tell you. Miss Richmond and I *were* engaged. It's been broken off. Her father is furious. She's in love with another man." Peter glanced at Roger's inscrutable eyes, blushed, glanced down again. "She has sacrificed everything for this other man. It's really stunning, the way she did it—and a lot more I can't tell you. And I do believe she'll stick—will not go back—though she's got next to nothing. You know her—know what a fine girl she is."

"Yes, indeed," said Roger cordially.

"She's at the Wolcott—if you care to call. I guess she's rather lonely, as all her old pals are shying off. You see, her father's a deadly dangerous sort—liable to do up anybody who sided with her."

Roger, his gaze upon a far, unseen country, was pale and somber.

"I do hope you'll look in on her, Wade," said Peter. "She'd appreciate it."

Wade's eyes slowly turned with his returning thoughts until they centered upon the eyes of young

Vanderkief. Suddenly Roger's face was illuminated by that splendid smile of his. He grasped Peter by the hand. "I'm glad to know you," said he. "And—I beg your pardon — for things I've thought about you."

"Oh, that's all right," cried Peter. "I'm not a dog in the manger, you know. And I tell you she's got a stiff stretch ahead of her—downright rough. Of course she's no fool. Still, it wouldn't be possible for any woman of her age and her bringing up to realize what she was bumping into, dropping out of her class, sacking her father and trying to scratch along on worse than nothing. When you've got tastes a little money's only an aggravation. Especially for her sort of woman. Won't you try one of my cigarettes?"

"Delighted," said Roger, taking one.

"Well, I must move on," proceeded Peter. "You don't mind my butting in?"

"Not in the least. It was a fine friendly—decent thing to do. . . . Would you like to see the picture?"

And without giving Peter time to reply, or himself a chance to repent the impulse, he flung aside the drapery over the easel in the middle of the room. He and Peter gazed in silence. It was a glorious vision of morning in the springtime. Upon lake and cataract, upon tree and bush and stone, sparkled the radiance

of the birthday of summer. That radiance seemed to
come from the figure of a young girl in a canoe, her
paddle poised for the stroke—an attitude of exquisite
grace, a figure alive in every line of flesh and drapery
—a face shedding the soft luster of the bright hopes
and dreams and joys that are summed up in the thrill-
ing word, youth. Roger was right in thinking it
his best work, his best expression of that intense
joy of life which he was ever striving to put upon
canvas.

Peter gave a long, furtive sigh. "Yes," he muttered, "she can look like that." He had seen her look
just so once—when she told him she loved the artist and
would never change. Queer, how anyone could so love
that she got happiness out of giving love, even though
it was unreturned. Queer—yet, there it was. Roger,
with a sudden gesture, recovered the canvas. Peter
stood motionless, staring at where the picture had been
—it was still there for him. He roused himself, looked
at the painter with frank admiration and respect.
"That's worth while!" said he. "No wonder she——"

Roger's frown checked him. But only for a moment; then he went on, in an awed undertone: "She's
more of a—a person than anyone I ever saw. If she'd
let me I'd be crazy about her. As it is, while I know I
can never get her, everything's stopped short with me

until I'm sure she's out of reach—married to some one else. I'm a better man for having known her, for having loved her."

Roger was standing with arms folded upon his broad chest—powerful arms bare to the elbow. He seemed lost in reverie.

"Thank you for showing me that," said Peter gratefully and humbly. "I'd wish to own it if it wasn't that—well, I'd never be able to get any peace of mind if I had it about. I'd stare at it till I went crazy."

Roger flushed a significant, a guilty deep red.

Peter got himself together with a shake of his big frame. "I'm off, now. You'll not say anything about my having called—not to her or anyone?"

"I do not see anyone," said Roger in a constrained voice.

"But you'll surely—" began Peter, but he halted on the threshold of impertinence. "Well—I hope you'll look in at the Wolcott and cheer her up. Good-by. Thank you again."

The young men shook hands with the friendliness of intimacy. Roger went with Peter to the door, where they shook hands again. As Peter was turning away he happened to glance down into the woods to the left. There, beating a hasty, not to say undignified retreat, was Daniel Richmond!

303

"Now what do you think of that?" cried Peter. "What the devil is *he* doing here?"

"I'm sure I don't know," said Roger indifferently.

"No doubt he recognized me," Peter went on. "He's got me scared to a panic—for fear he'll half ruin me—just out of a general insanity of meanness. If he asks you what I was doing here say I came to buy the picture. You don't know how much trouble he could make for me."

"I'll probably not see him."

"Do—for her sake, do," urged Peter. "Be civil to him. Try to soften him down. You ought to do it for her—honest, you ought."

"That's true," said Roger gravely.

Peter departed. Roger stayed on in the doorway. Presently Richmond reappeared, making his way slowly up the steep toward the studio. He arrived much out of breath, but contrived to put unmistakable politeness into his jerky tones as he gasped: "Good afternoon, Mr. Wade."

"How d'ye do, Mr. Richmond?" was Roger's civil rejoinder. His talk with Peter had put him in a frame of mind to bear and forbear, to do whatever he could toward ending the quarrel between father and daughter.

"I'd be greatly obliged—for a few—minutes of your time," said Richmond between breaths.

He looked old and worn and tired. Violent passions, especially violent temper, freely indulged, had played their wonted havoc. And these eroding emotions had deepened seam and gutter painfully. There had now appeared the gauntness in eye socket and under jawbone, about the saddest of the forewarnings of decrepitude and death that show in the human countenance with advancing age. Roger pitied him, this really superior man who had given his life furiously to plowing arid golden sands and was reaping ill health and unhappiness as his harvest. " Come in," said Roger.

When they were seated in the cool, airy workroom and had lighted, Richmond a cigar, Roger his pipe, Richmond glanced at the covered picture and said: " Is that it? "

" Yes," replied Roger, not in a tone that invited further conversation along those lines.

" I've come to see you about it," persisted Beatrice's father, apparently undiscouraged.

" I do not care to discuss it," said Roger.

" It is a picture of my daughter—painted for——"

" It is not a picture of your daughter," interrupted Roger, " and it was painted for my own amusement."

" My wife gave you the commission, with the idea of a surprise for me."

Roger was silenced.

" So," Richmond went on, " the picture belongs to us."

" No," said Roger quietly. " I purpose to keep it."

" You certainly have a strange way of doing business," said Richmond with resolute amiability.

" I don't do business," replied Roger.

Richmond waved his hand. " Oh—call it what you like. Artists paint pictures for money."

" I don't know about others," said Roger. " But I paint for my own amusement. And of my work I sell enough to enable me to live."

" Very fine—very fine," said Richmond, in the tone of a man who doesn't believe a word of it, but politely wishes to seem impressed. " I saw from the beginning of our acquaintance that you were an unusual man. I've thought about you a great deal "—with a sly smile —" naturally."

Roger made a slight inclination of his head.

" I owe you an apology for the way I acted the other day. And I make it. I lost my temper—a bad habit I have."

" Yes, it is a bad habit," said Roger dryly. " A particularly bad one for a man in your position, I should say."

306

"How in my position?" inquired Richmond, surprised.

"Oh, an independent man like me, who asks nothing of anybody, can afford that sort of thing. But you, who are dependent upon others for the success of your plans—that's very different."

"Um," grunted Richmond, little pleased but much struck by this new view of him as slave, not master. "Um." A long pause, with Richmond the more embarrassed because Roger's silence seemed natural and easy, like that of a statue or of a man alone. "I also —I also wish to say," Richmond resumed, "that on thinking the matter over I feel I did you an injustice in believing you—in accusing you—" He could not find a satisfactory word frame for his idea.

"In suspecting I was after your daughter and your money?" suggested Roger with an amused, ironic twinkle.

"Something like that. But, Mr. Wade, you are a man of the world. You can't wonder at my having such an idea."

"Not in the least," assented Roger.

"At the same time I do not blame you for being angry."

Roger smiled. "But, my dear sir, I was not angry. I didn't in the least care what you thought. Even if

307

you had succeeded in your vicious little scheme for robbing me of my competence, I still couldn't have been angry. It is so easy for a man to make a generous living if he happens not to have burdened himself with expensive tastes."

" That matter of the railway bonds—it will be adjusted at once, Mr. Wade. I was sorry the exigencies of a large operation forced me to—to———"

In his indignation Roger forgot the resolutions Peter had soothed and softened him into making. With his curtest accent he said: " What you did was contemptible enough. Why make it worse by lying? "

Richmond sprang to his feet. Roger rose toweringly, in his face a plain hope that his guest was about to depart. Richmond sat down again. " You have me at your mercy," cried he with a ludicrous mingling of attempt at politeness and frantic rage.

" I? " said Roger, laughing. " Oh, no. Neither of us can do the other any harm. I wouldn't if I could. You couldn't if you would. Don't you think we have had about enough of each other? "

" I have a favor to ask of you," said Richmond sullenly.

Roger hesitated, seated himself. There was a look in his visitor's eyes—a look of misery—that touched his heart.

"Mr. Wade," Richmond began again after a brief silence, "I am a man of very strong affections—very strong. Circumstances have concentrated them all on one person, my daughter Beatrice. They say everyone is a fool in at least one way. I am a fool about her."

Wade, inscrutable, was gazing at the drape over his painting.

"But," Richmond went on, "if she married against my will, much as I love her, foolish as I am about her, I would cut her off relentlessly."

"Then you don't love her," said Roger. "If you did you'd insist on her freely choosing the man she is to live with, the man who is to be the father of her children."

"Our ideas differ there," said Richmond stiffly.

"I am not surprised that she has left you," pursued Roger. "You have made her realize that you don't love her. And from what I know of her I doubt if you will ever get her back until you change your notions of what loving means."

Suspicion was once more sparkling in Richmond's wicked eyes. "You may be sure I'll not change, Mr. Wade," said he with a peculiarity of emphasis which even the simple-minded Roger could not fail to understand.

309

Roger laughed heartily. "At it again!" cried he. "Really, you are very amusing."

"Be that as it may," snapped Richmond, "I want you to know that I will never take her back—*never!*—until I am sure she has given you up. You may stake your life on that, sir. When I put my hand to the plough I do not turn back."

Roger leaned toward the unhappy man distracted by his own torturings of himself. "Will you believe me, sir," said he earnestly, "when I say I am deeply sorry that I have been the innocent cause of a breach between you and your daughter. Perhaps it is just as well that she has gotten away from you. It may result in her developing into the really fine person God intended her to be. Still, I wish to do all I can to heal the breach."

"That sounds like a man, Mr. Wade!" cried Richmond, all eagerness.

"I've been putting up with you this afternoon," pursued Roger, apparently not much impressed by this certificate of his virtue, "because I hoped to do something toward ending the quarrel between you two."

"You can end it," interrupted Richmond. "You can end it at once."

"Tell me how, and I'll do it," said Roger.

"She believes you wish to marry her."

"I am confident she never told you anything like that."

"She thinks you're afraid to marry her unless she brought the money to keep her in the style she's been used to."

"Impossible," said Roger.

"She tells me you refused her. But she still hopes."

Roger had become red and awkward. "Your daughter is something of a coquette," he stammered. "But I assure you you are wrong in thinking she— It's impossible for me to discuss this." He rose impatiently. "Your daughter does not wish to marry me. I do not wish to marry her. That's the whole story, sir. I must ask you to let me continue my work."

"If you *mean* that," urged Richmond, "you will go to her and tell her so. She's at the Wolcott—in New York City. You will tell her you do not love her and would not marry her—and she'll come home." The father's voice had grown hoarse and quavering, and in his face there was a piteous humility and wretchedness—such an expression as only a dethroned tyrant can have. "If you knew how her conduct is making me suffer, Mr. Wade, you'd not hesitate to do me— and her—this favor." That last word of abasement came in little more than a whisper.

Roger seemed to be debating.

"You must realize she is not a fit wife for you—she, brought up to a life of fashion and luxury. And she will never have a cent from me—not a cent!"

Roger had not been listening. "Can't do it," he now said. "Sorry, but I can't."

"You wish to marry her!" cried Richmond in the frenzy of impotence struggling at its bonds. "You hope!"

Roger, too full of pity for resentment, regarded the old man with friendly eyes. "Mr. Richmond,". said he, "I repeat I do not wish to marry anyone. I have made up my mind, with all the strength of what little good sense I may have, never to marry. I do not believe in marriage—for myself—for people who are doing the sort of thing I'm trying to do. You might as well accuse a Catholic priest of intending to marry."

"Fudge!" snorted Richmond.

Roger shrugged his shoulders. "This interview was not of my seeking. I wish it to come to an end."

"You refuse to tell her you will not marry her?"

"I refuse to make an impertinent ass of myself. If you wish your daughter back, sir, go and apologize for having outraged her finest feelings and ask her to come home unconditionally. I could not say to her what you request—for obvious reasons of good taste. If you had a sense of humor you'd not ask it. But I don't hesitate to give you my word that you need not have an instant's uneasiness lest your daughter and I marry."

"On your honor?"

"On my honor."

Richmond gazed at him with eyes that seemed to be searching every corner of his soul. "I believe you," said he at last. "And I am content." He had abruptly changed from suspicion and sneer and hardly veiled insult to his most winning friendliness and geniality. It was amazing how attractive his wizened and usually almost wicked face became. "It's been my experience," he went on to explain, "that human beings are at bottom exactly alike—in motives, in the things that appeal to them. Once in a while there is an exception. You happen to be one, Mr. Wade. I think you'll forgive me for having applied my principle to you. Where exceptions are rare it's most unwise for a practical man to consider them as a possibility."

Roger smiled amiably enough. "No matter," said he. "I hope you'll make it up with your daughter."

Richmond's face clouded, and once more that look of anguish showed deep in his eyes. "It'll just about kill me if I don't," said he.

"Go to her—like a father who loves," said Roger

gently. And once more the impulse came, too strong to resist, and he dropped the cover from the painting. But this time he did not look at the picture—at Beatrice Richmond as incarnation of a spring morning; he fixed his gaze upon her father. And the expression of that sad, passion-scarred face made him glad he had yielded to the impulse.

"I must have it!" said Richmond. "Name your own price."

"It is not for sale."

"I tell you I must have it."

"No—you can have her. I shall keep this."

Roger was gazing absently at his creation. Richmond, struck by some subtle accent in his words, glanced quickly at him.

"I'll take it with me—back to Paris," said Roger, talking aloud to himself.

"When do you go?" asked Richmond abruptly.

"Next week."

"For the summer?"

"For good," said Roger, covering the picture.

"I wish you every success," cried Richmond heartily. "You are an honest, sincere man."

The meaning of Roger's quizzical smile escaped him.

XVII

RICHMOND TRIES TO MAKE PEACE

It would hardly have been possible for anyone to hold crow in lower esteem as a repast than did Daniel Richmond; and, long though his career and many its ups and downs, seldom had he been called upon to eat it. But on those few occasions he had eaten like the wise man he was—as if it were a delicacy, as if it were his favorite dish; as if he were afraid some one would snatch away his portion should he linger over it. The vicissitudes of fortune had now swung crow round to him once more. He lost no time in setting about dispatching it.

At ten the next morning, when Beatrice descended to the parlor of the Wolcott in response to her father's name brought up to her in his hasty scrawl on one of the hotel's blank cards, she was greeted effusively. He did not give her a chance to be uppish and distant. He met her in the door, took her in his arms and kissed her fondly.

" It's been an age since I saw you," cried he, twinkling with good humor. "I'm amazed to find you still young."

She was quite taken aback, but succeeded in concealing it and in accepting his suggestion as to the dominant note of what she had assumed would be a trying interview. "How's mother—and the boys?" inquired she. "Much changed?"

"All well. Your mother holds together wonderfully."

There was no jest, however, but a moving earnestness in his eyes as they fixed upon her a hungry, devouring expression. And her own look at him strongly suggested the presence of a veil of tears. Neither had until now realized how much they cared about each other, how strong was the sympathy through similarity of character. He abruptly seized her and kissed her again, his fingers trembling as he passed them over her yellow hair. "I'm mighty glad to see you," said he. "Mighty glad."

"And I you," she replied, taking his hand and giving it an affectionate squeeze. And then she kissed him and openly wiped away her tears.

This outburst of nature on her part was a grave tactical blunder—for, in dealing with men of his sort, the guard can never be dropped; their habit of seeing and seizing advantage is too powerful ever to relax.

"'I'm mighty glad to see you,' said he. 'Mighty glad.'"

Upsetting to him though his agitation and delight were, he did not cease to be himself. The instant he saw how moved she was, how she was meeting his advances half way at least, if not more, he began to hope he could spare himself the hated dish of crow. So, although his napkin was tucked under his chin and his knife and fork were in air, eager for the festal attack, he did not proceed. He had intended his next words to be a sweeping apology. Instead, he said:

"I see you've been thinking things over, just as I have."

"Yes," replied she.

"We were both hasty. You inherit my disposition —and it's a rather difficult one." He was hesitatingly caressing her hand. "I wanted a boy with my sort of brain," he went on. "But it didn't turn out that way. You inherited, instead. Just as well, perhaps. I'd have broken with a boy like myself. But the feminine in you saves the situation. We can forgive each other without pride interfering. . . . I'm sorry for what I did, and I've no doubt you are. Let's forget it all and go home and begin again."

"You mean that, father?" cried she, tears again welling into her eyes. "Oh, you *do* love me! And I thought you didn't."

"This business has aged me ten years," said he,

317

thinking rapidly as he was still further encouraged by those tears. " I saw it myself when I shaved this morning."

Beatrice hung her head. For the moment she felt guilty. She—*she* had aged this loving, always-indulgent father!

This further evidence of feminine softness and affection encouraged him to the point of believing himself once more master. He said, in a forgiving tone: " But you didn't realize what you were doing. Well, you've had a valuable lesson, my dear, and you've got the intelligence to profit by it. How long will it take you to get ready? "

" Oh, not long. I've got some things to attend to, but I can do it at Red Hill just as well as here, I think."

" Go up and pack, and I'll come back in an hour." He rose. " What a weight this lifts off me! " And his appearance confirmed his words. " But I'm gladdest of all because it vindicates your good sense. I knew my daughter would see I was doing what was best for her, would see it just as soon as her intelligence regained control."

Beatrice had risen; at this last sentence she sat down again with a dazed expression. " I'm afraid I don't quite understand, father," said she, hesitatingly. " I'm afraid I misunderstood you."

Richmond saw he had gone too far—probably not much too far, but still beyond where her mood of penitence had carried her—as yet. "Let's not discuss disagreeable things," said he hurriedly. "Do your packing and let's get home. Once we get there everything else can be settled easily."

But Beatrice, after trying in vain to arrest his evading glance, kept her seat. "No, we must understand each other first," said she decisively.

"Now, Beatrice," protested her father at the door into the hall, "don't spoil your happiness and my own!"

"Listen to me, father. I've not changed my mind about Peter—not in the least."

"Oh—bother Peter!" exclaimed he good-humoredly.

"Do you still expect me to marry him?"

Richmond saw there was no dodging the issue. He met it squarely. "I'm sure you'll want to marry him. But I'm not going to force you—or try to."

"But listen. I haven't changed my mind about Roger, either."

"Well—well," said Richmond, still good-humored though not so easily. "It'd be foolish for us to quarrel about him. You say he has refused you."

"Yes—but I haven't given him up."

"That isn't a very nice way for a girl to talk—is it now, my dear?" said Richmond, laughing with some constraint.

"Why not?" said she.

"It's the man's place to do the courting and the proposing. And if the man doesn't want you I'm sure you've got too much modesty and pride to——"

"I don't know whether I have or not," interrupted Beatrice. "I've got a lot of you in me. I can't imagine anything I wouldn't do to get him if I thought it would help. And I haven't thought of much else but of different schemes to bring him round. I'm like you are when you see a railroad you want."

"But there's nothing you can do, Beatrice," remonstrated her father.

"No—it seems not," she assented despondently. "Oh, how it enrages me to be a woman! When a man sees a girl he recognizes as the very best for him, one he can't and won't do without, he goes after her—straight out—and everybody applauds. It ought to be so with a girl."

"God forbid!" cried Richmond, laughing.

"Oh, the men wouldn't be bothered as much as you seem to think. Not many of them are tremendously worth while. The women feel about most of them like——"

"Like they do about mashed potatoes in Indiana—don't care whether they're eating 'em or not?"

"Just so," laughed she.

Once more he was at the hall door. He turned for a last look and smile. "I'll be back in an hour, and out home we'll plan something to take your mind off this unappreciative man."

Beatrice looked disappointed. "I thought you were going to say plan something to bring him round. That's what we must do."

This was the fatal one prod too many at the leashed temper of Richmond. "Don't irritate me, Beatrice," he said sharply—a plea verging on a rebuke. "Please try to be a little tactful with me."

"I see you haven't changed at all," cried she, tears in her eyes again—hot tears of a very different kind from those before.

"I thought you wanted to go home," cried he, struggling with his temper.

"I do—if you are willing to grant me the dearest right a woman has—the right to select her own husband." She came closer to him, clasped her hands and laid them against his shoulder. And into his eyes gazed hers, innocent, anxious. "Oh, father, won't you be sensible—reasonable? I've got to live with him—not you."

"I'd do almost anything to please you, my dear. If he were in your class——"

"But that's just why I want him," cried she. "Do you think a man like that could grow up in my class?"

"There are lots of clever painters about—lots of 'em."

"I don't care anything about his painting," exclaimed she impatiently. "I don't know anything about it. I'm speaking of him as a man. A woman doesn't marry a talent—or a family—or a fortune. She wants a *man*. Of course, if she can't get a man, why, one of the other things is better than nothing. But *I* can get a *man*, father—if you'll help me!"

"Peter's almost as tall—and quite as handsome—and much more like your sort of looking man."

"Father—father—how can you! And you have a sense of humor, too!"

"It's fortunate for you, my dear, that Wade has the good sense to see he would be ill at ease out of his own class. If he were willing, and I were foolish, and you married him—how wretched you'd be when the awakening came!"

The girl turned sadly away. "You don't believe in love," she said with bitterness. "You don't believe in anything but money."

"I want to see my daughter happy," said Richmond with a melancholy, reproachful dignity that made her ashamed of herself.

"Yes—I know you do, father," said she. "But"—with a look of hesitation that might readily have been mistaken for weakness—"I see I must go my own way."

Richmond reflected that this did not mean much, as Roger Wade was firmly set against marriage. So he said, with hypocritical resignation: "Very well, my dear. Do as you like. All I want is you to come home."

Beatrice slowly shook her head. "I can't go," said she.

Her father stared, astounded; her expression made her words as far as possible from impulsive or careless.

"I see you haven't changed at all. If I went back the same trouble would break out again—only worse. Besides, what chance would I have to get him? You'd work against me secretly if you didn't openly. No—I don't trust you. I must make up my mind to shift for myself."

"What on earth are you talking about?" he ejaculated. "Are you stark mad?"

"No. I'm becoming sane," said she quietly. "Won't you sit down a minute?"

Richmond seated himself meekly. The fear that

had brought him there to apologize was chilling his hot temper.

"I left home partly because of Roger Wade," she proceeded to explain, "but not altogether. There was another reason—as strong—maybe stronger. You had opened my eyes to the truth about myself—to what a degraded position I was in."

"Degraded?" echoed he wonderingly. Then, somewhat like an alienist humoring an insane patient: "But go on, my dear."

"I had been imagining all along that I was free. I suddenly found that I wasn't free at all—that I had to do what you said—even about the things that meant my whole life—had to do as you ordered or lose all the things you had made necessities to me—all the luxury and the enjoyments and the friends even. I saw I wasn't anything in myself—nothing at all—and I had been going round with my head high, so proud and so pleased with myself! I understood why Roger Wade didn't think me worth while. I understood why you could treat me contemptuously."

"Is that all?" inquired her father, when she paused for a reflective silence.

"No—just a little more. So—I'm not going back home with you—not just now. I'm going on with the dressmaking."

" With the—*what?* "

" Oh, I forgot I hadn't told you," said she with a smile. " Valentine and I—and Monsieur Léry, whom she is marrying—are starting a dressmaking shop."

Richmond stood up straight, and his scanty hair and thick eyebrows seemed to be assisting materially in making him the embodiment of horrified amazement.

" Don't be alarmed, father. The name over the door is not to be Richmond or Beatrice, but Valentine —though, of course, I'll take part openly. I want everybody to know, because I intend to make loads and loads of money. You've no idea of the profits in fashionable dressmaking. Eighty—a hundred—a hundred and fifty per cent! "

" You are joking! "

She pretended to misunderstand. " No—fully that," she cried delightedly.

" Beatrice! I forbid it."

" But I'm not asking you to invest," laughed she. " In fact, we don't want any more capital or partners. Personally, I wish Léry were an employee instead of a partner. But Valentine would insist, I'm sure——"

" You will drive me mad! " exclaimed her father, throwing his arms about wildly. " This folly is worse than the infatuation for that artist. " And he started up, fumed about the room, sank exhausted and trembling into a chair. "You'll be the death of me!" he gasped.

"Now, do be reasonable, father," she urged. "Why shouldn't I use my talents for business and for dress and make myself rich? Don't talk to me about what people will think. I don't care. I've found out what people are worth. Why, even my friend, Allie Kinnear, hasn't been near me."

"I forbid it! I forbid it!" her father cried, shaking his fists in the air. And off again he went into one of his paroxysms of fury.

"But I'm of age."

"I'll have you locked up as insane! I'll have a commission appointed to take charge of your property!"

"When I showed them my plans for the shop I think they'd let me alone. We'll make barrels of money. New York hasn't seen such a shop as I'd run. The trouble with the dressmaking business is that no woman who really knows——"

He seized her by the arm, glared into her face. "This is an infernal scheme to bring me to terms! Has that artist put you up to it?"

"How absurd! I haven't seen him. I doubt if he knows I've left home. Father, since I seem not to be able to get him I've simply got to do something— something that will keep me so busy I shan't have time to think. For I'm not—as you imagine—the victim of a foolish girl's infatuation. I'm really in love, father dear—sensibly in love."

"No one is sensible who's in love," said he in a far gentler tone. His rages had about exhausted his strength. He was feeling an ominous feebleness of limb and heart that alarmed him. "Nobody's sensible who's in love," he repeated.

"Nobody's sensible who isn't—if they get half a chance," replied she. "It's the only thing in life."

And his haggard face and the hungry misery of his eyes contained no denial of her confident assertion. "Is there *nothing* that will induce you to come home, Beatrice?" he pleaded with the weakness of exhaustion. "I'll never speak of Peter—of marriage—again. I'll give you whatever income you want—in your own right."

"And Roger?"

Richmond winced; but those inward reminders of oncreeping old age, lonely and loveless if this girl turned from him, forbade him to draw back. "You think you could get him if I were to consent?"

"Perhaps." There was the ecstatic quiver of a newborn hope in her voice.

"That is, you would marry him, even though you were convinced he was a fortune hunter?"

"He might be afraid to undertake the support of as expensive a girl as I am. He doesn't dream how inexpensive I could be."

A long pause, he gazing at the floor, she anxiously watching him. "Well—I consent," burst from her father. His tone suggested a false admission wrung under torture.

Another long pause, she eying him dubiously, he avoiding her gaze. "I don't trust you," said she. "It's your own fault. You can't blame me. I couldn't ever trust you, after the thing you did against Roger —and your threats to Peter and to me."

"I am an old fool—a weak old fool!" he shouted, seizing his hat. "I wash my hands of you! I'm done with you!"

And out he bolted, running squarely into a woman who was just entering the parlor. He did not pause to apologize.

In the afternoon Mrs. Richmond came—beautifully dressed and diffusing a strong but elegant odor of concentrated essence of lilies of the valley. "I'd have been here long ago," she explained as she kissed and embraced her daughter and shed a few cautious tears, "but I didn't dare. This was my first chance. Your father has absolutely forbidden me. And I had always thought he was rather partial to you. But then, I might have known. He cares for nobody—for nothing —but those schemes and plans of his. You'd never believe he was the same man as the one I married. And he isn't. Success has turned his head."

"He was here this morning," said Beatrice.

"Here!" exclaimed her mother. "What for?"

"For me."

Jealousy sparkled in her mother's hastily veiled eyes. "Trying to get you into his power again," she sneered.

"I suppose so," said Beatrice. "Yes—that must have been it."

"Then you are coming home?"

"Oh, no."

The jealousy passed; the mother returned. "But, Beatrice—he has changed his will and has cut you off. He's leaving your portion to Hector."

Beatrice looked uncomfortable. "I shan't say I like that," said she, "for it'd be false. But I'm not coming home, just the same. There's been a great change in me, mother."

"You always were headstrong," said her mother. "I used to feel, when you were a baby, that the day would come when there'd be a clash between you and your father."

"Well—the clash is over. We'll let each other alone after this."

"But what is to become of you? Of course, I'll have something; and as long as I have anything—" Mrs. Richmond checked herself, flushed. "In fact, I have got a little, Beatrice. I put by in case there ever should be this kind of trouble between him and the children. I can let you have a good income—enough, with what you've got, to make a showing you needn't be ashamed of. Have you seen Mr. Wade?"

Beatrice put her arms around her mother and kissed her—tenderly, but with that carefulness which one woman never neglects in caressing another who has made a careful toilet. "If I need the money I'll tell you, dear," said she. "No, I haven't seen him. Have you?"

"Late yesterday afternoon. He was striding along the road—didn't see me."

"How was he looking?"

"Anxious and depressed, I thought."

Beatrice beamed. "You're not telling me that—just to make me feel good?"

"No—no, indeed. He looked almost haggard."

Beatrice kissed her mother again. There could not be the slightest doubt. Her mother, in the habit of siding with her children against their aggressive father and of protecting them from him, was moving in her direction. "Why don't *you* go to see him?" she boldly suggested.

"If your father should find out!"

"You've got the picture as an excuse. You know, father thinks we met Roger in Europe."

"Yes—yes—I had forgotten. . . . I don't know what possesses me! I can't understand myself, even thinking of helping you in such an absurd, idiotic thing as marrying a poor artist."

"A poor man—not a poor artist," laughed Beatrice.

"I suppose," went on Mrs. Richmond, "it must be for the pleasure of seeing your father defeated in something he has set his heart on. He has trampled me so often I'd like to see him humbled once."

"You ought to have seen him when I told him I was going into the dressmaking business."

"Beatrice!" cried her mother—and her expression of horrified amazement was a fit companion for that of Richmond.

"I'm going to make stacks of money," said Beatrice carelessly. "You know I've got taste—and a good business head."

"Didn't your father forbid you?" demanded her mother, quivering with agitation.

" Yes—and I reminded him I was of age."

" Why, it'll ruin us all!" wailed Mrs. Richmond. " Beatrice, I do believe you've lost your mind."

" Just what father said."

" Surely you won't do it, now that I've offered you a good income. You can have fifteen thousand—in addition to what you've got."

" And how would I pass the time?"

" Why, as you always have."

The peculiar, romantic—" crazy," her father called it—look drifted into the girl's face, completely transforming it. " Yes," replied she dreamily, " but that was before I knew Roger."

" What *shall* I do!" moaned Mrs. Richmond. She was anything but a keen observer, but she was woman enough to understand that look. " If you married him you'd give this up—wouldn't you?"

" I hadn't thought. Yes—I suppose I'd have to. Looking after him would take all my time."

" Then you *must* marry him!" cried her mother resolutely. " I shall see your father at once."

" You'll simply get yourself into trouble, mother dear."

" I'm not afraid of him now!" exclaimed Mrs. Richmond with militant eyes and nostrils. " He has made a fool of himself—and he knows it. I'll not have all I've

332

spent my life in building up torn down just because he is such a monstrous snob. Why should he object to a distinguished artist as a son-in-law? Why, Mr. Wade would be an addition to the family, socially."

And so on and on, Beatrice letting her mother rave herself into a fitting state of mind for a struggle with her husband. Whenever she paused Beatrice brought up the dressmaking to set her off again. And when she was about to leave Beatrice called in Valentine and presented her as " My partner, Miss Clermont." Mrs. Richmond was quite done for. Her daughter's maid treated as an equal—and become her daughter's business partner! " I'll telephone you to-night—or see you to-morrow," said she as she was leaving. She did not dare offend Beatrice by ignoring " Miss Clermont." So she made a bow that was a highly amusing specimen of those always amusing compromises which no sentient thing in the universe but the humorless human animal would attempt to carry off.

XVIII

FOR some time after her mother left Beatrice sat in a brown study, her ex-maid and partner seated across the table from her and not venturing to interrupt. At last, Beatrice said: "I don't understand it at all. I'd never have believed mother would take it that way."

"You could hardly expect her to be pleased, Miss Richmond," replied Valentine.

"Oh, I knew she'd blow up and sail into me," said Beatrice. "I'm puzzling over the way she acted about father. I never before knew her to revolt against him."

"Probably—when Mrs. Richmond sees him—" was Miss Clermont's highly suggestive, unfinished comment.

"No doubt," said Beatrice. "And yet— Mamma was mad through and through—fighting mad. I never saw her like that—with him. I shouldn't have believed it was in her. I suspect—I hope—she'll make trouble."

Beatrice was right in her diagnosis of her mother's rage. Mrs. Richmond was indeed fighting mad. Everything that lives, even a human being weakened

334

by luxury and by long and meek servitude, has its limit
of endurance, its point at which it will cease to run
or to cower and will fight to the last gasp. That limit,
that point had been reached by Mrs. Richmond. There
were many things she liked in varying degrees—her
children, society novels, half a dozen friends, her maid
Marthe, an occasional man—the Count d'Artois just
at that time. There were three things only to which
she was deeply attached—three besides herself. The
first was her youthful appearance, which she struggled
so assiduously to retain. The second was wealth, which
gave her so many delightful moral, mental and physical sensations. The third and dearest was social position. The mania of social position habitually seizes
upon persons of great affluence and small intelligence;
it manifests itself early, often in a grave form; but it
does not become virulent until middle life. With Mrs.
Richmond the mania was aggravated by her not having
been born to fashionable society. Patiently, resolutely,
toilsomely she had built herself up socially year by
year. She had endured humiliations, snubs, insults, as
a gallant soldier endures the blows and buffetings of
battle. And her virtue had been rewarded. She had
attained social position—not, indeed, security, for in
America social security is impossible; but an envied
rank among the very first, reasonably assured so long

as Richmond retained his wealth and no degrading scandal undermined and toppled. Like the prudent soul that she was, she remained sleeplessly vigilant lest some such scandal should come from an unexpected quarter.

There were obcure relations—vulgar—no, worse—positively low. True, everybody was cursed with such; but to Mrs. Richmond her own and her husband's impossible kin seemed more awful than anyone else's. Then, Richmond, industrious social climber though he was and as careful about matters of social position as any of the other big men of finance who graciously permitted their families to be fashionable—Richmond occasionally broke loose and offended by coarse and greedy snatching at wealth owned by persons of social power. Also, he occasionally almost overreached himself in his contempt for law and public opinion, and put in jeopardy his reputation. But this danger was not now haunting her as it once had. Through the constant infractions of Richmond and his like the moral code was no longer what it used to be, was a mere collection of old tatters. Pretty much everybody who socially was anybody despised it in private and professed public respect for it only out of habit and for the benefit of the lower classes.

Finally, there were the children. One could never tell what one's children would grow up into. Of the four, she had regarded the younger daughter as the safest because she was intensely proud, fond of social position, of fashionable luxury—fonder of them than of anything—except, perhaps, of having her own way where opposed. Yes, Beatrice would never cause her social anxiety. In the irony of fate it was she and only she who had become troublesome. The refusal to marry Peter Vanderkief was bad. The infatuation for an artist, eminent though he seemed to be—at least, in France—was worse. This dressmaking was worst. To Mrs. Richmond's excited fancy it seemed to foreshadow social downfall—not from the fashionable set, but from leadership in it. If there had been so much as a single previous generation of fashionable Richmonds, or if their own fashion were a matter of twenty years instead of a scant ten, the thing wouldn't matter. Beatrice would be regarded as eccentric—and eccentricity is a mark of aristocratic blood. But, in the circumstances, for Beatrice to become a dressmaker in partnership with a French maid and a chauffeur——

Mrs. Richmond burst in upon her husband at his office with her fury intact. Richmond knew at a glance that he had to deal with a revolt and a dangerous one. He showed that he understood all about its origin by saying as soon as his secretary had gone: " You've been to see Beatrice."

"She told you this morning that she was going into the dressmaking business?" said the wife, nostrils dilating, eyes blazing at him.

"Yes." And Richmond concentrated himself in a corner of his big chair. It looked like a gesture of shrinking, of timidity. In fact, it was simply his way of gathering himself together at the first onslaught of danger.

"Here in New York!"

"Yes."

"With Valentine!"

Richmond made a slight gesture of assent.

"And—*Léry!*"

Richmond from the corner of his chair stretched out one hesitating hand to the papers on the desk before him.

"What are you going to do about it?" demanded the wife in a low tone that sounded as if it had forced its way through clinched teeth.

Richmond leaned back in his chair, clasped his hands behind his big head, stared out of the window.

"What are you going to do about it?" repeated his wife.

Still no reply.

"Are you going to sacrifice all that I've spent so many years in building up?"

"You?" snapped Richmond, with contemptuous sarcasm. "What have *you* done?"

"I've made our social position—that's what I've done."

"You mean *I*'ve built it—my money and my power. People recognize us because they don't dare anger *me*." This in the voice of axiomatic truth.

But Mrs. Richmond was too angry—too alarmed. Panic has its courage more dangerous than valor's. "Look at the Galloways," cried she. "They've got more money than we have. Look at the Roebucks— more money than we have—and Roebuck a man you're afraid of."

"I'm afraid of nobody!" blustered he.

She answered this with a maddening, little, sneering laugh, and went on: "Look at the Fosdicks—and the Bellinghams—and the Ashforths. More money than we have."

"Yes—and they're received." But his tone was not all it might have been.

"You know the difference," said she, in open contempt of his flimsy evasion. "They're *in* but not *of*. We're both in and of. And why? . . . Why?" she repeated fiercely. "Why are we in and of, in spite of the enemies you've made—in spite of the shady things you've done—in spite of——"

"Now, see here, Lucy—I've not complained of your way of managing your side of the family affairs. You've done very well." This was said patronizingly, but with a mildness that, issuing from Daniel Richmond, made it sound almost like a whimper.

"And since I got the Earl of Broadstairs away from Sally Peyton and married him to Rhoda we've been right in the front rank. There aren't but two big families that still hold out."

"The Vanderkief marriage might have got them," said Richmond.

"If Beatrice starts up as a dressmaker—with those two servants——"

"But—what can *I* do?" he interrupted violently. "She's insane—insane!"

"It's you that are insane, Dan," cried his wife. "You knew the girl. You knew you'd made her hard to manage. Why did you goad her?"

"I suppose you'd have let her marry that painter fellow," sneered the husband.

"Anything but such a scandal as this," declared she. "And it's got to be stopped!"

Richmond shrugged his shoulders. "I offered to drop the Vanderkief marriage. I offered to take her back. I begged her to come back."

"But you didn't tell her she could marry Wade."

"Yes, I did!" confessed he. "Yes—I did even that."

Mrs. Richmond frankly showed her incredulity; and that there might be no doubt, she said: "I don't believe it."

"Do you think I've got no sense? I saw what the scandal would mean. Besides—" Richmond did not give his other reason. He was too ashamed of his weakness of love for the girl to expose it.

By this time Mrs. Richmond had recovered. "And is that *all* you've done?"

"All?" he cried. "*All?* What else could I do?"

"Get her the man."

"Get her the man?" repeated he, as if trying in vain to understand.

"She doesn't trust you—and you can't be surprised at that. You've got to get her the man. You've mismanaged this thing from the start. You've driven her on and on until now there's only the one chance left."

Richmond did not contradict this, even mentally. He said presently: "But I've talked with him and he won't have her."

Again Mrs. Richmond was taken by surprise—so much so that she said: "What did you say?"

Richmond showed his wild internal commotion.

341

With glittering eyes and teeth suggesting that they were about to gnash he all but hissed: "Are you getting deaf? I said I had talked with him, and he won't have her. I can't make the man marry her—can I?"

In her excitement, in her amazement Mrs. Richmond leaned forward and said slowly: "Did you go to him and give him permission to marry Beatrice?"

"No," Richmond confessed.

"Oh," said his wife with sarcasm, "you went to forbid him to marry her. Why do you deceive me when we're in such a dangerous position?"

"I didn't deceive you," growled he. "I went to make sure he didn't want to marry her. We got along all right."

Mrs. Richmond showed relief. "Then we're in a position to make advances to him."

"I'll make no more advances!" cried he defiantly—blustering defiance.

"I suppose you'd rather see the newspapers full of your daughter making dresses in partnership with a maid and a chauffeur," sneered Mrs. Richmond.

He winced as she jabbed surely at his one weak point—the weakness she knew so well; her knowledge of it had given her the courage to attack him. And she knew also that his one belief in her, his one use for her, was her skill as a social maneuverer.

" You'll do whatever is necessary," she went on. " I can't understand why you were so opposed to her marrying. He's young, but famous already. He'll be a help."

A long pause. Then: " Yes, he can paint," said Richmond absently, a queer look in his usually hard and wicked eyes.

" Of course he can. D'Artois told us so. I'll go ask him to dinner on my way home. If he accepts I'll telephone Beatrice to come down."

" Yes—that's a good idea—excellent," said Richmond. " I want to get this thing settled. It has unfitted me for business. A few weeks more of it and I'll go to pieces. Do whatever you like. I don't care, so long as you settle things." And he took up his papers to indicate that he had no more time to waste.

" I hope this will be a lesson to you," said she. " Next time any trouble comes with the children you'd better leave it to me."

Richmond muttered something into his papers. Mrs. Richmond issued forth in dignity and in triumph. No one, viewing her cold and haughty face, her beautiful, expensive toilet, her air throughout of the story-book aristocrat, would have believed her capable of participating in such a scene as she and her husband had just enacted. She was secure from suspicion of such vulgarities—secure behind the glamour of wealth and fashion that veils the Richmond kind of sordid lives and the sordid pursuits that engross them.

When Mrs. Richmond's auto stopped before Roger Wade's gate she saw him reading behind the leafy screen of the front veranda. She waited and watched a moment or so, but he did not glance up.

"Give the horn a squeeze or so," said she to the chauffeur.

At the sound of three sharp, imperious calls the artist slowly lifted his eyes. Mrs. Richmond, her face at the open window of her limousine, saw him observing her as one might a chance passer-by on the high-road. When he saw that she was seeing him he rose and advanced toward the gate at a pace that was neither fast nor slow—a pace somehow discouraging to Mrs. Richmond. She awaited him with a smile of the most flattering warmth.

"How do you do, Mr. Wade?" cried she as he opened the gate, and out went her gloved hand to meet his cordially. "You have treated me shamefully," she went on. "But one who is nobody must take whatever treatment a great man gives one and be grateful that it's no worse."

The big, dark man, looking extremely handsome in

his loose, white flannels, laughed amiably. He showed his good sense by attempting no reply. He simply stood waiting.

"I've stopped to ask you to dine with us to-morrow night—very informally," said she. "It'd be an enormous favor, as we're dreadfully dull."

"All this is very kind," said Roger, "but I can't come."

"Now, don't say that," urged she, her manner making her insistence seem polite—a manner of which she was admirably mistress. "Mr. Richmond told me this afternoon that I mustn't take no for an answer. He has developed a great admiration and liking for you. If you're not refusing just out of unneighborliness, perhaps you'll come day after to-morrow evening?"

"I'll be on the sea," said Roger. "I'm sailing Saturday morning."

"So suddenly!" cried Mrs. Richmond with an arresting agitation in her voice—obviously not the agitation of pleasure, but of alarm. "Then, you *must* come to-morrow evening. It is our last chance for better acquaintance."

"Oh, there's Paris," said Roger carelessly. His frank eyes were regarding her with a puzzled expression.

Mrs. Richmond flung away the last shred of pretense of merely social purposes. Her eyes pleaded and her voice implored as she said: " Mr. Richmond particularly wished to see you. Can't you arrange it— for to-morrow evening—or this evening? "

" Thank you. It's really impossible." And Roger's tone and manner were a courteous but final refusal of all that she was implying. " Will you trouble yourself with my adieux to Mr. Richmond and your daughter? "

" I'm so disappointed I hardly know what to say," cried Mrs. Richmond with pathetic appeal. " Do forgive my rudeness, but——"

" It's quite impossible for me to change my plans for the little time I have between now and Saturday morning." Roger was simply polite—not unfriendly, yet certainly not friendly.

Mrs. Richmond's handsome eyes veiled their anger behind a look of resigned regret. She dared not quarrel with him, must part with him on friendly terms. " I understand. I am dreadfully sorry. But—as you say, there's Paris. We haven't your address there, I believe."

" I have no address," said Roger. " I shall have to find a place."

" D'Artois will know," said Mrs. Richmond hastily,

to cover the almost blunt refusal to continue the acquaintance. "We can find out from him."

"I lead rather a secluded life there," was Roger's reply. "One must fight constantly against the temptations to distraction. But I needn't explain that to the wife of a busy man of affairs."

"No, indeed," cried she, with undiminished cordiality—and she did not find it difficult to be cordial to a man whose charm she was now feeling, hardly the less, perhaps the more, because he was defeating her will. "Still," she went on, "we'll venture to hope that you'll relent a little and not look on us altogether as intruders, Mr. Wade."

"You are too kind, Mrs. Richmond," said Roger. He made as much of a move toward turning away as politeness permitted.

"Again, I'm sorry—so sorry, about dinner," said Mrs. Richmond, once more extending her hand. She was all friendliness, all cordiality. "And I'll hope you and Fate will be kinder in Paris. Good-by. Mr. Richmond will be really distressed. And Beatrice——"

Roger's eyes shifted. A faint color crept into his cheeks.

"She will think you're a sadly negligent friend. She's at the Wolcott. If you are in town——"

"Unfortunately, I'll not be," interrupted Roger

347

curtly. " I'll have to trust to you to make my apologies."

Mrs. Richmond once more looked defeated. " Don't forget us," she pleaded.

" Thank you," said Roger embarrassed.

" Good-by."

Roger bowed. The machine got under way and disappeared in a cloud of dust while he went slowly and moodily back to the veranda to take up his book, but not to read it.

As Mrs. Richmond's auto swung into the terrace before the main entrance to Red Hill Richmond's auto departed, having just set him down upon the stone esplanade. He opened the door of the car for his wife. " Well? " said he sharply.

" He can't—that is, won't—come."

" I thought so."

" He's sailing."

" I know. Next week."

" No—Saturday."

Richmond startled. " Day after to-morrow? "

" And he wouldn't come either to-night or to-morrow night."

They walked in silence side by side into the house.

" He's a splendidly handsome man," said Mrs. Richmond. " Any woman would be proud to have him as her husband. And he has the air of a person-age. . . . I must telephone Beatrice."

"You must do nothing of the sort," ordered Richmond in the tone which, when he first had begun to use it with her, had made her feel like a servant. "You'll not tempt her to make a public fool of herself."

"You don't understand her," protested Mrs. Richmond.

"No matter. No telephoning. Small, timid people never can understand that a person of her sort has un-limited capacity for reckless folly."

"But what are we to do?" demanded his wife.

"I'll go to see him."

"To say what?"

"What circumstances may dictate after I get there," said her husband. "I'll go at once."

"Yes—yes. The time's very short," cried she.

"On the contrary, there's plenty of time."

And he turned on his heel and retraced his steps toward the door. Mrs. Richmond paused to look pityingly after him; he was slightly bent; his step had lost its spring. Only once before had she seen him so harassed—the time when he was trying to negotiate apparently impossible loans to save his fortune from ruin and himself from prison. She hated him with what she believed to be an implacable hate. In fact, she

349

hated him only because he would not let her love him;
he fascinated her, a woman of the sort that crave a
master and really love the servitude they profess to
loathe. She rejoiced in his defeats; she delighted to
waste his money where she could not sequester it. But
her soul did homage to him as its lord. She looked
after him longingly; she would have given a good part
of her possessions to be an unseen and unsuspected
spectator at the scene between him and Roger. For
she would have staked all she had on Roger's admin-
istering to him the defeat of his life.

XIX

Roger still seated on his front veranda behind the curtain of creepers, was not a little astonished to see that the solitary occupant of the runabout stopping at his gate was Beatrice's father. His astonishment did not decrease when the little big financier, advancing briskly up the gravel walk edged by flowering plants, hailed the first clear view of his face with a smile of the utmost geniality—the greeting of an old and dear friend.

" I've come about that picture," Richmond hastened to explain. " I wish—for my own sake—I'd seen it sooner. If you'll pardon an old man—at least, a much older man than yourself—for being quite frank —it has given me an entirely different opinion of you. It has made me very proud of my acquaintance with you. I know that's blunt—but it's sincere."

Roger was as fond of praise as the next human being. He had cultivated the philosophy of indifference only to uncritical censure. He blushed and stammered out some awkward words of thanks—certainly not the less awkward for the uneasiness Richmond's manner had raised within him.

"My wife and my daughter were quite right and I was wrong—stupidly wrong," continued Richmond. They were seated now. "I'm not an art expert—and not imagining I was or pretending to be has saved me thousands of dollars and a lot of fake art stuff. But, at the same time, a man who amounts to anything in any line always appreciates good work in every other line—whether he likes it or not. So—I want that picture. Isn't there anything I could say or do that would induce you to change your mind and let me have it?"

Roger's brow clouded again; a strange, absent look was in his eyes—the eyes of an artist, sensitive, sympathetic, penetrating, yet devoid of the least suggestion of craft. "I've been thinking that matter over," said he with an effort. "I have decided not to take the picture with me. So—you can have it—if you'll accept it."

"My dear Wade!" exclaimed Richmond, all enthusiasm. "But you must be generous with me. You must let me give you something in return. You know how burdensome a sense of unacquitted obligation is. All I have to give is money, unfortunately. You must let me give that. It is the right of you fellows to expect it from us fellows. It's our privilege to give it."

Roger, unaware of the many sides to the extraordinary man seated opposite him, was wholly unprepared for so adroit and graceful and sensible a speech. He could only make an impatient gesture and say with a decisiveness that seemed rude: "The picture has no money value. I'll have to insist on your taking it on my terms—or I'll give it to some one else. For I shall not carry it abroad with me."

"That brings me to the main reason for my coming," said Richmond, leaning forward, elbows on the broad arms of the chair.

Roger was all at sea again. With Richmond's request for the picture he had jumped to the conclusion that it was really the sole cause of the two visits of that afternoon and the two exhibitions of sultry affability. Now—what new complication was Richmond about to disclose?—what new obstacle was about to appear in his path back to peace and whole-hearted work?

The financier did not keep him long in suspense. "I want to persuade you not to go abroad," he proceeded. "Now—please hear me out! You are an American. Your proper place is here—your own country. It needs you, and you owe it the services of your genius."

Roger eyed his guest with candid suspicion. Guile

being foreign to his nature, he knew of its existence in his fellow-beings only as an incomprehensible but undeniable fact. He knew Richmond was a man of guile. Yet these sincere tones, these frank and friendly eyes— Also, what possible motive could the man have? Perhaps the picture had really converted him into a friend and admirer, unafraid now that there was no longer reason to suspect matrimonial designs.

"Don't affect a modesty a man of your abilities could not possibly feel," said Richmond, misunderstanding or pretending to misunderstand Roger's embarrassed silence. "Only mediocrity is modest, and it is the crowd of fools that compels us, who can do things and have sense enough to know we can, to pretend to be modest."

Roger laughed. "There's truth in that," said he. "Still, I'm sure my fate is a matter of importance only to myself." His expression settled to somberness again. "No, I shall go. Thank you, but I shall go."

"There is work for you here—big work," urged Richmond. "I shall see that you get it—that you don't have to wait for recognition and be wearied and disgusted by the stupid injustices that keep men of genius out of their own."

Roger's simple and generous face softened, for his heart was touched. "I see you understand," said he.

"I wish I could show my appreciation by accepting your offer. But I can't. I must go."

"I admit that the atmosphere over there is more congenial—much more congenial—to your sort of work. But you'll find us less unsympathetic than you think. Give us a trial, Wade."

Roger was entirely convinced now, and was deeply moved. "I wish I could, Mr. Richmond. But if I am to work I must go."

The older man leaned still farther toward the young man in his earnestness. "Why, you painted here one of the greatest pictures I've seen. Of course, my personal feeling may bias my judgment somewhat—for I am attached to my daughter as I am to no other human being "—Richmond's voice trembled, and there were tears in his eyes—" I'm a fool about her, Wade— a damn fool! . . . Excuse my gettting off the track. As I was saying, I may think the picture greater than it really is. But I know that it is really great— *great!* "

Roger tried to conceal his agitation.

"You painted it here. That means, you can do great work here. Did you ever paint a better picture in Europe? "

"No," admitted Roger.

"Then you ought to stay."

355

Roger rose, seated himself, lit a fresh cigarette. "Can't do it," he said curtly. "Let's say no more about it. Don't think me rude or unappreciative. But —you must take my decision as final."

"I'm older than you, Wade—twice as old. You are a young man, just starting. I'm about all in. So, I don't feel that I'm impertinent in pressing you."

Again Roger rose. This time he went to the edge of the veranda. At the steps he turned suddenly. "Don't think me unappreciative, sir," said he, "but this is painful to me—very painful."

Richmond put on a most effective air of apology. "I'm sorry—I beg your pardon—I did not mean to intrude upon your private affairs. I was assuming you were free. It never occurred to me that there might be obligations over there——"

"I *am* free!" cried Roger. "At least, I was. And I intend to be so again. But—enough of this—of me. I'll send you the picture— No, I'll see that it is sent on Saturday."

Richmond regarded the young man with the eyes of a father and a friend. He went up to him, laid one hand affectionately on his arm. "I know you don't want to leave America—give up your ambition—the one that brought you here, so d'Artois says. Tell me. Can't it be arranged somehow?"

" Impossible," said Roger.

Richmond laughed gently. " A word for boys and for old failures. . . . Can't you induce *her* to live on this side of the water? "

Roger looked puzzled.

" It's always a woman," said Richmond, eyes twinkling. " If she really cares for you she'll live wherever your career demands."

Roger's smile of exaggerated disdain revealed how much of the boy he was taking with him into the thirties. " You are mistaken," said he. " No woman has ever dominated my life." His face grew stern again and energetic. " And no woman ever shall! "

" That's right—that's right," heartily approved Richmond. " Woman in the wrong place in a man's life is almost as bad as if she were left out entirely. Almost—but not quite."

" I don't agree with you," said Roger.

" Did you ever happen to know a man who had left woman out altogether? " inquired Richmond.

" No—but I've seen many and many a life—an artist's life—wrecked by women—by marriage."

Richmond took advantage of Roger's averted face to indulge in a smile of satisfaction. He went on in a careless tone that had no relationship to the smile: " Probably those chaps wouldn't have amounted to much, anyhow. The man who has it in him to be wrecked by excess of any kind is bound to go under. Nothing can save him."

"No doubt," assented Roger, with assumed indifference. The point Richmond had just made was new, was impressive—appealed disquietingly to the young man's pride as well as to his intelligence. For the first time he looked upon his visitor as a dangerous man. He stood at the edge of the veranda in that expectant silence which compels a caller either to show cause why he should stay or to take himself off. Richmond covered his defeat and his embarrassment by returning to his chair and seating himself in the attitude of one far from the end of a leisurely and intimate visit. Roger could do nothing but reluctantly reseat himself. They smoked in silence a few minutes; then Richmond said reflectively:

"So—you're opposed to marriage?"

"Unalterably," said Roger.

"I remember now. You said that to me the other day when "—Richmond laughed with frank good humor—" when I was suspecting you of designs on my daughter—or, rather, on my fortune. How absurd that seems now. But I had some excuse. I didn't know you then. If I had I might not have been so well pleased by your views on matrimony."

As these words flowed fluently from Richmond's gracious tongue Roger cast at him a furtive glance of amazed suspicion.

"My older daughter," continued Richmond, "is a thoroughly worldly woman. She has married a title —and is as happy as a normal woman would be over getting the man of her heart's choice. But my other daughter——"

Roger moved uncomfortably in his chair. Could it be possible— No! No! Ridiculous! And yet—Preposterous! As little danger of it as of Roger himself giving in.

"Beatrice "—Richmond pronounced the name with tenderness—and tenderness now seemed as essentially one of his traits as hardness or cruelty or tyranny— "Beatrice is entirely different. But you know her. You artists read character. I needn't tell you she is delightfully unworldly—foolishly romantic—need I? "

"No," said Roger in a hurried, harried way.

"Your painting shows how thoroughly you understood—appreciated her. Wade, one of the finest things I ever knew a man to do was your refusal to take advantage of her inexperienced young imagination. It was noble—*noble!* "

Roger looked wretched. "I—I don't deserve that," was his stammering but vigorous protest. "My motive was altogether different—wholly selfish."

"Oh, come, now," cried the older man jocosely, "she's not so unattractive. A man less scrupulous, less honorable—might easily have fancied himself in love with her. You'll admit that—won't you?"

Roger was braced well back in his chair. "Yes," said he in a tone not remotely suggestive of terror.

"I didn't mean to embarrass you, Wade," laughed Richmond.

"Not at all—not at all," said Roger, his panic ludicrously obvious.

"So—it was really noble of you."

"I can't permit that, sir," said Roger. "My only motive was my determination never to marry."

"I don't like to hear you say that," said Richmond. "As the father of a daughter, as a man who wishes to see his daughter in the keeping of a man of the right sort—and how few such there are!—I don't like to hear any of those few declare against matrimony."

There was no misunderstanding the trend of this. Incredible though it seemed, the man had come round, was abetting his daughter in her willful whim of conquest! "I'm not opposed to marriage—for others," said Roger awkwardly. "I simply feel that it is not wise for me. If a man whose life is given to creative work marries a woman he loves he is content. It is the end of achievement, of ambition. Why strive after the lesser when what seems to him the greater has been achieved? If such a man marries unfortunately then the bitterness and the agitations destroy his ability to create. Happy marriage suffocates genius, unhappy marriage strangles it. Death inevitable—in either case."

The words were not unlike those he had used in describing his position to Beatrice. His manner—the tone, the look of the eyes, the expression of mouth and chin—made them seem entirely different, far more profoundly significant. A man, a serious man, rarely reveals his innermost self to a woman unless he and she have reached a far closer intimacy than Roger had permitted with Beatrice. But talking with Richmond, with another man, one who could and would understand and sympathize, Roger exposed a side of his nature of the existence of which Beatrice had only a faint intuition, no direct or definite knowledge. Richmond had been pushed by the portrait well toward conviction of Roger's high rank in the aristocracy he esteemed as a man among men. He was now wholly convinced. His daughter, he saw, had chosen more wisely than he knew.

"I see your point," said Richmond slowly, thoughtfully. "I see your point."

Roger showed his deep sense of relief.

" It is a good one—a very good one."

Roger's tension visibly relaxed.

" It is unanswerable," was Richmond's final, sweeping concession.

" Unanswerable," echoed the painter decisively, yet with a curious note of unhappiness.

" But," pursued Beatrice's father, " what would you do—if you fell in love? " And, ignoring the painter's confusion in the bursting of this bomb, he went on with an air of philosophic impartiality: " Love laughs at reason—at ambition—at calculation of every kind. Yes—I—about the last man in the world to be suspected of sentimentality—I say that love is supreme master."

Roger, with an air of youthful positiveness—cocksureness—made a gesture of strong dissent.

Richmond smiled, went on: " Yes, young man— *yes!* When love commands we all obey—you—I—*all*— we obey. We may squirm—struggle—but we surrender. What would you do if you fell in love? "

Roger leaned forward in his chair, looked firmly into the keen, kindly eyes of Beatrice's father. " I should fly," said he slowly.

The two men regarded each other steadily, each reading the other's mind. And again beneath the young and romantic handsomeness Richmond saw the man with whom his daughter was not yet acquainted—the man with the great character gracefully concealed behind the romantic-looking painter—a character in the making as yet, but having the imposing outlines that enable one to imagine something of the final form. At last Richmond said: "Yes—I believe—you—*could*—fly—and *would*."

Roger flushed and his gaze sank. "I should feel that I was false to all that means myself to me if I did not," said he. "No matter how I loved her I would fly."

"And she?" inquired Richmond. "What about her?"

Roger smiled faintly—a sardonic smile. "Women forget their caprices easily."

"Would *you* forget easily?" said the older man gently—he looked very old and very gentle and kind.

The handsome face of the young painter grew grave. "I'm afraid not," said he. "But if *I* could forget a—a reality, certainly she could forget a fancy."

No one—except perhaps his wife, with her memories of Richmond's ardent and generous youth when he had wooed and won her despite her father's misgivings about his poverty and her own misgivings about his size—but certainly no one else would have recognized the face of Daniel Richmond as he replied: " Not if she had, by some divine instinct, understood and appreciated such a rare man as you."

Roger's impatient gesture was almost angry. " I am not a man. I am a painter."

" And if she did not forget? " persisted Richmond in the same slow, insistent way, like conscience itself. " If it was not a whim? "

Roger stood up. " I don't grant your supposition," said he. " But, granting it, then at least I'd not have made a mess of her life and of my own. For if I were false to my art it would revenge itself by tormenting me. And the wife of a tormented man is not happy."

Richmond sat staring at the floor of the veranda. The wrinkles and seams and hollows in his face seemed to be deepening. After a few minutes of silence, disturbed by the irritating noisiness of a flock of sparrows, he said: " She refuses to come home. I offered to concede—everything. I'd be glad to let her have her way. But, as you say, it's impossible. She'll not come home. She blames me. I thought I was altogether to blame. I see I'm not. But—she blames me, and always will. And she'll not make it up with me." A long pause, then there came from him in a mere ghost of his normal voice: " And—it is killing me."

Roger sat motionless, gazing at the bed of sweet old-fashioned flowers before the veranda.

Richmond broke the long stretch of evening stillness: "Would you—would it be asking too much of you— If you saw her you might persuade her to make it up with me."

Roger did not move—did not reply. He had retreated deep within himself.

"I know it isn't fair to you—or to her—to ask it," went on her father's sad, monotonous voice, heavy with heartache. "I know that seeing her again would only make it harder for you to do what you've got to do—for I understand about those musts of ambition that make men like us relentless. And I know that seeing you again—and seeing even more clearly the man you are—would make it—impossible, perhaps, for her to forget. But—" Richmond paused long before adding— "I am an old man and—I have the selfishness of those who have not long to live."

Roger still neither moved nor spoke.

Richmond observed him for a while, rose with a painful effort. "Good-by," he said, extending his hand.

Roger stood, took his hand. "I'd do it if I could —if I were strong enough," he said. "It's humiliating, but I have to confess I am not."

"Think it over, Wade. Do the best you can for me."

And Richmond, his feet almost shuffling, went down the steps and down the walk and out through the gate. He climbed heavily into his runabout—was gone. Roger leaned against the pillar, staring into vacancy, until the old woman had twice called him to supper.

XX

BEATRICE LOSES

BEATRICE and Miss Clermont were finishing breakfast the following morning when Richmond came. As he entered the small sitting room with its bed folded away into a lounge he made no effort to conceal his feelings. In response to Beatrice's look of defiance he sent to her from his haggard face a glance of humble appeal—the look of the beaten and impotent tyrant— for the pride of the tyrant is not in himself, but in his power, and vanishes with it. "I'd like to see you alone," said he, ignoring Valentine as a servant.

"My partner, Miss Clermont," said Beatrice, in the tone of making an introduction.

Richmond's natural quickness did not fail him. He instantly repaired his mistake. "Miss Clermont," said he, bowing politely. Then, "Pardon my abruptness. I am much upset in mind."

Miss Clermont, who was now thoroughly adapted to her new rank, smiled politely and glided into the adjoining room, closing the door behind her. Said Beatrice: "You can't imagine how splendid she is. We shall make a fortune. I'm sure we shall. We have rented a shop—in Thirty-second Street—south side—three doors from Fifth Avenue. Frightful rent, but I insisted on beginning at the top."

" I saw Wade yesterday afternoon," said Richmond.

The animation died out of the girl's face. And with its animation departed most of its beauty, at least most of its charm.

" I practically asked him to marry you."

Her eyes lit up, immediately became dull again.

" He was polite—everything a man could be. But he—he will never marry."

" Until he loves," murmured Beatrice.

" There are men—" began Richmond.

" But they don't love!" exclaimed Beatrice.

" Perhaps so," said Richmond, who would not have ventured to discuss anything with her, however mildly. Also, no woman, no young woman could be expected to understand that marriage was not the one absorbing longing of every unattached man, as it was of every unattached woman. " Anyhow, he will never marry."

" Until he loves," repeated Beatrice.

Richmond was silent. He would not aggravate her unhappiness by telling her that Roger loved her.

" Is he still intending to go abroad? " she asked.

" To-morrow," replied her father.

" To-morrow!" Beatrice started from her chair, an expression of wild disorder flashing into her face. But she fought for and regained control, sat back quietly with a calm, " Oh, I thought it was to be next week."

" He has changed his plans."

The daughter was looking at the father with scrutinizing eyes, full of doubt. He saw it, said in the tone that carried conviction, " I have come over to your side. He is a much bigger man than I thought—or than you know."

" I know enough," said the girl.

" At any rate, I wanted him for a son-in-law. I did my best. I haven't anything he wants."

" Nor I," said Beatrice with a bitter, self-scorning laugh.

" He is opposed to marriage. He thinks——"

" He doesn't love," interrupted she. " That's the whole story. Well "—she made a gesture of dismissal —" now, let me tell you about the shop."

" He has sent——"

" Please!" said she imperiously. " No more about him."

" The picture—he promised to have it sent to Red Hill after he sailed. Instead, it came last night."

"Why did he do that?" demanded she swiftly.

"I asked him for it."

"No. I mean, why did he change his mind?"

"Oh, probably for no reason. That's a trifle."

She was sitting up, straight and alert. Her eyes were aglow with excitement. "He is sailing to-morrow instead of next week," she said rapidly. "Instead of taking my picture—our picture—his and mine—instead of taking it with him as he intended at first, he gives it to you. He first says he'll send it when he sails, then—after he has talked with you—he changes his mind and gets it out of the house—out of his sight—at once."

Richmond gazed at her with marveling eyes. She was clairvoyant—this wonderful daughter of his!

Her cheeks flushed, her eyes sparkled. Her words came joyfully tumbling over each other: "Why is he in such a hurry to sail—to get rid of *my* picture? Because he's *afraid!* He distrusts himself. He's fighting hard. He— Father, he loves me!"

"Beatrice," said Richmond tenderly, "he will never marry. He is a man of the unshakable sort—of my sort——"

Beatrice laughed. "You haven't changed in this affair—oh, no!"

Richmond smiled guiltily. "I should have said, he

is a man whose resolves haven't been shaken by age and by foolish paternal fondness long indulged."

"He is *afraid!* He is flying—flying from *love!*"

Richmond's face wore a look of deepest anxiety. "My dear, you will only distress yourself with false hopes. There are things about men—men like him—that you don't understand."

"Of course. But there are also other things that *you* don't understand, father dear."

"The picture is at home. Won't you come and see it?"

"I must see him first. I must dress and go at once." And she was up and was hastily gathering together the businesslike papers strewn upon the table among the breakfast dishes. "You'll excuse me, father——"

"I asked him to come and see you—to beg you to go home again."

She paused. "And he said?"

"He refused at first. As I was leaving—I hoped —he might."

She reflected. "No, he'll not come. Unless—but I'll take no chances."

"I know he was touched by my appeal," persisted her father. "Beatrice—go on with this dressmaking if you must. But—forgive me and let things be with us as they were before." He stretched out trembling hands toward her. "You're all I've got in the world— all I care for. I'm not ashamed or repentant for what I did. I did it because I thought it was for your good. But I'm sorry. I was mistaken."

"I do forgive you," said the girl, "though I don't like to say anything that sounds priggish and pious. But you can't expect me to trust you, can you, father?"

"I've tried to pay for those bonds, but he has sold them to some enemy of mine—and for a good price."

"Aren't you ashamed about the bonds?" said the daughter with a roguish smile.

"No," replied Richmond doggedly. "In the circumstances—what I believed and everything—that was the right move."

Beatrice laughed with a touch of her old mirthfulness, with all her old adoration of his skill and courage. "You are so different!" cried she. "Not a bit a hypocrite. We're friends again—until you try to undermine and ruin my dressmaking business."

"I'll give you all the capital you want," he eagerly declared.

"No—thanks," said she. "But—I'll tell you what you may do. You may buy a block of Wauchong bonds I happen to own."

" *You* did it? " cried he, delighted.

" You may have them at a hundred and fifty. I always try to make a reasonable profit on a deal."

" I'll send you a blank check."

She put her arms round him and kissed him. There was a trembling in his tight return embrace that sent a pang through her; for it suggested somehow his deep impelling thought—fear—of the eternal separation— the everlasting farewell, not far away from him and her at the most. " Father—dear," she murmured.

" Don't harass yourself, child—about him," he whispered. " Let me help you try to forget."

She drew away gently and looked at him, in her eyes a will which he now admitted—proudly—to be more unswerving than his own. Said she: " *You* didn't teach me to forget—or to give up, either."

He sighed. " I'll wait and take you to the ferry." And she went into her bedroom.

She had been dressing perhaps ten minutes when he rapped excitedly on her door. " What is it? " inquired she.

" He's come! " cried her father.

The door swung partly open and her face appeared at the edge. " Roger? Downstairs? "

" Yes—I answered the telephone from the office."

" I can't receive him up here. It's against the

rules. Yet I want— No—say I'll be down to the parlor immediately."

" But I'm here," suggested her father. " He could come up."

" He mustn't see you."

" I could wait in there—couldn't I? "

" Yes—the door is thick," reflected Beatrice aloud. " Yes—say he is to come up. Val—Miss Clermont has gone out. . . . No—I'll see him in the parlor."

And Beatrice closed the door. It was not many minutes before she opened it again—to appear bewitchingly dressed in a new spring toilet—and the styles that year were exactly suited to her figure. She was radiant, and her father's depressed countenance did not lessen her overflowing delight. " You can't deny that he loves me—can you? " cried she.

" No," replied Richmond. " The fact is, I saw he did yesterday."

" Why didn't you tell me? " demanded she.

" You guessed it. What was the use? " evaded he.

" Guess? " The girl laughed. " You call that guessing because you're merely a man. It was certainty—proof—plain as if he had said so. But then, I've known it for weeks. Now, keep well back in the elevator, dear, for he mustn't see you as I get out."

When the elevator was slowing for the parlor floor

Richmond caught his daughter's hand and pressed it convulsively. "Good luck!" he said in an undertone. "If you don't win to-day we'll follow him to France."

"To the ends of the earth," laughed she, kissing his hand and gayly pushing him back to a rear corner of the car.

The door closed behind her and the car resumed its descent; of all the thoughts boiling in Richmond's excited brain not one was related to the strangeness of his own conduct or to the amazing transformation in a cold, tyrannical nature. In fact, the transformation was apparent rather than real. The chase had ever dominated him—the passion for the chase. And it was dominating him now.

In the wall opposite the elevator, and the width of the rather wide room from it, was a long mirror. No man could well have been freer from physical vanity than this big, self-conscious Roger Wade. Beyond his human duty of making himself inoffensive to the eye in the matter of clothing, he did nothing whatever toward personal adornment. Yet as Beatrice advanced he was primping industriously and unconsciously. To occupy his agitated mind he was standing before the mirror smoothing his hair, arranging his tie, fussing with the hang of the big, loose, dark-blue suit that gave his splendid figure an air of freedom. Their eyes met in the glass. He did not turn, but gazed at her—and who would not have been charmed by a creature so redolent of springtime freshness, from the yellow roses in her hat, looking as if they were just from the garden, to the scrupulously neat effect of stockings and ties? She stood beside him, her yellow roses nodding in line with his ear. And they made a delightful picture—a rare harmony of contrasts and symmetries.

She laughed radiantly. " Chang! " she cried.

He was straightway so disconcerted that her amusement could not but increase. " Through primping? " mocked she.

" I think so," he replied. " I see you attended to all that thoroughly before you came down."

" Yes," said she with the air of half-serious, half-jesting complacency she could carry off so well. " I'm ready to the last button. Let's sit over there—by the window." Then, as they sat opposite each other: " Why are you so solemn? "

Again Roger had to struggle to keep himself in hand.

" Why do you avoid looking at me? " laughed she. And so glad was she to see him again that she had less difficulty than she had feared in hiding her anxiety, her feeling that she was playing her last stake in the game that seemed to her to mean lifelong happiness or lifelong wretchedness.

He colored, but contrived to smile and to look at her. It was an unsteady gaze, a grave smile. " I've come," said he, " because I wish to urge you to go back home. Your father and I——"

" Yes, I know," interrupted she. " Father has been here."

" And you're going back? "

" No—no, indeed. I've made the first step toward being independent. I'm going to keep on. Father's a dear, but he's not to be trusted. If he controls he tyrannizes. He might try not to do it, but he could not help himself. So—I'm to be a dressmaker."

" What nonsense, Rix! " exclaimed he. " There's nothing so detestable as an independent woman—a masculine woman."

" One that has a will of her own and proposes to the man if she happens to feel like it? " suggested she, with dancing eyes.

" Well—yes—if you insist on putting it that way."

" Woman, the weak, the foolish, the clinging—that's your ideal? " said she.

He nodded emphatically.

" Isn't it strange," said she absently, " that we never fall in love with our ideals? "

Roger stirred about in his chair, much embarrassed.

"I suppose it's part of our never—*never*—wanting to do what we ought—and never, never doing it if we can help."

Roger took his hat from the floor beside his chair, got ready to rise. "If you're determined on not going home I suppose it's useless for me to talk. But—your father is old—much older these last few weeks, Rix. If you could make it up with him——"

"Oh, but I have," cried she. "We are better friends than ever. I don't think we'll ever quarrel again."

The artist showed a rather conventional kind of pleasure. "I'm sincerely glad," said he. "I like him and I like you, and I'd have been sorry to go away feeling that you two were at outs."

"You're not a bit natural, Chang. You don't talk like yourself. What's the matter?"

"Probably I've got too much on my mind—the hurry of going so soon. That reminds me. I must say good-by. I've got such a lot to do."

Her face did not change, but her heart began to flutter wildly.

"You and your father are friends," proceeded he, his inward state showing only in the fact that he was absurdly repeating himself. "What I came to do is done. So I'll go—as that was my only reason for bothering you."

She gazed mockingly at him, shaking her head. "Oh, no—Chang. That wasn't why you came."

"I assure you it was. My only reason."

"You big, foolish Chang!" mocked she. "You don't know your own mind. Now, do sit down. That's better. Now—there you are, jumping up again. What *is* the matter?"

"I must be going."

"Is it really true that big men are more stupid? . . . No, that wasn't why you came. You came because——"

"Now, Rix," cried he angrily—for her eyes plainly foretold what was coming. "That joke has gone far enough—too far—much too far."

"What joke?"

"About your being in love with me."

"Whether or not it's a joke that I'm in love with you, it certainly is not a joke that *you* are in love with *me*."

He sat on the arm of his chair and smiled ironically. "Really?" said he.

"Really," declared she. "Shall I prove it to you?"

He stood. " I've no time. It's very pleasant dawdling here with you, but——"

She ignored his hand, concentrated on his eyes. " What else have you painted besides that picture? " asked she.

He blushed slightly. " I'm very slow at my work."

Her smile let him know that she was fully aware how heavily she had scored. " You came over to stay here in America," pursued she. " Yet, you are going back—never to return, you announce. Why? . . . You're not going through fear of father. No—don't pretend. Fear isn't in your line—fear of *men*. And you're not going through fear of me? You could easily bar me out—make it impossible for me to annoy you."

He had seated himself again. He was listening intently.

" You are going," she went on, " through fear of yourself." She laughed softly. " A regular panic, Chang! " she cried. " You didn't intend to sail till next week. You are running off in the morning—by the first steamer."

He made a faint effort to rise, gave it up, resumed the study of his hatband.

" You were going to take my picture with you," continued she.

" *Your* picture? " said he with feeble irony.

" *Our* picture," corrected she softly.

He waved the hat in a gesture of hopelessness.

" Then," proceeded she, " you changed your mind and decided to leave it. But you thought you wouldn't part with it until the last moment—to-morrow morning. Oh, Chang! Chang! "

" I found it more convenient to send it last night," said he with a brave effort at indifference.

" Convenient? " she laughed. " I can see you storming against your weakness, as you call it. I can see you resolving to be brave—to free yourself immediately. But your scheme didn't work. For the only result of not having the picture to say good-by to was that you had to come here and take one last look at the original."

He laughed aloud—a forced, mirthless laugh. " Same old Rix! " exclaimed he. " Of all the conceit! "

" Isn't it, though? " retorted she with a coquettish nod. " But it's the truth, too—isn't it? "

" I'd hate to destroy any illusion that seems to give you so much happiness."

" You couldn't, Chang. For " — softly — " I couldn't feel as I do toward you if I didn't know, with that deep, deep heart knowledge, that we are—like one."

He rose resolutely, in his eyes an expression that thrilled and frightened her. She had from time to time caught glimpses of the man of whom that was the expression, but only glimpses—when he was at work and unconscious of her presence. Now, somehow, the expression seemed to reveal this almost unknown man within the Roger she loved. However, she concealed her alarm.

"You see, I've proved that you do love me," said she. "But, Chang"—solemnly—"even though you do love me and I love you, what does it amount to—except for—for misery—unless we have each other?"

He slowly dropped to the chair again. He looked at her sternly, angrily. "It's the truth," said he. "I do love you. It is a whim with you—a caprice—a piece of willfulness. But with me"—he drew a long breath—"I love you. The only excuse for the way you've acted is that you're too young and light-hearted to know what you're about."

Her hands clutched each other convulsively in her lap. But she was careful to keep from her face all sign of the feeling those words inspired.

He laughed with bitter irony. "To that extent— you've had your way," he went on. "Get what satisfaction you can out of it—for, while you've conquered my heart, you'll not conquer my will. I am not yours to dispose of as you see fit. I can get over caring for you—and I shall."

"But *why*, Chang? *Why?* "

For answer he smiled mockingly at her.

" In your heart of hearts you don't believe for an instant it's a caprice with me. You know better, Chang." Sincerity looked from her eyes, pleaded in her voice.

But Roger held his ground stubbornly. " I know it is caprice," he said. " I'm not clean crazy with vanity, Rix. But even if you were in earnest—as much in earnest as you pretend—perhaps as you think—still, that wouldn't change things. We can't be anything more to each other than friends. In any other relation we'd be worse than useless to each other. You need a man of your own sort. If I tied up with any woman it'd be with one of my sort."

" I don't understand," said she. " It wouldn't be worth while for you to explain—for I couldn't understand. All I know is, we love each other."

" But marriage is a matter of temperaments. If you had less will I might compel you to go my way, to learn to like and lead my kind of life. If I had less will I might adapt myself to you—and become a comfortable, contemptible rich woman's nonentity of a husband. But neither of us can change—so, we part."

" I've thought of those things," said she, quiet and sweet and unconvinced. " I've gone over and over them, day and night. But—Chang, I can't give you up."

" That is to say, you don't care what becomes of me so long as you get your way."

She did not respond to his argumentative mood, but took refuge in woman's impregnable citadel. " I trust my instinct—what it tells me is best for us."

" You don't realize it," argued he desperately, " but you count on my love for you making me weak enough to adapt myself to your kind of life."

" I count on our love's making us both happy."

" You wish to marry me simply because you think I'm necessary to your happiness? "

" Yes—Chang. You are necessary to my happiness."

" And *my* happiness—have you thought of it? "

" I love you."

" And you feel that your love ought to be enough to make me happy? "

" Your love is all I need," replied she with sad gentleness.

" That's the woman's point of view," cried he. " I'll admit it's more or less mine, too—when I'm with you or have been thinking about you till my head's turned.

But—Rix "—he was powerfully in earnest now—
" while love may be all that's necessary to make a
woman happy, it isn't so with a man. For a man, love
is to life what salt is to food—not the food as it is
with a woman, but the thing that gives the food savor."

He paused. But she sat silent, her gaze upon her
hands folded listlessly in her lap. He went on: " You
have been indulging this whim of yours without giving
it a serious thought. Now, I want you to think—to
help me save us from the folly your willfulness and my
weakness are tempting us to commit. I want you to
ask yourself: ' What sort of life would Chang and I
lead together? Would I tolerate his devotion to his
work? Would I respect him if he gradually yielded
to my temptings and gave up his work? Whichever
way it turned out, wouldn't I either dislike or despise
him? ' "

" You—don't love me," she murmured.

" I do. But I'm not so selfish as your inexperience
and thoughtlessness make you."

She scarcely heard. She was gazing with all her
mind and heart at the new Chang revealed clearly for
the first time in the intense earnestness of this their
first profoundly and crucially serious talk. This was
the man her father had warned her about. There were
dark circles round her eyes as if they had been bruised,

and in them the look of present pain. He happened to glance at her. He saw—groaned. "No matter!" he cried. "I love you. I can't bear it. I'm weak—contemptibly weak where you're concerned. We'll surely fail—fail miserably. But we must go on, now. I had a presentiment—I was a damn fool to come here to-day. Yes—we've drifted too far. We must go on—over the falls."

He stopped, appalled by his own passionate outburst. She shook her head slowly. "No, we must not go on," said she.

Her tone instantly calmed his runaway passion; he stared in amazement.

"You really feel like that?" she went on—"feel it'd be weak and wrong for you to marry me?"

"I have told you the truth—about yourself and about me," was his reply. "You surely must see it."

She gave a long sigh, furtive, deep. But her voice was steady as she said sadly: "Then—we must give each other up."

"That is certainly best," promptly assented he. "You see now that you didn't want me, but only your own way."

"I see that we should not be happy. I don't understand your point of view. I suppose I'm not experienced enough. But I see you are in earnest—that it isn't just a—a notion with you. So—" From her face waned the last glimmer of its look of the spring-time. Her voice sank almost to a whisper—" I give up."

He stood with aggressive erectness. "Then—it is settled."

She nodded without looking at him. She could not trust herself to look. "I'll not bother you any more," said she.

He saw that he was victor—had gained his point. Yet never did man look or feel less the victor. He put out his hand; she let hers rest in it. "Good-by, Rix," he said with a brave attempt at philosophic calm. "This is much better than seeing our love end in a quarrel and a scandal—isn't it?"

"You go—in the morning?"

"Yes."

Her hand dropped to her lap. He looked steadily at her, with no restraint upon his expression, because her eyes were down. "Good-by," he repeated. He waited for a reply, but none came. With that long, sure stride of his, free and graceful, he went to the stairway and descended—and departed.

XXI

La Provence was due to sail in twenty minutes.
One whistle had blown; one of the gangways was casting off. Roger, with a suppressed excitement more
effective than any shouting or waving of fists, was su-
perintending the taking of his luggage from the ship.
" There's still one piece to come ashore—the old
leather trunk with brass nails," he said to the polite
chief steward. " It must be found. Double your efforts and I'll double your fee." He turned, found himself squarely facing Beatrice Richmond.

The color flamed in his face; it vanished from hers.
" You got my note? " she said. " And you are sailing
anyhow? "

" I did not get your note," replied he. " But I am
not sailing. . . . One moment, please." Then to the
chief steward: " There is also a note for me. I must
have it."

" Parfaitement, Monsieur." And the chief steward
raced up the gangway.

Roger and Beatrice stood aside in a quiet place,
a calm in the surging crowd of the voyagers and

388

their friends. Beatrice looked at him with that fine, frank directness which had been her most conspicuous trait in all her dealings with him. Said she: "In my note I asked you to take me on any terms or on no terms. All I wish is to be near you and to love you."

She spoke the words without any trace of emotion in either tone or manner—spoke them with a certain monotonous finality that gave them all the might of the simply genuine. And he answered in much the same way. "I am not sailing," said he, "because—because to love you and to have you—that's life for me. The rest isn't worth talking about."

"Not worth talking about," echoed she. "I don't know whether we'll be happy or not, but I do know it's my only chance to be anything but miserable."

"I don't know whether I could get over you or not," was his matching confession, "but I do know that I don't want to—and won't."

A moment's silence, with the two gazing up at the towering steamer through the great doors in the pier shed. Then his eyes turned to her, to look at her with an intensity that made her feel as if she had been suddenly seized in strong yet gentle arms and were being borne by mighty wings up and up and still up.

"Chang," she said between laughing and sobbing, "I must have been crazy yesterday to refuse you."

"No—you're crazy to-day. So am I. That is, I'm normal again—what's been normal for me ever since I knew you. And I hope the day'll never come when I'll be sane."

"Are you happy now?"

"Delirious."

"As we used to be when we were together by the cascade?"

"Like that—only a thousand times more so." And they gazed at each other with foolish-fond eyes, and from their lips issued those extraordinary sounds that seem imbecile or divine, according as the listening ears are attuned.

"Your father was right," said Roger. "Love is master." Again she was seeing the new and more wonderful and more compelling Chang. "I found that everything was going to stop stock-still if I went away from you."

The chief steward, bearing the note, and his assistants who had been collecting Roger's luggage around him, now appeared. Roger tore open the note, read its one brief sentence of unconditional surrender. Then he dismissed the men with fees so amazing to them that they thanked him with tears in their eyes. "But you really must be careful," cautioned Beatrice. "You know we've got no money to throw away."

Roger gave her a look that dazzled her. " I see you understand," said he. " Well, we may be happy in spite of all—all the difficulties."

She laughed. " I don't think, dear," said she, " that you're so weak as you fear, or I so foolish. . . . Maybe you'd like me to keep on with the dressmaking? "

He frowned in mock severity. " I don't want ever to hear of it again."

" Then you never shall," replied she with mock humility. " You want a meek slave—and you shall have one." Her lips moved with no sound issuing.

" What are you saying there? " demanded he.

" What Ruth said to Naomi." She gazed at him with ecstatic, incredulous eyes. " Have I *really* got you? " she said.

He looked at her with an amused smile. It died away slowly, and his gaze grew solemn. " That will depend on—you," he said.

She saw there was more than the surface meaning in the words; then she saw their deeper meaning—saw as clearly as an inexperienced girl may see, but only so clearly, the hidden reality of the man she had been striving to win, and would ever have to strive to keep. And beautiful was the light in her eyes as she murmured: " Love will teach me! "

He half turned away to hide the wave of emotion that almost unmanned him. When he spoke it was to say in a queer, husky voice: " Let me see the express-man about this luggage—then—we'll go to lunch somewhere."

" Let's go—in—" She halted, eyes dancing.

" In a cab? "

She blushed and laughed. " Isn't it about time? " said she, eyes full of that charming audacity of hers. " How well we understand each other! How congenial we are! "

" Wonderful, isn't it? " cried he. " I hope there have been other cases like ours—lots of 'em. But I doubt it."

She waited while he negotiated the return of the baggage to Deer Spring. When he rejoined her—or, rather, gave her his undivided attention, for he had not let her get so much as three feet away from him—she said: " Now I must telephone father."

" Oh, why hurry about that? "

" I must tell him not to engage passage for next Wednesday," explained she.

And they both burst out laughing.

(1)

THE END